£14

The Astonishing History of Troy Town

Sir Arthur Thomas Quiller-Couch

"This regiment of visitors." (Chapter VII)

THE ASTONISHING HISTORY OF TROY TOWN.

by

Arthur Thomas Quiller-Couch.

1914

TO CHARLES CANNAN.

My Dear Cannan,

It is told of a distinguished pedagogue that one day a heated stranger burst into his study, and, wringing him by the hand, cried, "Heaven bless and reward you, sir! Heaven preserve you long to educate old England's boyhood! I have walked many a weary, weary mile to see your face again," he continued, flourishing a scrap of paper, "and assure you that but for your discipline, obeyed by me as a boy and remembered as a man, I should never — no, never — have won the Ticket-of-Leave which you behold!"

In something of the same spirit I bring you this small volume. The child of encouragement is given to staggering its parent; and I make no doubt that as you turn the following pages, you will more than once exclaim, with the old lady in the ballad —

"O, deary me! this is none of I!"

Nevertheless, it would be strange indeed if this story bore no marks of you; for a hundred kindly instances have taught me to come with sure reliance for your reproof and praise. Few, I imagine, have the good fortune of a critic so friendly and inexorable; and if the critic has been unsparing, he has been used unsparingly.

Wargrave, Henley-on-Thames,
June 7, 1888

CONTENTS

CHAPTER I.

IN WHICH THE READER IS MADE ACQUAINTED WITH A STATE OF INNOCENCE; AND THE MEANING OF THE WORD "CUMEELFO".

"Any news to-night?" asked Admiral Buzza, leading a trump.

"Hush, my love," interposed his wife timidly, with a glance at the Vicar. She liked to sit at her husband's left, and laid her small cards before him as so many tributes to his greatness.

"I will not hush, Emily. I repeat, is there any news to-night?"

Miss Limpenny, his hostess and vis-a-vis, finding the Admiral's eye fierce upon her, coughed modestly and announced that twins had just arrived to the postmistress. Her manner, as she said this, implied that, for aught she knew, they had come with the letters.

1

The Vicar took the trick and gathered it up in silence. He was a portly, antique gentleman, with a fine taste for scandal in its proper place, but disliked conversation during a rubber.

"Twins, eh?" growled the Admiral. "Just what I expected. She always was a wasteful woman."

"My love!" expostulated his wife. Miss Limpenny blushed.

"They'll come to the workhouse," he went on, "and serve him right for making such a marriage."

"I have heard that his heart is in the right place," pleaded Miss Limpenny, "but he used—"

"Eh, ma'am?"

"It's of no consequence," said Miss Limpenny, with becoming bashfulness. "It's only that he always used, in sorting his cards, to sit upon his trumps—that always seemed to me—"

"Just so," replied the Admiral, "and now it's twins. Bless the man! what next?"

It was in the golden age, before Troy became demoralised, as you shall hear. At present you are to picture the drawing-room of the Misses Limpenny arranged for an "evening": the green rep curtains drawn, the "Book of Beauty" disposed upon the centre table, the ballad music on the piano, and the Admiral's double-bass in the corner. Six wax candles were beaming graciously on cards, tea-cakes and ratafias; on the pictures of "The First Drive," and "The Orphan's Dream," the photographic views of Troy from the harbour, the opposite hill, and one or two other points, and finally the noted oil-painting of Miss Limpenny's papa as he appeared shortly after preaching an assize sermon. Above all, the tea-service was there—the famous set in real silver presented to the late Reverend Limpenny by his flock, and Miss Priscilla—she at the card-table—

wore her best brooch with a lock of his hair arranged therein as a *fleur-de-lys*.

I wish I could convey to you some of the innocent mirth of those "evenings" in Troy—those *noctes Limpennianae* when the ladies brought their cap-boxes (though the Buzzas and Limpennys were but semi-detached neighbours), and the Admiral and his wife insisted on playing against each other, so that the threepenny points never affected their weekly accounts. Those were happy days when the young men were not above singing the "Death of Nelson," or joining in a glee, and arming the young ladies home afterwards. In those days "Hocken's Slip" had not yet become the "Victoria Quay," and we talked of the "Rope Walk" where we now say "Marine Parade." Alas! our tastes have altered with Troy.

Yet we were vastly genteel. We even had our shibboleth, a verdict to be passed before anything could hope for toleration in Troy. The word to be pronounced was "CUMEELFO," and all that was not *Cumeelfo* was Anathema.

So often did I hear this word from Miss Limpenny's lips that I grew in time to clothe it with an awful meaning. It meant to me, as nearly as I can explain, "All Things Sanctioned by the Principles of the Great Exhibition of 1851," and included as time went on—

Crochet Antimacassars.
Art in the style of the "Greek Slave."
"Elegant Extracts," and the British Poets as edited by Gilfillan.
Corkscrew Curls and Prunella Boots.
Album Verses.
Quadrille-dancing, and the *Deux-temps*.
Popular Science.
Proposals on the bended Knee.
Conjuring and Variety Entertainments.
The Sentimental Ballad.
The Proprieties, etc., etc., etc.

The very spirit of this word breathed over the Limpenny drawing-room to-night, and Miss Priscilla's lips seemed to murmur it as she gazed across to where her sister Lavinia was engaged in a round game with the young people. These were Admiral Buzza's three daughters, Sophy, Jane, and Calypso—the last named after her father's old ship—and young Mr. Moggridge, the amusing collector of customs. They were playing with ratafias for counters (ratafias were *cumeelfo*), and peals of guileless laughter from time to time broke in upon the grave silence of the whist-table.

For always, on such occasions, in the glow of Miss Limpenny's wax candles, Youth and Age held opposite camps, with the centre table as debatable ground; nor, until the rubber was finished, and the round game had ended in a seemly scramble for ratafias, would the two recognise each other's presence, save now and then by a "Hush, if you please, young people," from the elder sister, followed by a whispered, "What spirits your dear girls enjoy!" for Mrs. Buzza's ear.

But at length the signal would be given by Miss Priscilla.

"Come, a little music perhaps might leave a pleasant taste. What do you say, Vicar?"

Upon which the Vicar would regularly murmur—

"Say, rather, would gild refined gold, Miss Limpenny."

And the Admiral as invariably broke in with—

"Come, Sophy! remember the proverb about little birds that can sing and won't sing."

This prelude having been duly recited, the Misses Buzza would together trip to the piano, on which the two younger girls in duet were used to accompany Sophia's artless ballads. The performance gained a character of its own from a habit to which Calypso clung, of counting the time in an audible aside: as thus—

Sophia (singing): "Oh, breathe but a whispered command."
Calypso: "One, two, three, four."
Sophia: "I'll lay down my life for thee!"
Calypso: "One, two, three, four."

—the effect of which upon strangers has been known to be paralysing, though we who were *cumeelfo* pretended not to notice it. But Sophy could also accompany her own songs, such as, "Will you love me then as now?" and "I'd rather be a daisy," with much feeling. She was clever, too, with the water-colour brush, and to her we owe that picture of " *H.M.S. Calypso* in a Storm," which hangs to this day over the Admiral's mantelpiece.

I could dwell on this evening for ever; not that the company was so large as usual, but because it was the last night of our simplicity. With the next morning we passed out of our golden age, and in the foolishness of our hearts welcomed the change.

It was announced to us in this manner—

The duets had been beaten out of Miss Limpenny's piano—an early Collard, with a top like a cupboard, fluted in pink silk and wearing a rosette in front; the performers, on retiring, had curtseyed in acknowledgment of the Vicar's customary remark about the "Three Graces "; the Admiral had wrung from his double-bass the sounds we had learnt to identify with elfin merriment (though suggestive, rather, of seasick mutineers under hatches), and our literary collector, Mr. Moggridge, was standing up to recite a trifle of his own—"flung off" —as he explained, "not pruned or polished."

The hush in the drawing-room was almost painful—for in those days we all admired Mr. Moggridge—as the poet tossed back a stray lock from his forehead, flung an arm suddenly out at right angles to his person, and began sepulchrally—

"Maiden" —

(Here he looked very hard at Miss Lavinia Limpenny.)

"Maiden, what dost thou in the chill churchyard
Beside yon grassy mound?
The night hath fallen, the rain is raining hard
Damp is the ground."

Mrs. Buzza shivered, and began to weep quietly.

"Maiden, why claspest thou that cold, cold stone
Against thy straining breast?
Tell me, what dost thou at this hour alone?
(*Persuasively*) The lambs have gone to rest.
The maiden lifted up her tearful gaze,
And thus she made reply:
'My mother, sir, is—'"

But the secret of her conduct remains with Mr. Moggridge, for at this moment the door opened, and the excited head of Sam Buzza, the Admiral's only son, was thrust into the room.

"Maiden, what dost thou in the chill churchyard—"

"I say, have you heard the news? 'The Bower' is let."

"What!"

All eyes were fixed on the newcomer. The Vicar woke up. Even the poet, with his arm still at right angles and the verse arrested on his lips, turned to stare incredulously.

"It's a fact; I heard it down at the *Man-o'-War* Club meeting, you know," he explained. "Goodwyn-Sandys is his name, the Honourable Goodwyn-Sandys, brother to Lord Sinkport—and what's more, he is coming by the mid-day train to-morrow."

The poet's arm dropped like a railway signal. There was a long pause, and then the voices broke out all together—

"Only fancy!"

"There now!"

"'The Bower' let at last!"

"An Honourable, too!"

"What is he like?"

"Are you sure?"

"Well, I never did!"

"Miss Limpenny," gasped the Admiral, at length, "where is your Burke?"

It lay between the "Cathedrals of England" and "Gems of Modern Art"; under the stereoscope. Miss Lavinia produced it.

"Let me see," said the Admiral, turning the pages. "Sinkport—Sinkport—here we are—George St. Leonards Goodwyn-Sandys, fourth baron—H'm, h'm, here it is—only brother, Frederic Augustus Hythe Goodwyn-Sandys, b. 1842—married—"

"Married!"

"1876—Geraldine, eighth daughter of Sheil O'Halloran of Kilmacuddy Court, County Kerry—blank space for issue—arms: gules, a bar sinist—Ahem! Well, upon my word!"

"I'm sure," sighed Mrs. Buzza, after the excitement had cooled a little—"I'm sure I only hope they will settle down to our humble ways."

"Emily," snapped her husband, "you speak like a fool. Pooh! Let me tell you, ma'am, that our ways in Troy are not humble!"

Outside, in Miss Limpenny's back garden, the laurestinus bushes sighed as they caught those ominous words. So might Eden have sighed, aware of its serpent.

CHAPTER II.

HOW AN ADMIRAL TOOK ONE GENTLEMAN FOR ANOTHER,
AND WAS TOLD THE DAY OF THE MONTH.

Next morning, almost before the sun was up, all Troy was in
possession of the news; and in Troy all that is personal has a public
interest. It is this local spirit that marks off the Trojan from all other
minds.

In consequence long before ten o'clock struck, it was clear that some
popular movement was afoot; and by half-past eleven the road to the
railway station was crowded with Trojans of all sorts and
conditions—boatmen, pilots, fishermen, sailors out of employ, the
local photographer, men from the ship-building yards, makers of
ship's biscuit, of ropes, of sails, chandlers, block and pump
manufacturers, loafers—representatives, in short, of all the staple
industries: women with baskets—women with babies, women with
both, even a few farmers in light gigs with their wives, or in carts
with their families, a sprinkling from Penpoodle, across the
harbour—high and low, Church and Dissent, with children by the
hundred. Some even proposed to ring the church bells and fire the
cannon at the harbour's mouth; but the ringers and artillerymen
preferred to come and see the sight. As it was, the "George" floated
proudly from the church tower, and the Fife and Drum Temperance
Band stood ready at the corner of East Street. All Troy, in fact, was
on tip-toe.

Meanwhile, as few in the crowd possessed Burke or Debrett, the
information that passed from mouth to mouth was diverse and
peculiar, but, as was remarked by a laundress in the crowd to a
friend: "He may be the Pope o' Rome, my dear, an' he may be the
Dook o' Wellington, an' not a soul here wud know t'other from
which no mor'n if he was Adam. All I says is—the Lord send he's a
professin' Christian, an' has his linen washed reg'lar. My! What a
crush! I only wish my boy Jan was here to see; but he's stayin' at

9

home, my dear, cos his father means to kill the pig to-day, an' the dear child do so love to hear'n screech."

The Admiral, who happened by the merest chance to be sauntering along the Station Road this morning, in his best blue frock-coat with a flower in the buttonhole, corrected some of the rumours, but without much success. Finding the throng so thick, he held a long debate between curiosity and dignity. The latter won, and he returned to No. 2, Alma Villas, in a flutter, some ten minutes before the train was due.

By noon the crowd was growing impatient. But hardly had the church clock chimed the hour when the shriek of a whistle was heard from up the valley. Amid wild excitement a puff of white smoke appeared, then another, and finally the mid-day train steamed serenely into the station.

As it drew up, a mild spectacled face appeared at the window of a first-class carriage, and asked —

"Is this Troy?"

"Yessir — terminus. Any luggage, sir?"

The mild face got out. It belonged to the only stranger in the train.

"There is only a black portmanteau," said he. "Ah, that is it. I shall want it put in the cloakroom for an hour or two while I go into the town."

The stranger gave up his ticket — a single ticket — and stepped outside the station. He was a mild, thin man, slightly above middle height, with vacant eyes and a hesitating manner. He wore a black suit, a rather rusty top-hat, and carried a silk umbrella.

"Here he comes!"

"Look, that's him!"

"Give 'un a cheer, boys."

"Hip, hip, hoor-roar!"

The sound burst upon the clear sky in a deafening peal. The stranger paused and looked confused.

"Dear me!" he murmured to himself, "the population here seems to be excited about something—and, bless my soul, what a lot of it there is!"

He might well say so. Along the road, arms, sticks, baskets, and handkerchiefs were frantically waving; men shouting and children hurrahing with might and main. Windows were flung up; heads protruded; flags waved in frenzied welcome. The tumult was stupendous. There was not a man, woman, or child in Troy but felt the demonstration must be hearty, and determined to make it a success.

"What *can* have caused this riot?"

The stranger paused with a half-timid air, but after a while resumed his walk. The shouts broke out again, and louder than ever.

"Welcome, welcome to Troy! Hooroar! One more, lads! Hooroar!" and all the handkerchiefs waved anew.

"Bless my soul, what *is* the matter?"

Then suddenly he became aware that all this frantic display was meant for *him*. How he first learnt it he could never afterwards explain, but the shock of it brought a deathly faintness.

"There is some horrible mistake," he murmured hoarsely, and turned to run.

He was too late. The crowd had closed around him, and swept him on, cheering, yelling, vociferating towards the town. He feebly put up a hand for silence—

"My friends," he shouted, "you are—"

"Yes, yes, we know. Welcome! Welcome! Hip-hip-hoo-roar!"

"My friends, I assure you—"

Boom! Boom! Tring-a-ring—boom!

It was that accursed Fife and Drum Temperance Band. In a moment five-and-twenty fifers were blowing "See, the conquering hero comes," with all their breath, and marching to the beat of a deafening drum. Behind them came a serried crowd with the stranger in its midst, and a straggling train of farmers' gigs and screaming urchins closed the procession.

Miss Limpenny, at the first-storey window of No. 1 Alma Villas, heard the yet distant din. With trembling fingers she hung out of window a loyal pocket-handkerchief (worn by her mother at the Jubilee of King George III), shut down the sash upon it, and discreetly retired again behind her white blinds to watch.

The cheering grew louder, and Miss Limpenny's heart beat faster. "I hope," she thought to herself, "I hope that their high connections will not have given them a distaste for our hearty ways. Well as I know Troy, I think I might be frightened at this display of public feeling."

She peeped out over the white blinds. Next door, the Admiral was fuming nervously up and down his gravel walk. He was debating the propriety of his costume. Even yet there was time to run up-stairs and don his cocked hat and gold-laced coat before the procession arrived. Between the claims of his civil and official positions the poor man was in a ferment.

12

"As a man of the world," Miss Limpenny soliloquised, "the Honourable Frederic Goodwyn-Sandys cannot fail to appreciate our sterling Admiral. Dear, dear, here they come! I do trust dearest Lavinia has not put herself in too conspicuous a position at the parlour window. What a lot of people, to be sure!"

The crowd had gathered volume during its passage through the town, and the "Conquering Hero" was more distractingly shrill than ever. The goal was almost reached, for "The Bower" stood next door to Alma Villas, and was divided from them only by a road which led down to the water's edge and the Penpoodle ferry boat.

"Why, everybody is here," said Miss Limpenny, "except, of course, the Vicar. There's Pharaoh Geddye waving a flag, and blind Sam Hockin and Mrs. Hockin with him, I declare, and Bathsheba Merryfield, and Jim the dustman, and Seth Udy in the band—he must have taken the pledge lately—and Walter Sibley and a score I don't even know by sight. And, bless my heart! that's old Cobbledick, wooden leg and all! I thought he was bed-ridden for life. But I don't see the arrivals yet. I wonder who that poor man is, in the crowd—it can't be—and yet—Why, whatever is the Admiral doing?"

For Admiral Buzza had opened his front gate and deliberately stepped out into the road.

The stranger, dishevelled, haggard and bewildered, had long since abandoned all attempts at explanation and fallen into a desperate apathy, when all at once a dozen voices in front cried "Hush!" The band broke off suddenly, and the cheering died away.

"Make way for the Admiral!" "Out of the road, there!" "The Admiral's going to speak!" "Silence for the Admiral!"

The stranger looked up and saw through the opening in the crowd a little man advancing, hat in hand. He had a red face, and the importance of his mission had lent it even a deeper tint than it usually wore: his bald head was fringed with stiff grey hair: he was clothed in "pepper-and-salt" trousers, a blue frock-coat and waistcoat, and carried a large bunch of primroses in his buttonhole. His step was full of dignity and his voice of grave politeness, as he began, with a bow —

"Though not the accredited spokesman of my fellow-citizens here, I am sure I shall not be deemed presumptuous" (cries of "No") "if I venture to give expression to some of the kindly sentiments which I am sure we one and all entertain upon this auspicious occasion." (Loud cheers.) "For upwards of twenty years I have now resided in this beautiful and prosperous—I think I may use these words" ("Hear, hear!") "this beautiful and prosperous little town, and it is therefore with the more sincere pleasure" (here the Admiral laid his hand upon his waistcoat) "that I bid you welcome to Troy." (Frantic cheering.) "We had hoped—I say we had hoped—to have seen your good lady also among us to-day: but doubtless when 'The Bower' is prepared—the—ahem! the bird will fly thither."

Vociferous applause followed this impromptu trope, and for some moments the Admiral's voice was completely drowned.

"I hope and trust," he went on, as soon as silence was restored, "that she enjoys good health."

The stranger looked more perplexed than ever.

"But be that as it may—be that, I say, as it may, my pleasant duty is now discharged. In the name of my fellow-Trojans and in my own name I bid you a hearty welcome to 'The Bower.'" (Loud and continuous cheering, during which the Admiral handed his card with a flourish, and mopped his brow.)

"I can assure you," replied the stranger after a pause, "that I am deeply sensible of your kindness—" (The cheering was renewed.) "While conscious," he went on, "that I have done nothing to deserve it. In point of fact, I think you must all be labouring under some ridiculous delusion."

"What do you mean, sir?" gasped the Admiral. "Do you mean to say you are not the new tenant of this delightful residence?" Then the speaker waved his hand in the direction of "The Bower."

"Certainly I am not."

"Then, damme, sir! who are you?" cried the Admiral, whose temper was, as we know, short.

"My name is Fogo," replied the stranger. "Here is my card—Philip Fogo—at your service."

Even Miss Limpenny, with the first-floor window of No. 1 timidly lifted to admit the Admiral's eloquence; even the three Misses Buzza, arranged in a row behind the parlour blinds of No. 2, and gazing with fond pride upon their papa; even Mrs. Buzza, nervously clasping her hands on the upper storey;—could not but perceive that something dreadful was happening. The Admiral's face turned from crimson to purple; he positively choked.

The situation needed a solution. A wag among the crowd hit upon it.

"Tell th' Admiral, some of 'ee: what day es et?"

"Fust of April!" cried a voice, then another; and then—

Then the throng broke into roar upon roar of inextinguishable laughter. The whole deluded town turned and cast its April folly, as a garment, upon the Admiral's shoulders. It was in vain that he stamped and raved and swore. They only held their sides and laughed the louder.

The credit of Trojan humour was saved. With a final oath the Admiral dashed through his front gate and into the house. The *volgus infidum* formed in procession again, and marched back with shouts of merriment; the *popularis aura* of the five-and-twenty fifers resumed the "Conquering Hero," and Mr. Fogo was left standing alone in the middle of the road.

CHAPTER III.

OF A BLUE-JERSEYED MAN THAT WOULD HOIST NO MORE
BRICKS; AND A NIGHTCAP THAT HAD NO BUSINESS TO BE
WHERE IT WAS.

No one acquainted with the character of that extraordinary town will
be surprised when I say that, within an hour after the occurrences
related in the last chapter, Troy had resumed its workday quiet. By
two o'clock nothing was to be heard but the tick-tack of mallets in
the ship-building yards, the puffing of the steam-tug, the rattle of
hawsers among the vessels out in the harbour, and the melodious
"Woo-hoo!" of a crew at capstan or windlass. Troy in carnival and
Troy sober are as opposite, you must know, as the poles. Fun is all
very well, but business is business, and Troy is a trading port with a
character to keep up: for who has not heard the bye-word—
"Working like a Trojan"?

At two o'clock on this same day a little schooner lay alongside the
town quay, busily discharging bricks. That is to say, a sunburnt man,
blue-jerseyed and red with brick-dust, leisurely turned a windlass
which let down an empty bucket and brought it up full. Another
blue-jerseyed man, also sunburnt and red with brick-dust, then
pulled it on shore, emptied and returned it; and the operation was
repeated. A choleric little man, of about fifty, presumably the
proprietor of the bricks, stood on the edge of the quay, and swore
alternately at the man with the windlass and the man ashore.

"Look 'ere," said the man at the windlass, after a bit. "Stop cussin'.
This ain't a hurdy-gurdy, and if you expec's music you'll have to toss
us a copper."

The owner of the bricks swore worse than ever.

Round went the windlass as leisurely as might be and another bucketful was hoisted ashore. The man on deck spat on his hands, and broke into cheerful song:—

> "Was you iver to Que-bec,
>   Bonnie laddie, Hieland laddie
> Was you iver to Que-bec,
> Rousing timber over the deck?
>   Hey my bonny laddie!
> Wur-roo! my heart's—"

The rage of the little man found extra vent.

"Look here, Caleb Trotter," he concluded, after a full minute of profanity, "how do you think I'm to get my living and pay a set of lubberly dolts like you?"

Caleb paused with his hand on the windlass, and suggested retrenchment of the halfpenny a week hitherto spent in manners. "'Cos, you see, all this po-liteness of yourn es a'runnin' to waste," he explained with fine irony.

But before the next load was more than three-parts hoisted, Caleb's patience was exhausted. What he did was simple but decisive. He removed his hold; the handle whizzed violently round, and the bucket of bricks descended to the hold with a crash.

"Now I tell 'ee straight. Enough's enough; an' I han't got time, at my time o' life, to be po-lite to ivery red-faced chap I meets. You can pay me or no, as you likes; but I'm off to get a drink. An' that's all about et; an' wen 'tes over, 'tes over, as Joan said by her weddin'."

With this Caleb stepped ashore, spat good-naturedly, put his hands in his pockets, and went off whistling.

At this moment Mr. Fogo, who had been on the quay long enough to hear this altercation, touched him softly by the arm.

"You said you were going to have a drink, I believe. May I go with you? I wish to ask you a few questions."

"You said you were going to have a drink,
I believe. May I go with you?"

"Sutt'nly, sir," said Caleb with a stifled grin, as he recognised the hero of the morning. "I generally patronises the 'King o' Prooshia' for beer. It won't make your hair curl, nor yet prevent your seein' a hole dro' a ladder: but perhaps neither o' these is your objec'."

Mr. Fogo, a little bewildered, replied modestly that he pursued neither of these aims. Caleb led the way across the quay, and they ascended the steps of the "King of Prussia" together.

"My object," said Mr. Fogo timidly, as they were seated together in the low-roofed parlour before two foaming mugs—"My object was this. In the first place, I like your look."

"Same to you, sir," said Caleb, and acknowledged the compliment with a draught, "though 'tes what my gal said afore she desarted me for a Rooshan."

"Are you a single man, then?"

"To be sure, sir."

"So much the better—but I will talk of that presently. I, too, am a single man, with rather peculiar tastes. One of these is solitude. I had heard of Troy as a place where I was likely to find this, though my experience of this morning—"

Fig4.

"Never mind, sir. Accidents will happen even in the best reggylated families. You was took for another, which has happened even to Bible characters afore this—though Jacob's the only one I can call to mind just now."

"Still, I should be sorry to go back with the knowledge that my journey has been in vain. But I must have solitude at any price, and the reason why I am consulting you is that you might possibly know of a house to let in this neighbourhood, where I could be alone and secure against visitors."

Caleb scratched his head.

"I'm sure, sir, 'tes hard to say. Troy's a powerful place for knowin' what your neighbour's got for dinner, and they *do* say as the Admiral's telescope will carry dro' a brick wall."

Mr. Fogo's face fell.

"Stop a bit," said Caleb more brightly. "About livin' inside o' the town, now—es that a shiny cannon?"

"A what?"

"A shiny cannon—which es the same as to say, won't et do elst?"

"Oh, a *sine-qua-non*," said Mr. Fogo; "no, I am not particularly anxious to live in the town itself."

"Wud the matter of a mile up the river be out o' the way?"

"Not at all."

"An' about rent?"

"Within reasonable limits, that would not matter."

"Then my advice to you, sir, es to see the Twins about et."

Mr. Fogo's mild face looked more puzzled than ever. He removed his spectacles, wiped and resumed them.

"For any reasonable object," he said, "I am ready to see any number of twins—much as I dislike babies—"

But here Caleb interrupted him by bursting into a roar of laughter which lasted for half a minute.

"Babbies! Well I—ho! ho!—'scuse me, sir—but aw dear, aw dear! Babbies! Bab—" Here he slapped his thigh and broke into another roar, at the end of which he grew fairly black in the face.

"Bless yer innocent heart, sir! They'm a matter o' six foot high, the both—and risin' forty. Dearlove's their name—and lives up the river 'long wi' their sister—Peter an' Paul an' Tamsin (which es short for Thom-a-si-na), an' I've heerd tell as the boys came nigh to bein'

20

chrisn'd Sihon an' Og, on'y the old Vicar said he'd be blowed fust—very free wi' his langwidge was th' ould Vicar."

"I should fancy so," said Mr. Fogo; "but you'll excuse me if I don't quite see, yet, why you advise me to call on these people."

"No offence, sir. On'y they owns Kit's House, that's all."

"I see; and Kit's House is the place you have in your mind."

"That's et, sir."

"And these Dearloves, where do they live?"

"Furder up the river by two mile."

"Could you row me up this afternoon to see them?"

Caleb Trotter rose, and drew the back of his hand across his mouth.

"Wi' all the pleasure in life, sir, as Uncle Zachy said when he gi'ed his da'ter in marriage."

In less than ten minutes Caleb had brought his boat round to the quay. Mr. Fogo stepped in, and was presently seated in the stern and meditatively listening while Caleb rowed—and talked—"like a Trojan."

Here we may leave them for a while and return to the Admiral, whom we left in the act of plunging furiously into his own house. It was not the habit of that fiery little tar to hide his emotions from the wife of his bosom.

"Emily!" he bellowed, "Em-i-ly, I say! Come down this instant."

The three Misses Buzza at the parlour window knew the tone, and shuddered: Mrs. Buzza, up-stairs, heard, trembled, and obeyed.

"Yes, darling. What is it?"

"Fill the warming-pan at once. I'm going to bed."

"To bed, love!"

"Yes, to bed. Don't I speak plainly enough? To bed, ma'am, to bed, and at once."

"You are upset, dearest; be cool, I implore you."

"Be cool! Be coo'—Don't hector me, ma'am, but fetch that warming-pan at once. I'll teach you about being cool! Sophy, pull off my boots."

They obeyed. The warming-pan was brought—an enormous engine, big enough to hold the Admiral himself—and the bed heated. The Admiral undressed, and, himself a warming-pan of rage, plunged between the sheets. It was a wonder the bed-clothes were not on fire.

"Pull down the blind, and bring me something to eat!"

"Yes, love."

"And be quick about it. Can't you see I'm starving?"

It is true that the Admiral's excitement had interfered with his breakfast that morning, but it was none the less difficult to read starvation upon his face. Mrs. Buzza obeyed, however; and presently returned with the liver-wing of a fowl.

"You call that a dinner for a hungry man, I suppose! Bring me some more!"

"My dear, I didn't know you wanted a dinner."

"Confound it, ma'am! must I put dress-studs in my night-shirt to convince you I want to dine? Bring me some more!"

"There is no more fowl, dear. I kept this from yesterday's as a tit-bit for you."

"What is for dinner to-day?"

"Boiled beef: but you said expressly that dinner was to be late to-day, in consequence of the arrivals, and it is not nearly done yet."

"I don't care, bring it!"

The mention of the arrivals sent the Admiral up to a white heat again.

"But, my—"

"Bring it!"

It was brought. The Admiral had two helpings, and then a glass of grog.

"Go."

Mrs. Buzza withdrew. Left to himself, the Admiral tossed, and turned, and fumed, and swore, lay still for a while, and then repeated the process backwards. After a time the bed-clothes began to prick him, and the heat to become a positive torture. He leapt out, and tore at the bell-rope, until it came away in his hand—just as his wife reappeared.

"Will you kindly inform me what the devil's wrong with this bed? Who made it?"

"Selina, dear."

"Then will you kindly give Selina a month's notice on the spot? Do you hear? On the spot—What's that?"

The Admiral rushed to the window and pulled up the blind. He was just in time to see a close carriage and pair dash past and pull up at "The Bower."

A moment afterwards, Miss Limpenny, from the first-storey window of No. 1, saw the carriage door open, and a tall gentleman emerge. The tall gentleman was followed by a lady, whom even at that distance Miss Limpenny could see to possess a remarkably graceful figure. A small youth in livery sprang down from beside the coachman and helped to lower the boxes, whilst the new arrivals passed into the house where the charwoman, Mrs. Snell, stood smearing her face with her apron, and ducking in frenzied welcome.

The Honourable Frederic Augustus Hythe Goodwyn-Sandys and his wife, instead of arriving by train, had posted from Five-Lanes Junction.

There was no public demonstration. They might as well have come in the dead of night. Miss Limpenny was almost the sole witness of their arrival, and Miss Limpenny's observations were cut short by a terrible occurrence.

She had taken stock of the Honourable Frederic, and pronounced him "aristocratic-looking"; of the Honourable Mrs. Frederic's travelling-dress, and decided it to be *Cumeelfo*; she had counted the boxes twice, and made them seven each time; she was about to count the buttons on the liveried youth, when —

To this day she sinks her voice as she narrates it. She saw — the unseemliness, the monstrous indelicacy of it! — she saw — the nightcap and shoulders of Admiral Buzza craning out of the next-door window!

What happened next? Whether she actually fainted, or merely kept her eyes shut, she cannot clearly remember. But for weeks afterwards, as she declares, the sight of a man caused her to "turn all colours."

It was significant, this nightcap of Admiral Buzza—as the ram's horn to Jericho, the Mother Carey's chicken to the doomed ship. It announced, even as it struck, the first blow at the old morality of Troy.

CHAPTER IV.

OF CERTAIN LEPERS; AND TWO BROTHERS,
WHO, BEING MUCH ALIKE, LOVED THEIR SISTER,
AND RECOMMENDED THE USE OF GLOBES.

I must here clear myself on a point which has no doubt caused the reader some indignation. "We remarked," he or she will say, "that, some chapters back, the Admiral described Troy as a 'beautiful little town.' Why, then, have we had no description of it, no digressions on scenery, no word-painting?"

To this I answer—Dear sir, or madam, no one who has known Troy was ever yet capable of describing it. If you doubt me, visit the town and see for yourself. I will for the moment suppose you to do so. What happens?

On the first day you take a boat and row about the harbour. "Scenery!" you exclaim, "why, what could you have more? Here is a lovely harbour flanked by bold hills to right and left; here are the ruined castles, witnesses of the great days when Troy sent ships to carry the English army to Agincourt; here axe grey houses huddled at the water's edge, hoary, battered walls and quay-doors coated with ooze and green weed. Such is Troy, and on the further shore quaint Penpoodle faces it, where a silver creek, dividing, runs up to Lanbeg; further up, the harbour melts into a river where the old ferry-boat plies to and from the foot of a tiny village straggling up the hill; further yet, and the jetties mingle with the steep woods beside the roads, where the vessels lie thickest; ships of all builds and of all nations, from the trim Canadian timber-ship to the corpulent Billy-boy. Why, the very heart of the picturesque is here. What more can you want?"

On the second day you will see all this from the harbour again, or perhaps you will cross the ferry and climb the King's Walk on the opposite bank; you will see it all, but with a change. It is more lovely, but not the same.

On the third day you will cast about in your mind to explain this; and so in time you will come to find that it is the spirit of Troy that plays this trick upon you. For you will have learnt to love the place, and love, as you know, dear sir or madam, is apt to affect the eyesight.

The eyes of Mr. Fogo, as Caleb pulled sturdily up with the tide, were passing through the first of these stages.

"This," he said at length, reflectively, "is one of the loveliest spots I have looked upon."

Caleb, in whom humanity and Trojanity were nicely compounded, flushed a bright copper-colour with pleasure.

"'Tes reckoned a tidy spot," he answered modestly, "by them as cares for voos an' such-like."

"There, now," he went on, after a pause, and turning round, "yonder's Kit's House, wi' Kit's Cottage, next door. You can't see the house so plain, 'cos 'tes behind the trees. But there 'tes, right enough."

"Is the cottage uninhabited, too?"

"Both on 'em. Ha'nted they *do* say. By the way, I niver axed 'ee whether you minded ghostes?"

"Ghosts?"

"Iss, ghostes. This 'ere place was a Lazarus one time, where they kept leppards."

"Leopards? How very singular!" murmured Mr. Fogo.

"Ay, leppards as white as snow, as the sayin' goes."

"Oh, I see," said Mr. Fogo, suddenly enlightened. "You mean that this was a Lazar-house."

"That's so—a Lazarus. The leppards used to live there together, and when they died, they was berried at dead o' night down at thicky spit you sees yonder. No one had dealin's wi' 'em nor went nigh 'em, 'cept that they was allowed to make ropes. 'Tesn' so many years that the rope-walk was moved down to th' harbour mouth."

Caleb stopped rowing, and leant forward on his paddles.

"These 'ere leppards in time got to be quite a happy famb'ly—'cept, of course, they warn't happy, 'cos nobody wudn' have nuthin' to say to 'em. Well, the story goes as one on 'em got falled in love wi' by a very nice gal down in Troy, and one fine day she ups an' tells her sorrowin' parents that she's agoin' to marry a leppard. 'Not ef we knows et,' says they; 'we forbids the banns'; and wi' that they went off to bed thinkin' as they'd settled et. 'But,' says Parson Lasky—"

"Who was he?" interrupted Mr. Fogo.

"On'y a figger o' speech, sir, and nothin' to do wi' the yarn, as the strollin' actor said when his theayter cotched a-fire. Wot I meant was, that very night the gal gets a boat an' rows up to Kit's House, arter leavin' a letter to say as she'd drownded hersel'. An' there she lived in hidin', 'long wi' the leppards for the rest of her days, which, by the tale, warn't many, an' she an' her sweetheart was berried in wan grave." Caleb paused for breath.

"And the ghosts?" said Mr. Fogo, much interested.

"Some ha' seed her rowin' about here in a boat, o' dark nights; and others swear to seein' all the leppards a-marchin' down wi' her corpse to the berryin'-ground. Leastways, that's the tale. Jan Spettigue was the last as seed 'em, but as he be'eld three devils on his own chimbly-piece the week arter, along o' too much rum, p'r'aps he made a mistake. Anyways, 'tes a moral yarn, an' true to natur'. These young wimmen es a very detarmined sex, whether 'tes a leppard in the case or a Rooshan."

Mr. Fogo had fallen into a reflective silence.

"'Tes a thousand pities this 'ere place should be empty, wi' a lean-to Crystal Pallis—by which I means a conserva-tory, sir—an' gardens, an' room for a cow, an' a Pyll o' ets own—"

"A what?"

"Pyll, sir, otherwise a creek—'c, r, double e, k—an arm o' the sea,' as the spellin' book says."

A curious fascination stole over Mr. Fogo as he looked earnestly at the house round which these memories hung. Standing on an angle formed by the bending river, and the little creek, and behind a screen of trees—elms almost too old to feel the sap of spring, a chestnut or two, and a few laurels and sombre firs, that had cracked with their roots the grey garden wall and sprawled down to the beach below— the stained and yellow frontage looked down towards the busy harbour, as it seemed with a sense of serene decay, haunted but without disquietude, like the face of an old lady who has memories and lives in them, though she deigns to contemplate a life from which her hopes, with her old friends and lovers, have dropped out. Perhaps Mr. Fogo had some sympathy with this mood; for Caleb, after waiting some time for his reply, took to his paddles again with a will, and presently the boat, sweeping round a projecting rock, passed into a very different scene.

Here the river, shut in on the one side with budding trees to the water's edge, on the other with bracken and patches of ploughed land to where the cliffs broke sheer away, stretched for some miles without bend or break. Far ahead a blue bank of woodland closed the view. Not a sound disturbed the stillness, not a sail broke the placid expanse of water.

But a true Trojan must still be talking. Presently Caleb resumed.

"'Tes a luvly spot, as you said, sir. Mr. Moggridge down at the customs—he's a poet, as maybe you know—has written a mint o' verses about this 'ere place. 'Natur', he says:—"

> "Natur' has 'ere assoomed her softest garb;
>   'Ere would I live an' die

"—which I calls a very touchin' sentiment, an' like what they says in a nigger song."

With such conversation Mr. Trotter beguiled the way until they came abreast of a tiny village almost buried in apple trees and elms. On the opposite bank, a thin column of blue smoke was curling up from among the dense woodland.

Caleb headed the boat for this smoke, ran her nose on the pebbles beneath a low cliff, and stepped out.

"'Ere we are, sir."

"But I don't see any house," said Mr. Fogo, perplexed.

"All in good time, sir," replied Mr. Trotter, and having fastened up the boat, led the way.

A narrow flight of steps, hewn out of the rock, led up to the little cliff. At the top, and almost hidden by bushes, stood a low gate. Thence the path wound for a space between walls of budding hazel, and at its end quite unexpectedly a tiny cottage burst upon Mr. Fogo's view.

Little dreaming that the owner of Kit's House could live in such humility, he was considerably surprised when Caleb stepped up and struck a rousing knock upon the door.

It was opened by a comely girl with a white apron pinned before her neat stuff gown, and a face as fresh and healthful as a spring day.

"Why, Caleb," she cried, "who would have thought it? Come inside; you're as welcome as flowers in May."

"And you," replied Caleb gallantly, "are a-lookin' so sweet as blossom. Here's a gentlem'n come to call upon 'ee, my dear. An' how's Peter an' Paul? Brave, I hopes."

"Both, thank you, Caleb," said the maiden, curtseying without embarrassment to Mr. Fogo. "Won't you come in, sir?"

It was noticeable that Mr. Fogo at this point became very nervous, but he crossed the threshold in answer to this invitation. Mr. Trotter followed.

The fragrant smoke of a wood fire filled the room in which Mr. Fogo found himself. It was a rude kitchen, with white limeash floor, and for ceiling, a few whitewashed beams and the planching of the bedroom above. All was scrupulously clean. In the flickering obscurity of the chimney depended a line of black pot-hooks and hangers; a trivet and a pair of bellows furnished the hearth; from the capacious rack hung a rich stock of hams and sides of bacon, curing in the smoke; an English clock stood in one corner, a tall cupboard in another, and a geranium in the window-seat. Along the side opposite the door, and parallel to a dresser of shining crockery, ran a strong deal table. Some high-backed chairs, a pair of brass candlesticks with snuffers, a book or two, a few old hats, and a lanthorn, on various pegs, completed the furniture of the place.

But Mr. Fogo's gaze was riveted on two men who rose together at his entrance from the table where they were seated, side by side, at their tea.

Both tall, both adorned with crisp curls of black hair—with clean-shaven, mahogany faces, and the gentlest of possible smiles, the twins came forward to greet the stranger. So appallingly alike were

31

they that Mr. Fogo felt a ridiculous desire to run away, nor could help fancying himself the victim of a disordered dream.

The Twins advanced upon him simultaneously with outstretched horny palms. He noticed that even their dress was precisely similar, with the single exception that one wore a red, the other a yellow bandanna handkerchief loosely knotted about his throat.

The Twins advanced upon him simultaneously.

"You'm kindly welcome, sir," said the Twin with the red bandanna; and the Twin with the yellow neck-cloth murmured "kindly welcome," like an echo.

"Stop a bit," interposed Caleb, "let's do a bit of introducin'. This here es Mr. Fogo, gent, as es thinkin' of rentin' Kit's House, and es come for that puppos'. That there es Peter Dearlove—him wi' the red neckercher; likewise Paul Dearlove—him wi' the yaller. An', beggin' yer pardon for passin' over the ladies, this es Tamsin Dearlove (christ'n'd Thomasina), dearly beloved sister o' the same," concluded Caleb, with a sudden recollection of having read something like this on a tombstone.

Tamsin curtseyed, and the two horny palms were again presented. Not knowing which to take first,

Mr. Fogo held his umbrella between his knees and gave them a hand a-piece.

"I am afraid, Mr.—" He hesitated with a suspicion that he ought to say "Messrs."

"Dearlove," suggested Caleb; "an' reckoned a purty name, too."

"I am afraid, Mr. Dearlove," repeated Mr. Fogo, compromising matters by staring hard between the Twins, "that we have interrupted you."

"Not at all, sir," said Peter. "Sit down, sir, ef you'm not proud. Tamsin, bring a cup for the gentleman. A piece o' pasty, sir? Tamsin es famous for pasties."

Mr. Fogo, remembering that, with the exception of the mug of beer at the "King of Prussia," he had not broken his fast since the morning, and seeing also that the hospitality was anxiously sincere, complied. In a few moments both he and Caleb were seated before a steaming pasty.

Tamsin poured out the tea. She was a full twenty years younger than her brothers, as could be seen notwithstanding their boyish look, which came from innocence and clean-shaven faces. It was pleasant to see their almost fatherly pride in her. Mr. Fogo noted it vaguely, but an inexplicable nervousness seemed to have overtaken him since entering the cottage.

"I came," he said at last, "to inquire about Kit's House, which I hear is to let."

"Thankin' you kindly, sir," answered Peter; "an' I won't say but what we shall be glad to let et. But Paul and I ha' been puttin' our heads togither, and we allow 'tes for Tamsin to say."

Here he looked at Paul, who nodded gravely and repeated, in his former mechanical tone, "for Tamsin to say."

Mr. Fogo looked more distressed than ever.

"I beg your pardon, I'm sure," he began, with a quick glance at the girl, who was quietly pouring tea; "I did not know."

"No offence, sir. On'y, don't you see, 'tes this way. Kit's House es a gran' place wi' a slaty roof an' a I-talian garden, and a mighty deal too fine for the likes of Paul an' me. But wi' Tamsin 'tes another thing. We both agree she ought to be a leddy—not but what she's a better gal than tens o' thousands o' leddies—an' more than once we've offered to get her larnt the pi-anner an' callysthenics, an' the use o' globes, an' all such things which we knows to be usual in gran' sussiety; on'y she sticks to et to bide along wi' we. God bless her! I say, an' a rough life et must be for her."

Tamsin turned away towards the fireplace, and became very busy among the pot-hooks and hangers. Her brother pulled out a red handkerchief—a fellow to the one around his neck—mopped his face and proceeded—

"Well, as I was a-saying, seein' she was bent on bein' wi' us, Paul and me allowed to each other that we'd set up in fine style at Kit's House, so as not to rob her of what es her doo: that es to say—one of us wou'd live down there wi' a car'ge and pair o' hosses, and cut a swell wi' dinner parties an' what-not, while the other bided here an' tilled 'taties, turn and turn about. But she wudn' hear o' that, neither. She's a terrible stubborn gal, bless her!"

"We shou'd ha' been slow at larnin' the ropes, just at fust," he resumed after a moment's silence, "not bein' scholards, partikler at the use o' globes, which I *have* heerd es diffycult, though very entertainin' in company when you knows how 'tes done. But we was ready to try a hand—on'y she wudn' have et, an' so et has gone on. But, beggin' your pardon, sir, and hopin' no offence, she shall give her answer afore 'tes too late. Eh, Paul?"

34

"You have spoken, Peter," said the other twin, very slowly, "like a printed book. Let Tamsin speak her mind about et."

The girl came forward from the fireplace, and Mr. Fogo, as he stole a glance at her, could see that her eyes were red.

"What do 'ee say, Tamsin? Must we let Kit's House, or shall we leave th' ould place an' go an' make a leddy of 'ee?"

Tamsin's reply was to fall on her knees before the speaker and break into a fit of weeping.

"Don't ask me, don't ask me! I don't want to be a lady, an' I *won't* leave you. Don't ask me, my dear, dear brothers!"

Peter stroked the dark head buried in his lap, while Paul blew his nose violently in a yellow bandanna, and replied to Mr. Fogo.

"Very well, sir, so be et. There's the key of Kit's House yonder on the nail. Ef you likes to look over the place, one of us will follow you presently, and then, supposin' et to be to your likin', us can talk over terms."

CHAPTER V.

HOW AN ABSENT-MINDED MAN, THAT HATED WOMEN,
TOOK A HOUSE BY THE WATER-SIDE,
AND LIVED THEREIN WITH ONE SERVANT.

"Well, sir," said Caleb Trotter, when the boat was pushed off, "what do 'ee think of 'em?"

Mr. Fogo, whose wits had been wool-gathering, came to himself with a start. "I think they are very good people."

"You may say that! The likes o' those Twins you won't see again, not ef you live to be a hundred. Seems to me," he went on reflectively, "that Natur', when she turned out the fust, got so pleased wi' herself that she was bound to try her hand at a dooplicity, just to relieve her feelin's."

"A what?"

"A dooplicity, sir, otherwise another of the same identical."

"Oh, I see."

"Iss, sir. 'Tes like that rhyme about the Force o' Natur' what cudn' no furder go, and you can't do 't agen, not ef you try all you know."

"You are fond of poetry, I see," said Mr. Fogo, with a smile.

"Puffec'ly dotes on et, sir."

"Have you ever composed any yourself?"

"Once 'pon a time, sir," said Caleb, pausing in his work, and leaning forward very mysteriously. "Ef you cares to hear, I don't mind tellin' 'ee; on'y you must gi' me your Davy you won't let et out to nobody."

Mr. Fogo gave the required promise.

"Well, 'twas in this way. Once 'pon a time, me an' old Joe Bonaday was workin' a smack round from Bristol. The *Betsy Ann* was her name, No. 1077 o' Troy. Joe was skipper, an' me mate; there was a boy aboard for crew, but he don't count. Well us got off Ilfrycombe one a'ternoon—August month et was, an' pipin' hot—when my blessed parlyment, says Molly Franky—"

"Who was she?"

"Another figger o' speech, sir, that's all. Well, as I was a-sayin', on a sudden, lo and be'old! the breeze drops dead. Ef you'll believe me, sir, 'twas calm as the Sar'gossa Sea. So there we was stuck—the sail not so much as flappin'—for the best part o' two hour; at the end o' which time (Joe not bein' a convussational man beyond sayin' 'thankye' when he got hes vittles) I was gettin' a bit dumb-foundered for topicks to talk 'pon. 'Cos, as for the weather, there 'twas, an', as Joe remarked, 'twasn' going to move any more for our discussin' of et, nor yet cussin' for that matter."

"I see."

"Well, sir, we was driven at last to singin' a hymn to keep our speerits up. Leastways, the boy an' me sang, an' Joe beat time. Then says Joe, 'Look 'ere, I'm a-goin' to allee-couchee ef et lasts like this.' 'Well,' I says, for I was gettin' desprit, 'have 'ee ever tried to make poetry?' 'No,' says he, 'can't say I have.' 'Well,' I says, 'I've oft'n wanted to. Let's ha' a shy. You go aft and think of a verse, an' I'll go forra'd an' make another, an' then us'll see which sounds best.' 'Done,' says he, an' off he goes.

"Well, I sits there for mor'n an hour, thinkin' hard, and terrable work I found et. At last Joe shouts across, 'Hav'ee done? Time's up'; and I told 'un I'd done purty middlin'. So us stepped amidships, and spoke out what us had made."

Caleb made a long pause.

"I should like to hear the verses, if you remember them," said Mr. Fogo.

"Should 'ee now?" Caleb asked with fine modesty. "Well, I don't mind, on'y you mus'n' expect 'em to be like Maister Moggridge's. Mine went thicky way." He recited very slowly, with a terrific rolling of syllables:—

> "See her glidin' dro' the water,
>   Far, far away!
> Many a true heart's niver to be found.

"The last line alludes to my gal wot had recently e-loped wi' the Rooshan," Caleb explained.

"Was that all?"

"That was all o' mine, sir, but Joe's was p'ints better. Just listen:—"

"Fare thee well, Barnstaple steeple,—"

"(He was a Barnstaple man, sir, was Joe)—"

> "Fare thee well, I say,
>   Never shall I see thee, once agen, a long time ago."

"Well, sir, we was just a-goin' to step back an' have another shy, when the breeze sprang up a'most as sudden as et fell, and the consikence es, sir, that I've niver made no more poetry from that day to this."

The sun was getting low, as Mr. Fogo and Caleb stepped ashore on the ruined quay at Kit's House, not far from the spit of land where the lazars were buried. Kit's Cottage stood plain to see at a short distance from the water, but Kit's House lay to the right, behind its screen of laurels and elms. A narrow flight of steps and a path along the cliff's edge brought the visitors to the front door.

It was a long, low house, with pointed windows on the upper storey, and a deep verandah shading the ground-floor rooms. It faced the south, and although few flowers were out, the ruined garden was luxuriant with decay. One could see where the old Lazar-house had been overlaid with the taste of more recent inhabitants, but, as Caleb said, no one had lived here now for a dozen years or more. The walls were smeared with green vegetation; the iron gate creaked heavily with rust. On the roof the stonecrop flourished, and the swallows had built their nests about the chimneys.

Indoors it was as bad. Rich papers hung and rotted from the walls; rats scampered about the floors overhead; a smell of damp and mouldiness pervaded every room.

"Deary me, sir!" said Caleb in despair, "I'd no idee 'twas as bad as this, or I wou'dn' have mentioned the place to 'ee."

An old barrel stood on end before the French-window of the drawing-room. Mr. Fogo seated himself on this, and gazed meditatively out on the mellow glory of the evening.

"Caleb," he said very quietly, after a while, "I think I shall take this house."

"You will, sir?"

"I fancy there will be no difficulty in arranging about the rent. And now I want to speak with you on another question. You are a single man, you say. Have you any employment?"

"Why, sir, I mostly picks up my livin' on the say, on'y I thought as how I'd like a spell ashore for a change; but the end o' that you saw for yourself this very a'ternoon."

"Do you think that for a pound a week you could look after me?"

"I'd like the chance."

"That would exclude your food and clothes."

Caleb hesitated for a moment, and then said, with Trojan independence—

"You beant' a-goin' to rig me out in a yaller weskit an' small-clothes wi' a stripe down the leg, by any chance?"

"I was proposing that you should dress exactly as you do at present."

"Then done wi' you, sir, an' thank 'ee. When be I to enter on my dooties?"

"At once."

"An' where, sir?"

"Here."

"Be you a-goin' to sleep the night in this moloncholy place?"

"Certainly."

"Very well, sir. Please yoursel', as Dick said to the press-gang. An' what be I to do fust?"

Mr. Fogo perhaps did not hear the question, for he was gazing out at the falling shadows: when he spoke again it was upon another subject.

"It is right that you should know," said he, "the kind of life you will be wanted to lead. In the first place, I am extraordinarily subject to fits of abstraction—absence of mind, in other words. It is an affection to which my style of life has made me particularly prone: it has led me before now into absurd, and sometimes into dangerous situations.

"I *have* heard tell," said Caleb, "of an old gentl'm'n as carefully tucked hes umbrella in bed an' put hissel' in the corner. Es that the style o' thing, sir?"

"It is something similar," said his master, "and within certain limits I should expect you to look after me and as far as possible prevent such accidents: however, I shall not, of course, expect you to have more than one pair of eyes. My tastes are simple—I read a little, sketch a little, botanise, dabble in chemistry, am fond of carpentering—boat-building especially. My very absence of mind makes me indifferent to surroundings. In short, I am a mild man."

Mr. Fogo got off his barrel, went to the window, sighed softly, and returned. Something in his manner imposed silence on Caleb.

"We shall live here alone," he resumed. "It is even possible that, to ensure solitude, I shall rent the cottage as well, and install you there. Above all things, remember," with sudden sternness, "that no woman is to come near this house—I shall even expect you to do your utmost to prevent their landing on the quay below. That, I think, is all. I now wish you to row down to the station and get my portmanteau. After that, with this money procure a couple of hammocks, besides provisions and whatever will be necessary for the night, not forgetting soap and candles. To-morrow we will take in further stock."

Caleb was about to make some answer when the garden gate creaked heavily, and Peter Dearlove appeared in the dusk outside the window; so he merely took the money, touched his forelock by way of acknowledging his new employment, and retired. But it was noticeable that once or twice on his way to the boat he had to pull himself up and think a bit. Arrived on the quay, too, he stood for a moment or so beside the boat in profound meditation.

"Come, Caleb Trotter!" he exclaimed, suddenly jumping in and seizing the paddles; "this sort o' thing won't do, nohow. Here you be paid for lookin' arter a gentl'm'n as wanders in hes wits, and fust news es, you be doin' the same yoursel'. 'Tes terribul queer, though," he added, and with that began to row towards town with an energy that set the boat quivering.

When he returned, in less than two hours' time, he found Mr. Fogo with a barrel full of water and the stump of a decayed broom, washing out the back kitchen. The Twin had gone.

"Here we be, sir. Pound o' candles, pound o' tea, two loaves o' bread, knives, forks, two cups, three eggs—one on 'em smashed, in my trowsy pocket—saucepan, kettle, tea-pot, an' a hunk o' cold beef as salt as Lot's wife's elbow. That's the fust load. There's more in the boat, but I must ax'ee to bear a hand wi' thicky portmanty o' youm, 'cos 'tes mortal heavy. I see'd Jan Higgs's wife a-fishin' about two hundred yards from the quay, on my way up, an' warned her to keep her distance. There's a well o' water round at the back, an' I've fetched a small sack o' coal, and ef us don't have a dish o' tay ready in a brace o' shakes, then Tom's killed an' Mary's forlorn."

With the statement of which gloomy alternative Mr. Caleb Trotter broke into a smile of honest pride.

"Caleb," said Mr. Fogo from his hammock in the back kitchen at about eleven o'clock on the same night.

"Aye, aye, sir."

"Are you comfortable?"

"Thank'ee, sir, gettin' on nicely. Just a bit Man-Fridayish to begin wi', but as corrat as Crocker's mare."

"What did you say?"

"Figger o' speech agen, sir, that's all. Good-night, sir."

"Good-night, Caleb."

42

Mr. Fogo settled himself in his hammock, sighed for a second time and dropped asleep.

CHAPTER VI.

HOW CERTAIN TROJANS CLIMBED A WALL OUT OF
CURIOSITY; AND OF A CHARWOMAN THAT COULD GIVE NO
INFORMATION.

Meanwhile, curiosity in Troy was beating its wings against the
closed doors of "The Bower." The early morning train next day
brought three domestics to supplement the youth in buttons, and
supplant the charwoman. Miss Limpenny, in *deshabille* (but at a
decent distance from the window), saw them arrive, and called
Lavinia to look, with the result that within two minutes the sisters
had satisfied themselves as to which was the cook, which the
parlour-maid, and which the kitchen-maid.

Later in the day, a van-load of furniture arrived, though "The
Bower" was already furnished; but, as Miss Limpenny said, in all
these matters of comfort and refinement, "there are degrees." On this
occasion the Admiral, who had been prevailed upon to leave his bed,
executed a manoeuvre the audacity of which should have
commanded success.

He crossed the road, and opened a conversation with the driver.

But success does not always wait on the brave. The van-driver
happened to have a temper as short as the Admiral's, and far less
reverence.

"Good-morning," said the Admiral, cheerily.

"Mornin'."

"What's a-foot to-day?"

"Same as yesterday—twelve inches."

The Admiral was rather taken aback, but smiled, nevertheless, and persevered.

"Ha, ha! very good. You are a wit, I perceive."

But the driver's conversation teemed with the unexpected.

"Look 'ere, Ruby-face! give me any more of your sass an' I'll punch yer 'ed for tuppence."

This was conclusive. The Admiral struck his flag, re-crossed the street, went indoors, and had it out with Mrs. Buzza. Indeed, at the end of half-an-hour that poor lady's feelings were so overwrought, and, in consequence, her sobs so loud, that the Admiral had perforce to get out his double-bass and play a selection of martial music to prevent Miss Limpenny's hearing them on the other side of the partition.

All this happened early in the afternoon. Towards five o'clock Miss Limpenny, who had only left her post twice, and on each occasion to snatch a hurried meal, was rewarded for her patience. The front door of "The Bower" opened, and Mr. and Mrs. Goodwyn-Sandys appeared, dressed, as Miss Limpenny could see, for a walk.

"Now, I wonder," reflected that kind soul, "which direction they will take. Personally, of course, I should prefer them to pass this window; but I hope I can subdue private inclination to public spirit, and for Troy's sake I hope they will visit the Castle first. The salubrity of the air, as well as the expansiveness of the view, would be certain to impress them favourably. Dear, dear! I wish I could advise them. Should they take the direction of the town, I know by experience they will be apt to meet with an effluvium of decaying fish, and I should *so* like their stay among us to be begun under pleasant auspices."

But almost before Miss Limpenny had concluded these reflections, the strangers had determined on the direction. They turned neither towards the Town nor up the hill towards the Castle and the harbour's mouth; but down the little road which led to Bower Slip and the Penpoodle Ferryboat.

"Gracious me!" exclaimed Miss Limpenny; "they are going to take a boat."

The words were scarcely out of her mouth, when she was seized with a sudden idea—an idea so alluring, yet so bold withal, that the blood flew from her cheeks. She made a step forward, paused, took another step, and returned to the window. The strangers had turned down the road and were out of sight.

For a full minute she stood there, tapping her foot.

"I will," she said, with sudden determination. "I will!" On Miss Limpenny's maiden lip the words were as solemn as though she spoke them at the altar. "I will,—and—I don't care what happens!"

Awful words! Awful in themselves, more awful from such lips, but surely most awful as making the second-step in the moral decadence of Troy!

Yet I would not have my readers too excited. They were words to shudder at, indeed; but the immediate consequences were not bloody— they were only to a limited degree tragic. It must be remembered that the magnificence of all actions is relative to the performer, nor would I seek to exalt Miss Limpenny to the level of a Semiramis or a Dido; only, when I say that she bore a great soul in a little body, I say no more than that she was a Trojan.

In short, Miss Limpenny did not, as the reader may have expected, take a boat and pursue after the strangers. What she did was simply to descend swiftly to the front hall, take down from its stand an antique, brass-bound telescope of enormous proportions, and with it make her way swiftly to the back door.

The back gardens of Alma Villas ran parallel to each other, and were terminated by a high wall, with a quay-door apiece, a tall ladder leading from the door straight down to the water. At the end of the garden, and built against this wall, in each case a stone terrace with a flight of steps allowed any one who chose to climb, and even perform a limited promenade while enjoying a full view of the harbour beyond.

It was to this flight of steps that Miss Limpenny, with a prayer on her lips and the telescope under her arm, made her way.

Both terrace and steps were rickety to a degree. To help you to estimate her conduct at its full temerity I may mention that Miss Limpenny had never attempted the climb before in her life. But whatever qualms she may have felt, they did not appear in her behaviour. Gingerly, but without hesitation, and clutching the telescope, which impeded her as an ice-axe the rock-climber, she essayed all the perils of this maiden ascent.

Five minutes' stiff climbing, as they say in the *Alpine Journal*, brought her to a point where she could take breath and look about her. Despite her terror, the excitement and the light breeze now blowing over the *arete* of garden wall, had brought a flush to her cheek. But scarcely had she resumed and set her foot upon the summit, when the flush suddenly faded, and left her blanched as snow.

For there, not a foot to her right, and above the crest of the partition wall, rose another telescope, the exact counterpart of her own!

The Spectre on the Brocken was nothing to this.

She clutched at the rotten stones and panted for breath. Slowly, very slowly, the rival telescope was tilted up against the harbour-wall; very slowly it rose in air. Then came a pair of hands—of blue cuffs— and then—the crimson face of Admiral Buzza soared into view, like the child's head in *Macbeth*.

He did not see her yet, being absorbed in adjusting the telescope. Terror-smitten, too fearful to advance or retreat, clinging to the telescope with one hand as a drowning mariner might grasp a spar, and clutching with the other at the crumbling wall, Miss Limpenny stood arrested, wildly staring, scarce venturing to breathe.

The Admiral's telescope was tilted into position, and the Admiral half-turned his head before applying his eye to the hole.

She could not help it. In spite of all her efforts to repress it, a little gasping squeal of affright broke from her. The Admiral, with a start, withdrew his eye quickly from the glass, and looked over the wall.

"Damnation!" (This was the Admiral, by the way.)

What happened exactly at this moment will never be known. Whether a stone underfoot gave way, or whether the Admiral's voice brought down a *serac* of rotten wall, is not clear. There was a rumbling sound, an oath or two—and then both telescope and Admiral disappeared, with a crash, from view.

Miss Limpenny screamed, dropped her telescope, which went rattling down the steps, cowered desperately against the wall, shut her eyes, screamed again, trod on a tilting slab, hung for a moment, toppled, clutched wildly at space, and shot, with a rush and shower of stones, straight to the very bottom.

Miss Lavinia Limpenny, who, startled by the screams, had rushed to the window and witnessed the last stages of the catastrophe, was out in a minute. Tenderly raising her sobbing sister, she assisted her back to the house, and attended to the bruises with a combination of arnica, vinegar, and brown paper. On the other side of the wall the Admiral lay for some time and bellowed for help, until his frightened family bore him in, and attempted to put him to bed.

But mark the heroism of the truly great. In spite of his late treatment at the hands of his fellow-citizens—treatment which still rankled— here was no Coriolanus to depart in a huff to Antium. The Admiral had a duty to perform, a service due to this ungrateful Town, and on the subject of going to bed he was adamant.

"Cease, Emily. Your tears, your protestations are in vain. Stop, I tell you! Get me my uniform."

Surely some desperate, some decisive step was contemplated when the Admiral ordered out that gold-laced coat and cocked hat that once had shone in the Blue Squadron of Her Majesty's Navy. What could this stern magnificence portend?

The Admiral had made up his mind. He was going to interview Mrs. Snell, the charwoman.

It was a pretty fancy, and one not without parallel in the history of famous men, that inspired him at his crisis to assume his bravest attire. There is to my mind a flavour in the conceit—a bravado lifting the action above mere intrepidity into actual greatness. Nor in this little Iliad are there many figures that I regard with more affection than that of Admiral Buzza at his garden gate waiting for Mrs. Snell.

When at length she issued from "The Bower" and came down the road, the effect of the gold lace was rather striking. She dropped her bundle and her lower jaw together.

"Lawks, sir! how you did frighten me, to be sure! I thought it was the devil!"

This was hardly what the Admiral had expected. He beckoned with his forefinger mysteriously. Mrs. Snell advanced as though not quite sure that her first fright was unfounded.

"Mrs. Snell," inquired the Admiral, in a whisper, "what are they like?" He pointed melodramatically towards "The Bower" as he asked the question.

Again the unexpected happened. Mrs. Snell burst into loud and hysterical sobbing.

"Don't 'ee, sir! don't 'ee! I can't abear it. Not a thing can you do to please 'em, an' the Honorubble Frederic a-dammin' about the 'ouse

49

fit to make your flesh creep. An' that though he might 'ave ate his dinner off the floor, gold studs an' all, as I told 'un at last. For 'twasn't in flesh and blood, sir—not to be ordered this way an' that by a whipper-snapper whose gran'mother I might 'a been, though he 'as got three rows o' shiny buttons on 'is stummick, which is no cause for a proud carriage toward them as 'asn't, nor callin' 'em slow-coaches and names which I won't soil my tongue wi'—an' so I said. Aw dear! aw dear!" And here Mrs. Snell's passion again found vent in violent sobs and cries.

"Hush! Confound it! Hush! I tell you. You'll have the whole town out."

"I beg your pardon, sir—boo-hoo!—but it isn't in natur', sich wickedness in 'igh places, an' pore Maria sick at 'ome wi' the colic an' a leak in the roof you might put your cocked 'at through, an' very fine it looks, sir, beggin' your parding agen, which is all vexashun o' sperrit on a shillin' a day an' your vittles, let alone bein' swore at 'till you dunno whether you be 'pon your 'ed or your 'eels."

With this Mrs. Snell picked up her bundle and marched off down the road. She was quite hopeless, the Admiral determined, as he watched her retreating figure and heard her sobs borne back to him on the evening air. Well, well! it had been another reverse—but not a defeat. His face cleared again as he turned to re-enter the house.

"Let me see: to-morrow is Sunday. They will probably be at church. In the afternoon, though it involve the loss of my usual nap, I will consider. On Monday I will act."

Even the strangers themselves, as they walked up the aisle of St. Symphorian's Church, Troy, on the following morning, could not but perceive something of importance to be in the wind. That the church should be full was not unusual, for in those days Sunday Observance was the rule among Trojans. But on this particular day the Wesleyan and Bible Christian chapels must have been sadly depleted, so great was the crush; and, besides, there was the unwonted magnificence of dress, the stir caused by the simultaneous turning of some hundred bonnets as the Goodwyn-Sandys entered, the audible whispering as they took their seats, the nervousness of the Vicar, who twice dropped his spectacles over the reading desk and once over the pulpit. On this last occasion one of the glasses was broken, and the sermon in consequence became, towards the end, a trifle involved. All this made the service rather hysterical.

Tell me, my Muse, thou who sittest at the tea-table and rejoicest in the rattling of cups: Who were they that attended St. Symphorian's Church on this Sunday morning? First, there were the Misses Limpenny, in black tabbinet dresses and lace shawls; a cameo brooch adorned the throat of each, and from her waist a reticule depended. These first directed the gold-bound optic glass at the strangers' pew. Behind them sat the Doctor and his wife, the one conspicuous for his black stock, the other for a shawl of Paisley workmanship. Next, the Harbour-master, tall Mr. Stripp, with his daughters Tryphena and Tryphosa; nor would Mrs. Stripp have been absent had she not been buried some years before. Yellow-haired were both the daughters, and few knew better the prevailing fashion in dress; these whispered concerning Mrs. Goodwyn-Sandys' costume. By them sat Mr. Moggridge, the poet, good at the responses, and Sam Buzza, his friend, whom few Trojans excelled in casting glances at the female congregation. Then, most gorgeous and bravest of all, the Admiral: he wore again his gold-laced coat, but the cocked-hat rested underneath the seat, and none could fathom the import of his gaze. By him sat his three daughters, a-row, in straight-backed dresses of like cut and colour, and peeped over their prayer-books; and Mrs. Buzza, timorous, in bright green satin. But of the throng of Trojan men and women, not though I had a hundred mouths, etc., etc.

"Her dress must have cost nine shillings a yard if it cost a penny," said Miss Limpenny when they were outside in the open air. She looked at the ground as she said so, for she could forget neither the Nightcap nor the Telescope.

The Admiral was silent.

"She is very lovely," remarked Mrs. Buzza, "and did you remark how the Vicar paused in the Litany when he came to 'all the Nobility'?"

"I was particularly careful to pray for Lord Sinkport," said Calypso, innocently.

Still the Admiral was silent. That afternoon Mrs. Buzza, stealing softly into the back parlour lest she should disturb her lord, was amazed, in place of the usual recumbent form with a bandanna over its face, to find him sitting up, wide awake, and staring gloomily.

"My dear—" she began in her confusion.

The Admiral turned a Gorgon stare upon her, but made no answer. Under its petrifying influence she backed out without another word, to communicate with the girls upon the portent.

This mood of the Admiral's lasted all day. Next morning, at breakfast, he looked up from his bacon, and observed, with the air of a man whose mind is made up—

"Emily, see that the girls have on their best gowns by eleven o'clock sharp. I am going to pay a call."

Consternation sat on every face. Sam Buzza paused in the act of breaking an egg.

"At 'The Bower'?" he asked.

"At 'The Bower.'"

Mrs. Buzza clasped her hands nervously. The girls turned pale.

"Oh, very well," said Sam, tapping his egg. "I shouldn't wonder if I turned up while you were there."

He was a light-haired, ungainly youth, of about twenty, with a reputation for singing a comic song. It was understood that the Admiral designed him for College and Holy Orders, but meanwhile time was passing, and Sam sat "with idle hands at home," or more frequently, in the bar of the "Man-o'-War."

"You!" exclaimed his father.

"Well, I don't see what there is in that to be surprised about," replied the youth, with an aggrieved air. "I met the Honourable Frederic smoking a cigar out on the Rope-walk last night. His cigars are very good; and he asked me to drop in soon and try another. He isn't a bit stuck-up."

The Admiral's feelings were divided between annoyance at the easy success of his son, and elation at finding the stranger so unexpectedly affable. He rose.

"Girls, remember to be punctual. I will show this town of Troy that I am not the man to be laughed at."

CHAPTER VII.

OF A LADY THAT HAD A MUSICAL VOICE,
BUT USED IT TO DECEIVE.

Many of the advantages that wait upon the readers of this history are, I should hope, by this time obvious. Among them must be reckoned the privilege of taking precedence of Admiral Buzza—of paying a visit to "The Bower" not only several minutes in advance of that great man, but moreover on terms of the utmost intimacy.

Shortly before eleven on Monday morning the Honourable Frederic Augustus Hythe Goodwyn-Sandys was shaving contemplatively. He was a tall, thin man, with light, closely cropped hair, a drooping moustache that hid his mouth, and a nose of the order aquiline, and species "chiselled." For the present the lower half of his face was obscured with lather. His dress—I put it thus in case Miss Limpenny should read these lines—was that usually worn by gentlemen under similar circumstances.

Mr. Goodwyn-Sandys was just taking his first stroke with the razor, when the creaking of the garden gate caused him to glance out of window. The effect of this was to make him cut his cheek; whereupon he both bled and swore simultaneously and profusely.

On the gravel walk stood Admiral Buzza with his three daughters.

Again the great man was in full dress. Behind him in Indian file advanced Sophia, Jane, Calypso, each in a straight frock of vivid yellow surmounted by a straw hat of such enormous brim as to lend them a fearful likeness to three gigantic fungi. As far as the hats allowed one to see from above, each wore sandal-shoes, and carried a small green parasol, neatly folded.

Mrs. Goodwyn-Sandys rose to receive them.

At the sight of this regiment of visitors, Mr. Goodwyn-Sandys paused with razor in air and blood trickling down his chin. The Admiral marched resolutely up the path and struck three distinct knocks upon the door.

It was opened by the youth in buttons.

The Admiral produced a sheaf of visiting cards and handed them to the page, as if inviting him to select one, note it carefully, and restore it to the pack.

"Is the Honourable Frederic Goodwyn-Sandys or the Honourable Mrs. Goodwyn-Sandys at home?"

Words cannot do justice to the Admiral's tone.

The regiment was marched into the drawing-room, where Mrs. Goodwyn-Sandys rose to receive them.

She was undeniably beautiful; not young, but rather in that St. Martin's Summer when a woman learns for the first time the value of her charms. Her hair was of a glossy black, her lips red and full, her figure and grey morning gown two miracles. But on her eyes and voice you shall hear Mr. Moggridge, who subsequently wasted a deal of Her Majesty's time and his own paper upon this subject. From a note-book of his, the early pages of which are constant to a certain Sophia, I select the following—

"TO GRACIOSA, WALKING AND TALKING."
> Whenas abroad, to greet the morn,
>   I mark my Graciosa walk,
> In homage bends the whisp'ring corn;
>   Yet, to confess
>   Its awkwardness,
> Must hang its head upon the stalk.
>
> And when she talks, her lips do heal
>   The wound her lightest glances give.

> In pity, then, be harsh and deal
>> Such wounds, that I
>> May hourly die
> And, by a word revived, live!

All this was very shocking of Mr. Moggridge; for Mrs. Goodwyn-Sandys was not *his* Graciosa at all. But it was what we were fated to come to, in Troy. And Graciosa's voice and smile were certainly inspiring.

Let us return to "The Bower." The Admiral having presented his daughters, and arranged them in line again, cleared his throat and began—

"Though aware that, as judged by the standard of the best society, this visit may be condemned as premature, I have thought right to stifle such apprehensions in my anxiety to assure you of a welcome in Troy—I may say, an open-armed welcome."

Here the Admiral actually spread his arms abroad. His hostess retreated a step.

"My daughters,—Calypso, I perceive an errant curl—my daughters, madam, will bear me out when I say that only excess of feeling prevents their mother from joining in this—may I call it so?—this ovation."

(In point of fact, Mrs. Buzza had been judged too red in the eyes to accompany the Admiral.)

"Ever since I beheld you and your husband—whom I do not see" (here the Admiral stared ferociously under a table), "but who, I trust, is in health—for the first time in church yesterday"— (Oh, Admiral Buzza!)—"I have been forcibly reminded of an expression in one of our British poets, which runs—Sophia, how the devil does it run?"

Neither of the Misses Buzza had the faintest idea. Their father's efforts to remember it were interrupted by Mrs. Goodwyn-Sandys, who begged them, with a charming smile, to be seated.

"My husband," she said, "will be down in a minute or two. It is really most kind of you to call; for, as strangers, we are naturally anxious to hear about the place and its people."

Her voice, which was low and musical, came with the prettiest trip upon the tongue. There was just the faintest shade of brogue in it— for instance, she said "me husband"—but I cannot attempt to reproduce it.

Upon this hinted desire for information, the Admiral bestowed his cocked-hat under the chair, and began—

"Our small town, ma'am, may be viewed in many aspects—as an emporium of commerce, a holiday centre, or a health resort. In our trade you would naturally, with your tastes, find little interest. It is rather our scenic advantages, our romantic fortresses, our river (pronounced by many to equal the Rhine), our mild atmosphere—"

"On the contrary, I take the greatest interest in your trade."

The Admiral lifted his brows and smiled, as one who would imply "You are kind enough to say so, but really, with your high connections, that can hardly be seriously believed." What he said was—

"It is indeed good of you to interest yourself in our simple tastes. We are (I confess it) to some degree—ahem!—mercantile, and as citizens of Troy esteem it our duty to acquaint ourselves (theoretically) with the products of other lands. To this end I have had all my daughters carefully grounded in the 'Child's Guide to Knowledge.' Jane, my dear, what is Gamboge?"

"A vegetable, gummy juice, of a most beautiful yellow colour, chiefly brought from Gambodia in the East Indies," repeated Jane, with a glance at her gown.

"You see, ma'am," explained her father with a wave of the hand, "it is a form of instruction in which the rawness of the material is to some extent veiled by a clothing of picturesque accessories. This will be even more noticeable in the case of Soy. Calypso, inform Mrs. Goodwyn-Sandys of the humorous illusion under which our seamen labour with regard to Soy."

But at this point the door opened, and Mr. Samuel Buzza entered, with Mr. Goodwyn-Sandys himself.

The introductions were gone through; the Admiral let off another speech of welcome, and plunged with the Honourable Frederic into a long discussion of Troy, its scenery and neighbourhood; the three girls sat bolt upright, each on the edge of her chair; and their brother took his hostess' extended hand with a bashful grin.

"Ah, Mr. Buzza, I am interested in you already—my husband has been telling me how he met you."

"Proud to hear it," muttered Sam.

"Oh, yes. I hope we shall be great friends. It is so kind of you all to call."

Sam asked her not to mention it; and looked at his father, whose face was by this time purple with conversation.

"I say, ain't the old boy enjoying himself, though!" he remarked in a sudden burst of confidence. "What do you think of him?"

Mrs. Goodwyn-Sandys smiled sweetly, and replied that the Admiral was "so thorough."

"Thorough old duffer, you mean. Look at him. What with his gold spangles and his talking to Mr. Goodwyn-Sandys, he's as proud as a cock on a wall."

His hostess laughed. "You are very frank," she said.

"That's me all over," replied Sam, evidently pleased. "You see, I ain't polite—not a ladies' man in any way."

"There I am sure you do yourself injustice."

"No, 'pon my word! I never had any practice."

"What, not among all the charming girls I saw in church yesterday? Oh, Mr. Buzza, you mustn't tell me *that*." A look from the dark eyes accompanied this sentence.

Now, very few young men of Sam's stamp greatly mind being considered gay Lotharios. So that when he repeated that "'Pon his word he wasn't," he also turned his neck about in his collar for a second or so, smiled meaningly, and altogether looked rather pleased than not.

"I'm afraid you are a very sad character, Mr. Buzza."

"No, really now."

"And are deceiving me horribly."

"No, really; wouldn't think of it."

"Sam!" broke in the Admiral's voice in tones of thunder.

"Yes, sir."

"How does Mr. Moggridge describe the 'Man-o'-War' Hotel?"

"Says the beer's falling off, sir. It *did*, once upon a time, taste of the barrel, but now he'll be hanged if it tastes of anything at all. It ought—"

"Don't be a fool, sir! I mean in that poem of his from 'Ivy Leaves: or, Tendrils from Troy.'"

"Beg pardon, sir, I'm sure. Let me see—"

Before he could recall it, Sophia finished the quotation, timidly. "I think, papa, I can remember it:—"

> 'And thou,
> Quaint hostel! 'neath whose mould'ring gable ends
> In amber draught I slake my noonday thirst...'

"Something like that, I think, papa."

"Ah, to be sure: 'mould'ring gable ends,' a most accurate description. It used to belong to—" and the Admiral plunged again into a flood of conversation.

"You must bring this Mr. Moggridge and introduce him," said Mrs. Goodwyn-Sandys to Sam. "He is a Collector of Customs, is he not? Do you think he would recite any of his verses to me?"

"By the hour. But I shouldn't advise you to ask him. It's all about my sister."

"Which?"

"The eldest there—Sophy's her name—and don't judge from appearances; the family diet is not hardware."

"Hush, sir! you must not be rude. That reminds me that I ought to go and speak to them."

"You won't get anything out of them. If you want a subject, though, I'll give you the straight tip—lambs. I've heard them talk about lambs by the hour. Say they are nice and soft and woolly: that'll draw them out."

"You are a great quiz, I perceive."

"No, really, now, Mrs. Goodwyn-Sandys."

"But, really yes, Mr. Buzza. I shall have to cure you, I see, before I can trust my husband in your company."

She rose and left him to his flutter of pleased excitement. Oh, Sam! Sam! To fall from innocence was bad enough, but to fall thus easily!

In a few moments and with charming tact, Mrs. Goodwyn-Sandys had drawn the Misses Buzza into a lively conversation; had told Sophy of some new songs; and had even promised them all some hints on the very latest gowns, before Sam Buzza, weary of silence, called across the room—

"I say, dad, what do you think is the news about the seedy-looking fellow you treated by mistake to all that speechifying?"

The Admiral looked daggers, but Sam was imperturbable.

"Ho, ho! I say, Mr. Goodwyn-Sandys, the governor took him for you, and welcomed him to Troy in his best style-flower in his buttonhole and all—'twas as good as a play. Well, the fellow has taken Kit's House."

"Kit's House!"

"Yes, and lives there all alone, with Caleb Trotter for servant. I'd advise you to call, now that you've got your Sunday best on. I'm sure he'd like to thank you for that speech you made him."

"Be quiet, sir!"

"Oh, very well; only I thought I'd mention it. I'm afraid I must be going, Mrs. Goodwyn-Sandys." Sam held out his hand.

"Must you? Good-bye, then," she said, "but remember, you have to come and be taught innocence."

"Oh, I'll remember, never fear," answered Sam, and departed.

The Admiral also rose.

"I trust," he said, "that this may be the beginning of a pleasant intimacy. My wife will be most happy to give you any information concerning our little town that I may have omitted. By the way, how is Lord Sinkport? I really forgot to ask. Quite well? I am so glad. I was afraid the gout—Come, Sophy, my dear, we have trespassed long enough. Good-morning!"

He was gone. Scarcely, however, could his host and hostess exchange glances before he reappeared.

"Oh, Mrs. Goodwyn-Sandys, that quotation—I have just remembered it. It was, 'Welcome, little strangers!' The original, I believe, has the singular—'little stranger'—but the slight change makes it more appropriate. 'Welcome, little strangers!' Good-morning!"

O Troy, Troy! Scarcely had the garden gate creaked again, when Mr. and Mrs. Goodwyn-Sandys looked at each other for a moment, then sank into arm-chairs, and broke into peals of the most unaffected laughter.

"Nellie, hand me a cigar. This beats cock-fighting."

"Whist, me dear!" answered the lady, relapsing into honest brogue, "but Brady is the bhoy to know the ropes."

"I believe you, Nellie."

Outside the garden gate the Admiral had fallen into a brown study.

"I perceive," he said, at length, very thoughtfully, "that wine and biscuits have gone out of fashion, as concomitants of a morning call. In some ways I regret it; but they are evidently people of extreme refinement. Sophy, how badly your gown sits."

"Why, it was only yesterday, papa, that you praised it so!"

"Did I? H'm! Well, well, now for the boat."

"The boat, papa?"

"Certainly, Sophy; we are going to call at Kit's House."

CHAPTER VIII.

HOW A CREW, THAT WOULD SAIL ON A WASHING-DAY, WAS
SHIPWRECKED: WITH AN ADVERTISEMENT AGAINST
WOMEN.

It was a bright April morning, and the Admiral's boat, as it swept
proudly past the little town, cast a wealth of bright reflection on the
water. Inhabitants of Troy, sitting at their windows, and overlooking
the harbour, caught sight of the yellow dresses, the blue coat with its
gold lace, and the red face beneath the cocked-hat, and whispered to
each other that something was in the wind.

Jane and Calypso rowed—for the Trojan maidens in those days were
not above pulling an oar, and did not mind blisters—while Sophia
sat in the bows, her mushroom hat "a world too wide" for the little
green parasol hoisted above it. The Admiral himself held the tiller
ropes, and occasionally gave a word of command. It was a gracious
spectacle.

But as the boat drew clear of the jetties with their press of vessels,
and Kit's Cottage hove in sight, the Admiral's eyes, which were fixed
ahead, grew suddenly very large and round.

"This is very extraordinary!" he muttered, "very extraordinary
indeed!"

"What is it, papa?" and the three Misses Buzza simultaneously
turned their mushroom hats to look.

"I cannot tell, Sophia; but to me it appears as if these people were—
not to put too fine a point upon it—washing."

It was quite true. On the little beach, Mr. Fogo, with his sleeves
turned up and a large apron pinned around him, was standing
before a huge tub, industriously washing. The tub rested on a couple

of stools. A little to the left, Caleb Trotter, with his back turned to the river, was wringing the articles of male costume which his master handed him, and disposing them about the shingle to dry.

Washing-day

The Admiral had chosen a washing-day for his first call at Kit's House.

The approach of the boat was at first unperceived; for Caleb, as I said, had his back turned to it, and Mr. Fogo's spectacles were bent over his employment.

"Really," murmured the Admiral, as his eye travelled over the beach, "anything more indelicate—Why, Miss Limpenny might be rowing this way for anything they know. Hi, sir!"

Still grasping the tiller-lines, the Admiral stood up on the stern seat and shouted.

At the sound Mr. Fogo raised his spectacles and blandly stared through them at the strangers. Caleb started, turned suddenly round, and came rushing down the beach, his right hand frantically waving them back, his left grasping a pair of—(Oh! Miss Limpenny!)

"Hi! you must go back. Go away, I tell 'ee!" he gesticulated.

"What on—"

"Go away; no females allowed here. Off with 'ee this moment!"

"Put down those —s, sir," yelled the Admiral.

"Sarve 'ee right: no business to come: 'tes Bachelor's Hall, this, an' us don't want no womankind trapesin' here: so keep your distance. Go 'long!" And Caleb began to wave again.

"Sir," cried the Admiral, appealing to Mr. Fogo, "what is the meaning of this extraordinary reception?"

"Eh? What?" said that gentleman, who apparently had fallen into a fit of deep abstraction. "I beg your pardon. I did not quite catch—"

"What is the meaning of all this, sir?" The Admiral was scarlet with passion.

"Oh, it's quite right, I believe—quite right. Caleb will tell you." As he gave this astonishing answer in a far-away tone, Mr. Fogo's spectacles rested on his visitor for a moment with a smile of deepest benevolence. Then, with a sigh, he resumed his washing.

The Admiral positively danced with rage.

"There, what did I tell 'ee?" exclaimed Caleb triumphantly. "That's your answer, and now you can go 'long home. Off with 'ee!"

The Admiral's reply would probably have contained some strong words. It was arrested by a catastrophe.

During this altercation the tide had been rising, and carried the boat gently up towards the little beach. As the Admiral opened his mouth to retort, the boat's nose jarred upon a sunken heap of pebbles. The shock was slight, but enough to upset his equilibrium. Without any warning, the Admiral's heels shot upwards, and the great man himself, with a wild clutch at vacancy, soused backwards— cocked-hat and all—into the water.

The three Misses Buzza with one accord clasped their hands and uttered dismal shrieks; the three mushroom hats shook with terror. Mr. Fogo looked up from his washing.

"Papa! oh, save him—save our dear Papa!"

There was no danger. Presently a crimson face rose over the boat's stern, blowing like a grampus. A pair of dripping epaulets followed; and then the Admiral stood up, knee-deep in water, and swore and spat alternately.

How different from that glittering hero, at sight of whom, not an hour before, the Trojan dames at their lattices had stopped their needlework to whisper! Down his nose and chin ran a pitiable flood; his scanty locks, before so wiry and obstinate, lay close against his ears; his gorgeous uniform, tarnished with slime, hung in folds, and from each fold poured a separate cascade; the whole man had become suddenly shrunken.

Speechless with rage, the little man clambered over the stern and shook his fist at the wondering spectacles of Mr. Fogo.

"You shall repent this, sir! You shall—Jane, push the boat off at once!"

But even the dignity of a fine exit was denied the Admiral. The boat was by this time firmly aground, and he was forced to stand, forming large pools upon the stern-board, while the grinning Caleb pushed her off. And still Mr. Fogo looked mildly on, with his hands in the wash-tub.

"Do you hear me, sir? You shall repent this!" raved the Admiral.

"Now, don't 'ee go upsettin' yourself again, 'cos wance es enough. An' 't'ain't no good to be vexed wi' Maaster, 'cos he don't mind 'ee. 'Tes like Smoothey's weddin'—all o' one side. Next time, I hopes you'll listen when you'm spoken to."

And with a chuckle, Caleb sent the boat spinning into deep water. Scarce daring to look at their father, the Misses Buzza plunged their oars into the brine, and the Admiral, still shaking his fist, was borne slowly out of sight. At last even his language failed upon the breeze.

Caleb quietly returned to his work.

"Thicky Adm'ral," he observed, contemplatively, after a silence of a minute or so, "puts me in mind o' Humphrey Hambly's ducks, as is said to look larger than they be."

He paused in the act of wringing a shirt, to look at Mr. Fogo.

The next instant the shirt was lying on the shingle, and Caleb had sprung upon his master, taken him by the shoulders, and was shaking him with might and main.

"Come, wake up! Do 'ee hear? What be glazin' at?"

"Eh? Dear me!" stammered Mr. Fogo, as well as he might for the shaking. "What's all this?"

"Axin' your pardon, sir," explained Caleb, continuing the treatment, "but 'tes all for your good, like ringin' a pig. You'm a-woolgatherin'; wake up!"

Mr. Fogo came to himself, and sat down upon a log of timber to rearrange his thoughts and his spectacles. Caleb stood over him and sternly watched his recovery.

"You are quite right, Caleb: my thoughts were wandering. Your treatment is a trifle rough, but honest. Are those extraordinary people gone?"

"Iss, sir; here they were, but gone—like Jemmy Rule's larks."

"I beg your pardon?"

"Figger o' speech, sir. They be gone right enough—Adm'ral Buzza in full fig, and a row o' darters in jallishy buff. I sent 'em 'bout their bus'ness. Look 'ee here, sir: ef you'll promise to sit quiet and keep your wits at home, I'll run down to town for a happord o' tar."

"Tar, Caleb?"

"Iss, sir, tar!" and with this Caleb turned on his heel and strode away across the shingle. In a moment or two he had untied his boat from the little quay, and was pulling down towards Troy Town.

When he returned, it was with a huge board, a pot of tar, and a brush. He looked anxiously about the beach, but Mr. Fogo was nowhere to be seen. "Drownded hissel'," was Caleb's first thought, but his ear caught the sound of hammering up at the house. He walked indoors to see that all was right.

"How be feelin'?" he asked, putting his head in at the dining-room door.

Mr. Fogo laid down the mallet with which he had been nailing a loose plank in the flooring, and looked up.

"All right, Caleb, thank you."

"I was afear'd you might be none compass agen."

70

"What?"

"None compass—Greek for 'mazed.' Good-bye for the present, sir."

Caleb borrowed a hammer, a nail or two, and a spade, and descended again to the beach. Here he chose a spot carefully, and began to dig a large hole in the shingle. This finished, he turned to the board, and spent some time with the brush in his hand and his head on one side, thinking. Then he began to paint vigorously.

Half-an-hour later, a tall post with a board on top stood on the beach at Kit's House. On the board, in letters six inches long, was tarred the following inscription:—

TAKE NOTICE.

ALL WIMMEN
FOUND TRAPESING ON THIS
BEECH WILL BE DEALT
WITH ACCORDING
TO THE LAW.

Above this notice jauntily rested the Admiral's cocked-hat, which had drifted ashore further up on the shingle—an awful witness to the earnestness of the threat and the vanity of human greatness.

Caleb stood in front of his handiwork and gazed at it with honest pride for some minutes; then went into the house to fetch Mr. Fogo forth to look. He was absent for some minutes. When he returned with his master, their eyes were greeted with a curious sight.

On the spit of shingle, and staring open-mouthed at the notice, stood the Twins, their honest faces expressing the extreme of perplexity. A few yards off the shore, in their boat, waited Tamsin, and leant quietly on her paddles.

Staring open-mouthed at the notice.

At the sight of her, Caleb's face fell a full inch; but he led his master down and planted him resolutely in front of the board. Mr. Fogo stared helplessly from it to the Twins.

"Mornin', sir," said Peter, after a long pause. His face wore a deepened colour, and he smiled awkwardly.

"Good-morning," replied Mr. Fogo.

"A fine mornin'," repeated Peter, with a long gaze at the board, "an' no mistake."

There was another long interval, during which everybody stared hard at the Notice.

"'Tes a powerful fine mornin'," Peter re-asserted very slowly, "ef so be as your station in life es in noways connected with turmuts. Ef 'tes the less us says about the mornin' the better." With this observation Peter looked hard at Mr. Fogo, as if the ball of conversation now lay in that gentleman's hands.

"What do 'ee think o' this 'ere Notice?" broke in Caleb.

Paul twitched his yellow bandanna and smiled evasively.

"'Tes very pretty writin', sir, sure-ly," he replied, addressing Mr. Fogo. "Nice thick down-strokes, an' all as it shou'd be."

"Uncommon fash'nubble et makes the beach look, sir, a'ready," added Peter.

Some mental reservation seemed to lurk behind this criticism. Mr. Fogo looked dubiously from the Twins to Caleb, who stood with his eyes fixed on his handiwork.

"Axin' your pard'n, sir, an' makin' so free as to mention et," began Peter at length, pulling off his hat and twirling the brim between his fingers, "but us was a bit taken aback, not understandin' as fash'nubbleness was to begin so smart; or us wou'dn't have introoded—spesh'ly Tamsin. Tamsin was thinkin' this mornin' as a pound of fresh butter might be acceptable to the gentl'm'n down at Kit's House, wi' ha'f a dozen fresh eggs or so, 'cos her Minorcy hen began to lay agen last week, an' the spickaty Hamburg as allays lays double yolks; an' Paul an' me agreed you wudn' be above acceptin' a little present o' this natur', not seemin' proud, an' Tamsin shou'd bring et hersel', the eggs bein' hers in a manner o' speakin'. But us was not wishful to introod, sir, an' iver since us seed the board here, her's been keepin' her distance in the boat yonder; on'y us stepped ashore to larn ef there was anything us cou'd do to make things ship-shape an' fitty for 'ee."

At the end of this long address, Peter, whose mahogany face was several shades deeper, pulled up, and resumed his hat.

"Ship-shape an' fitty—not wishful for to introod. That's so, Peter," echoed his brother.

Mr. Fogo looked at the pair helplessly, and again at Caleb, whose eyes were obstinately averted.

"Caleb!"

"Sir."

"Ask Miss Dearlove if she would mind stepping ashore."

With a sudden brightening of face, Caleb called her name. Tamsin looked up.

"Ef 'ee please, you'm to come ashore, to wance!"

The girl rowed a couple of strokes, grounded the boat, and stepped lightly ashore with a big basket and an unembarrassed glance at the Notice.

"There's a few young potatoes at the bottom," she said, with a curtsey, as she handed her gift to Mr. Fogo. "They're the earliest and best anywhere in these parts. Can you cook potatoes?" she asked, suddenly turning to Caleb. Beneath her sun-bonnet her pretty cheek was flushed, and her chin thrust forward with just a shadow of defiance.

"Iss, to be sure," grinned Caleb. "Why, us does our own washin'."

Tamsin's eyes travelled without bashfulness over the array upon the beach.

"Pretty washing, I expect!" She walked up and took some of the clothes into her hand. "Look here—not half-wrung—and some fallen in the mud and dirtied worse than ever."

With fine contempt she moved among the clothes, wrung them, spread them out again, and even returned with some to the wash-tub. Like four whipped schoolboys the males looked on as she tucked up the sleeves of her neat print gown.

"Soap, too, left to float in the wash-tub, and—salt water I declare! Caleb, empty this and get some soft water from the old butt by the back door. Oh, you poor, helpless baby!"

Mr. Fogo, though the words were not spoken to him, winced and turned to stare abstractedly at the river.

"Sir," said Caleb from his hammock that night, "cudn' 'ee put in a coddysel?"

"A codicil?"

"Iss, just to say, 'No wimmen allowed but Tamsin Dearlove—us don't mind she.' Wudn' that do, sir?"

"I'm afraid not, Caleb. By-the-bye, how does your Notice run? 'All women found trespassing will be—'"

"Dealt wi' 'cordin' to the law, sir."

"Dear me, Caleb!" murmured Mr. Fogo, "but I trust that under no circumstances should I deal with a woman otherwise than according to the law."

CHAPTER IX.

OF A TOWN THAT WOULD LAUGH AT THE GREAT. AND HOW A DULL COMPANY WAS CURED BY AN IRISH SONG.

We left the Misses Buzza engaged in rowing their papa homewards. The Three Queens as they steered King Arthur to Avilion can have been no sadder pageant. It is true the Misses Buzza grieved for no Excalibur, but the Admiral had lost his cocked-hat.

Picture to yourself that procession: the journey past the jetties; the faces that grinned down from overhanging hulls, or looked out hurriedly at casements and grew pale; the blue-jerseyed Trojan lounging on the quay, and pausing in his whistle to stare; the Trojan maidens gazing, with arrested needle; the shipwrights dropping mallet and tar-pot; the ferrymen resting on their oars; the makers of ship's biscuit rushing out, with aprons flying, to see the sight; the butcher, the baker, the candle-stick maker—each and all agog. Then imagine the Olympian mirth that ran along the waterside when Troy saw the joke, and, hand on hip, laughed with all its lungs.

But even this was not the worst: no, nor the crowd of urchins that followed from the landing-stage and cheered at intervals. It was when Admiral Buzza looked up and spied the face of Mrs. Goodwyn-Sandys at an upper window of "The Bower," that the cup of his humiliation indeed brimmed over.

Mrs. Buzza, "tittivating" at the mirror, heard the stir, and, presentient of evil, rushed down-stairs. She saw her lord restored to her, dear but damp. Yet she "nor swooned, nor uttered cry:" she simply sat violently and suddenly down upon the hall-chair, and piteously stared.

"Emily, get up!"

She did so.

"You are wet, my love," she ventured timorously.

"*Wet!* Woman, is this the time for airy *persiflage?*"

"My love," replied Mrs. Buzza, meekly, "nothing was further from my thoughts."

The Admiral glared upon her for a moment, but the retort died upon his lips. He flung his hands out with an appealing gesture and something like a sob.

"Emily," he cried, hoarsely, "Troy has laughed at me again. Put me to bed."

O forgiving heart of woman! In a moment her arms were about him, and her tears mingling with the general dampness of the Admiral's costume. Then, having wept her fill, she smiled a little, dried her eyes, and put the Admiral to bed.

Out of doors Troy still laughed at the mishap. The whole story was soon related (with infinite humour) by the unfilial Sam. Down at the "Man-o'-War," in the bar-parlour, for seven days it formed the sole topic of discussion; and Mr. Moggridge (who ought to have respected Sophia's father) even wrote a humorous ode upon the theme, beginning—

"Ye gods and little fishes…"

and full of the quaintest conceits. For seven days, from dawn to nightfall, the river off Kit's House was crowded with boat-loads of curious gazers, and the Steam-Tug Company (Limited) neglected its serious business to run special excursions to the scene of the catastrophe.

The Trojan maidens especially would stare at the Notice by the half-hour (that being the time allowed by the Steam-Tug Company), and hope, with much blushing and giggling, to catch a glimpse of Mr. Fogo. But the hermit remained steadily indoors.

Meanwhile the Admiral sulked in bed, and nursed his ill-humour. On Tuesday he was strangely softened and quiet; but:—

On Wednesday he recovered, and began to bully his wife as fiercely as ever.

On Thursday he broke the bell-rope again, and the servant gave warning.

On Friday he threatened to make his will, and refused his food.

On Saturday he was still fasting.

On Sunday he ate voraciously, drank four glasses of grog, and threw the wash-hand basin out of window.

On Monday Mrs. Buzza revolted, and took herself off, with the girls, to Miss Limpenny's party.

Yes. Miss Limpenny had mustered courage to put on her best brooch and call at "The Bower" with Lavinia. Nor did her daring end here; it took the form of a little three-cornered note on that very evening, and on the next morning Mr. and Mrs. Goodwyn-Sandys accepted.

"Have great pleasure in accepting," read Miss Limpenny to her sister. "The very words. I'm sure it's most affable."

"We must have cheesecakes—the famous cheesecakes—of course," reflected Miss Lavinia, "and a dish of trifle, and jellies, and—oh, Priscilla!"

"What, Lavinia?"

"Do you think a Tipsy Cake would be unbecoming?"

Miss Limpenny knit her brows over this bold proposal.

"I disapprove of the name," she said. "It has always seemed to me a trifle—ahem!—'fast,' if I may call it so. Still, we need not mention its name at supper, and the taste is undeniably grateful. But, Lavinia, I was thinking of a more important matter. Who are to be asked?"

"Why not everybody, Priscilla dear?"

"The Simpsons, for instance? It is true his father was a respectable solicitor, and even Mayor of Devonport I have heard, but Mr. Simpson's taste in *badinage* is such as I cannot always approve. It is very well in Troy here, where everybody knows them, but the Goodwyn-Sandys are certain to be most particular, and, Lavinia, that crimson gown of hers!"

"It *is* bright," assented Miss Lavinia.

"And the Saunders! What a pity the girls cannot be invited without the boys."

"The boys have always come before, Priscilla."

Miss Limpenny groaned. "To meet an Honourable, Lavinia!"

The leaven was working.

However, on the following Monday everybody was assembled in the little drawing-room. The Vicar was there in evening dress; the doctor and his wife; Mr. Simpson and Mrs. Simpson in the crimson gown; the Saunders boys in carpet slippers (at sight of which Miss Limpenny went hot and cold by turns); the Misses Buzza in book-muslin, with ultramarine sashes and bronze shoes laced sandal-wise; their mother in green satin and deadly terror lest the Admiral's voice should penetrate the party-wall. Mr. Moggridge was frowning gloomily in a corner at some humorous story of Sam Buzza's telling. In short, with the exception of their Admiral, all Trojan society had gathered to do honour to the new-comers.

Miss Limpenny, nervously toying with her best brooch, rose in a flutter as the door opened and admitted them.

"So afraid we are late! but the clocks at 'The Bower' have not yet recovered from their journey."

Mrs. Goodwyn-Sandys gazed calmly about her. There was a rustle throughout the room; two pink spots appeared on Miss Limpenny's cheeks; she stumbled in her words of welcome. The Vicar frowned and looked puzzled.

Mrs. Goodwyn-Sandys wore a low-necked gown!

It was a shock; but it passed. She was wonderfully pretty, all admitted, in her gown of a rich amber satin draped with delicate folds of black lace; around her white throat a diamond necklace glistened. How well I can remember her as she stood there toying with a button of her glove! And how mean and dowdy we all looked beside this glittering vision!

The Honourable Frederic Augustus Hythe Goodwyn-Sandys meanwhile stared at us all calmly but firmly through his eye-glass. I saw young Horatio Saunders meet that gaze and sink into his carpet slippers. I saw Mr. Moggridge frown terribly, and cross his arms. Sam Buzza came forward—

"Ah, how d'ye do? How d'ye do, Mrs. Goodwyn-Sandys? Looking round for the governor? He's been in bed for a week."

I think we all envied Samuel Buzza at this moment.

"Ah, nothing serious, I hope?" drawled Mr. Goodwyn-Sandys.

"Serious, ha, ha! Haven't you heard—"

"Sam, dear!" expostulated Mrs. Buzza.

"All right, mother. He can't hear," and Sam plunged into the story.

The ice was broken. In a few moments a whist party was made up to include the Honourable Frederic, and Miss Limpenny breathed more freely. Mr. Moggridge was led up by Sam, and introduced.

"Ah, indeed! Mr. Moggridge, I have been so longing to know you."

Sam looked a trifle vexed. The poet simpered that he was happy.

"Of course I have been reading 'Ivy Leaves.' So mournful I thought them, yet somehow so attractive. How *did* you write it all?"

Mr. Moggridge confessed amiably that he "didn't quite know."

"Let me see; those lines beginning—"

'O give me wings to—to—'

"I forget for the moment how it goes on."

"'To fly away,'" suggested the bard.

"Ah, exactly; 'to fly away.' So simple—just what one *would* wish wings for, you know. It struck me very much when I read it. When did you think of it, Mr. Moggridge?"

The poet blushed and began to look uncomfortable.

"Ah! you are reticent. Excuse me; I ought not to probe a poet's soul. Still, I should like to be able to tell my friends—"

"The—the fact is," stammered Mr. Moggridge, "I—I thought of them— in—my bath."

Mrs. Goodwyn-Sandys leaned back and laughed—a pretty rippling laugh that shook the diamonds upon her throat. Sam guffawed, and by this action sprang that little rift between the friends that widened before long into a gulf.

"I shall ask you to copy them into my Album. I always victimise a lion when I meet one."

This was said with a glance full of compensation. Mr. Moggridge tried to look very leonine indeed. Across the room another pair of eyes gently reproached him. Never before had he tarried so long from Sophia's side. Poor little heart! beating so painfully beneath your dowdy muslin bodice. It was early yet for you to ache.

"Oh, ah, Dick Cheddar—knew him well," came in the sonorous tones of the Honourable Frederic from the whist-table. "So you were at College with him—first cousin to Lord Stilton—get the title if he only outlives the old man—good fellow, Dick—but drinks."

"Dear me," said the Vicar; "I am sorry to hear that. He was wild at Christchurch, but nothing out of the way. Why, I remember at the Aylesbury Grinds—"

Miss Limpenny, who did not know an Aylesbury Grind from a Bampton Lecture, yet detected an unfamiliar ring in the Vicar's voice.

"He fought a welsher," pursued the Vicar, "just before riding in a race. 'Rollingstone,' his horse was, and Cheddar's eyes closed before the second fence. 'Tom,' he called to me—I was on a mare called Barmaid—"

I ask you to guess the amazement that fell among us. He—our Vicar— riding a mare called Barmaid! Miss Limpenny cast her eyes up to meet the descent of the thunderbolt.

"Lord Ballarat was riding too," the Vicar went on, "and young Tom Beauchamp, son of the Bishop—"

"Died of D.T. out at Malta with the Ninety-ninth," interpolated the Honourable Frederic.

"So I heard, poor fellow. Three-bottle Beauchamp we called him. I've put him to bed many a time when—"

It was too much.

"In the Great Exhibition of 1851," began Miss Priscilla severely.

But at this moment a dreadful rumbling shook the room. The chandeliers rattled, the egg-shell china danced upon the what-not, and a jarring sensation suddenly ran up the spine of every person in the company.

"It's an earthquake!" shouted the Honourable Frederic, starting up with an oath.

Miss Limpenny thought an earthquake nothing less than might be expected after such language. Louder and still louder grew the rumbling, until the very walls shook. Everybody turned to a ghastly white. The Vicar's face bore eloquent witness to the reproach of his conscience.

"I think it must be thunder," he gasped.

"Or a landslip," suggested Sam Buzza.

"Or a paroxysm of Nature," said Mr. Moggridge (though nobody knew what he meant).

"Or the end of the world," hazarded Mr. Goodwyn-Sandys.

"I beg your pardon," interposed Mrs. Buzza timidly, "but I think it may be my husband."

"Is your husband a volcano, madam?" snapped Mr. Goodwyn-Sandys, rather sharply.

Mrs. Buzza might have answered "Yes," with some colour of truth; but she merely said, "I think it must be his double-bass. My husband is apt in hours of depression to seek the consolation of that instrument."

"But, my dear madam, what is the tune?"

"I think," she faltered, "I am not sure, but I rather think, it is the 'Dead March' in *Saul*."

There was no doubt of it. The notes by this time vibrated piteously through the party-wall, and with their awful solemnity triumphed over all conversation. Tones became hushed, as though in the presence of death; and the Vicar, in his desperate attempts to talk, found his voice chained without mercy to the slow foot of the dirge. He tried to laugh.

"Really, this is too absurd—ha! ha! *Tum-tum-tibby-tum*." The effort ended in ghastly failure. *Thrum-thrum-tiddy-thrum* went the Admiral's instrument.

Miss Limpenny grew desperate. "Sophia," she pleaded, "pray sing us one of your cheerful ballads."

Sophia looked at Mr. Moggridge. He had always turned over the pages for her so devotedly. Surely he would make some sign now. Alas! all his eyes were for Mrs. Goodwyn-Sandys.

"I will try," she assented with something dangerously like a sob.

She stepped to the "Collard" at a pace remorselessly timed to the "Dead March," and chose her ballad—a trifle of Mr. Moggridge's composition. It would reproach him more sharply than words, she thought. A cloud of angry tears blurred her sight as she struck the tinkling prelude.

> "A month ago Lysander prayed To Jove,
>   to Cupid, and to Venus—"

Thrum-thrum-thrum went the double bass next door. Mr. Moggridge looked up. How thin and reedy Sophia's voice sounded to-night! He had never thought so before.

> "That he might die, if he betrayed
> A single vow that passed between us."

"Sweetly touching!" murmured Mrs. Goodwyn-Sandys.

Sophia pursued—

> "O careless gods, to hear so ill,
>   And cheat the maid on you relying;
> For false Lysander's thriving still,
>   And 'tis Corinna lies a-dying."

"Is that all?" asked Mrs. Goodwyn-Sandys as Sophia with flushed cheeks left the piano.

"That is all—a little effort not worth—"

"Oh, it is yours! But," with a sweet smile, "I ought to have guessed. You must write a song for me one of these days."

"Do you sing?" cried the delighted Mr. Moggridge.

Sam, who had been waiting for a chance to speak, shouted across the room—"I say, Miss Limpenny, Mrs. Goodwyn-Sandys will sing if you ask her."

After very little solicitation, and with none of the coyness common to amateurs, she seated herself at the instrument, quietly pulled off her gloves, and dashed without more ado into a rollicking Irish ditty.

> "Be aisy an' list to a chune
> That's sung uv bowld Tim, the dragoon;
>   Sure, 'twas he'd niver miss
>   To be stalin' a kiss—

> Or a brace—by the light uv the moon,
>> Aroon,
> Wid a wink at the man in the moon!"

"Really!" murmured Miss Limpenny. The keys of the decorous "Collard" clashed as they had never clashed before. The guests, at first shocked and startled, began to be carried away with the reckless swing of the music. The Vicar stared for a moment, and then began gradually to nod his head to the measure.

"You must sing the last line in chorus, please," said Mrs. Goodwyn-Sandys from the piano—

> "Wid a wink at the man in the moon!"

It was sung timidly at first. Nothing daunted, the performer plunged into the next verse—

> "Rest his sowl in the arms uv owld Nick!
> For he's gone from the land uv the quick:
>> But he's still makin' luv
>> To the leddies above,
> An' be jabbers! he'll tache 'em the thrick,
>> Avick,
> Niver fear but he'll tache 'em the thrick!"

There was no doubt this time. By the spirit of her mad singing, by some demon that rode upon her full and liquid voice, the whole company seemed possessed. Miss Limpenny looked furtively towards the Vicar. He was actually joining in the chorus! And what a chorus! She put her mittened palms to her ears, such a shout it was that went up.

> "'Tis by Tim the dear saints'll set sthore,
> And 'ull thrate him to whiskey galore;
>> For they've only to sip
>> But the tip uv his lip,
> An' bedad! they'll be askin' for more,

86

> Asthore,
> By the powers! they'll be shoutin' 'Ancore'!"

It was no longer an assembly of dull and decent citizens: it was a room full of lunatics yelling the burden of this frantic Irish song. Laughingly, Mrs. Goodwyn-Sandys rested her finger on the keys and looked around. These stolid Trojans had caught fire. There was the little Doctor purple all above his stock; there was the Vicar with inflated cheeks and a hag-ridden stare; there was Mr. Moggridge snapping his fingers and almost capering; there was Miss Limpenny with her under-jaw dropped and her eyes agape. They were charmed, bewitched, crazy.

Mrs. Goodwyn-Sandys saw this, and broke into a silvery laugh. The infection spread. In an instant the whole room burst into a peal, a roar. They laughed until the tears ran down their cheeks; they held their sides and laughed again. She had them at her will.

There was no more wonder after this. At supper the talk was furious and incessant; Miss Lavinia spoke of a "tipsy-cake," and never blushed; the Vicar took wine with everybody, and told more stories of Three-bottle Beauchamp; even Sophia laughed with the rest, although her heart was aching—for still her poet neglected her and hung with her brother on the lips of Mrs. Goodwyn-Sandys. I saw him bring the poor girl's cloak in the hall afterwards and receive the most piteous of glances. I doubt if he noticed it.

Outside, the Admiral's double-bass was still droning the "Dead March" to Miss Limpenny's laurestinus grove. It was the requiem of our decorum. Long after I was in bed that night I heard the voice of Mr. Moggridge trolling down the street—

> "An' be jabbers! he'll tache 'em the thrick!"

Mrs. Goodwyn-Sandys had "taught us the trick," indeed.

CHAPTER X.

OF ONE EXCURSION AND MANY ALARUMS.

"Caleb!" said Mr. Fogo on the morning after Miss Limpenny's party.

"Aye, aye, sir!" Caleb paused in his carpentering to look up.

"It is a lovely morning; I think I will take my easel and go for a walk. You are sure that the crowds have gone at last?"

"All gone, sir. Paice and quiet at last—as Bill said when he was left a widow. Do 'ee want me to go 'long wi' 'ee, sir?"

"No, thank you, Caleb. I shall go along the hills on this side of the river."

"You'd best let me come, sir, or you'll be wool-gatherin' and wand'rin' about till goodness knows what time o' night."

"I shall be back by four o'clock."

"Stop a minnit, sir; I have et. I'll jest put that alarmin' clock o' yourn in your tail-pocket an' set et to ha'f-arter-dree, an' that'll put you in mind when 'tes time to come hom'. 'Tes a wonnerful in-jine, this 'ere clock," reflected Caleb as he carefully set the alarum, "an' chuck-full o' sense, like Malachi's cheeld. Lor', what a thing es Science, as Jenifer said when her seed the tellygrarf-clerk in platey buttons an' red facin's to his breeches. Up the path, sir, an' keep to the left. Good-bye, sir! Now, I'd gie summat," soliloquised Caleb as he watched his master ascend the hill, "to be sure of seein' him back safe an' sound afore nightfall. Aw dear! 'tes a terrable 'sponsible post, bein' teetotum to a babby!"

With this he walked back to the house, but more than once halted on his way to ponder and shake his head ominously.

Mr. Fogo meanwhile, with easel and umbrella on his arm, climbed the hill slowly and with frequent pauses to turn and admire the landscape. It was the freshest of spring mornings: the short turf was beaded with dew, the furze-bushes on either hand festooned with gossamer and strung with mimic diamonds. As he looked harbourwards, the radiance of sky mingling with the glitter of water dazzled and bewildered his sight: below, and at the foot of the steep woods opposite, the river lay cool and shadowy, or vanished for a space beneath a cliff, where the red plough-land broke abruptly away with no more warning than a crazy hurdle. Distinct above the dreamy hum of the little town, the ear caught the rattle of anchor-chains, the cries of an outward-bound crew at the windlass, the clanking of trucks beside the jetties; the creaking of oars in the thole-pins of a tiny boat below ascended musically; the very air was quick with all sounds and suggestions of spring, and of man going forth to his labour; the youthfulness of the morning ran in Mr. Fogo's veins, and lent a buoyancy to his step.

By this time the town was lost to view; next, the bend of Kit's House vanished, and now the broad flood spread in a silver lake full ahead. On the ridge the pure air was simply intoxicating after the languor of the valley. Mr. Fogo began to skip, to snap his fingers, to tilt at the gossamer with his umbrella, and once even halted to laugh hilariously at nothing. An old horse grazing on an isolated patch of turf looked up in mild surprise; Mr. Fogo blushed behind his spectacles and hurried on.

He had gone some distance when a granite roller lying on the ploughed slope beneath a clump of bushes invited him to rest. Mr. Fogo accepted the invitation, and seated himself to contemplate the scene. The bush at his back was comfortable, and by degrees the bright intoxication of his senses settled to a drowsy content. He pulled out his pipe and lit it. Through the curls of blue smoke he watched the glitter on the water below, the prismatic dazzle of the clods where their glossy surface caught the sun, the lazy flap-flap of a heron crossing the valley, and he heard along the uplands the voice (sweetest of rural sounds, and, alas! now obsolete) of a farm-boy

chanting to his team, "Brisk and Speedwell, Goodluck and Lively" —
and so sank by degrees into a soothing sleep.

When he awoke and looked lazily upwards, at first his eyes
encountered gloom. "Have I been sleeping all day?" was his first
thought, not without alarm. But under the darkness a bright ray was
stealing. Mr. Fogo put up his hand and encountered his umbrella,
carefully spread over his face for shade.

This was mysterious; he could swear the umbrella was folded and
lying at his side when he dropped asleep. "It must be Caleb," he
thought, and stared around. No Caleb was in sight, but he noticed
that the sun was dropping towards the west, and noticed also, not
fifty yards to the left, and quietly cropping a tuft of bushes, a red
bull.

Now Mr. Fogo had an extreme horror of bulls, especially red bulls,
and this one was not merely red, but looked savage, to boot. Mr.
Fogo peered again round the corner of his umbrella. The brute
luckily had not spied him, but neither did it seem in any hurry to
move. For twenty minutes Mr. Fogo waited behind his shelter, and
still the bull went on cropping.

It was already late, and the brute stood full in the homeward path to
Kit's House. It was only possible to make a circuit around the ridge,
as the cliff's edge cut off a *detour* on the other side. Weary of waiting,
Mr. Fogo cautiously rose, pushed his easel under the bushes, and
began to creep up towards the ridge, holding his umbrella in front of
him as a screen. This was rather after the fashion of the ostrich,
which, to avoid being seen, buries its head in the sand; nor was it
likely that the beast, if irritated at sight of a man, would acquiesce in
the phenomenon of an umbrella at large, and strolling on its own
responsibility. But as yet the bull's back was towards it.

Stealthily Mr. Fogo crept round. He had placed about seventy yards
between him and the animal, and had almost gained the summit
when a dismal accident befell.

"Cl'k—Whir-r-r-r-roo-oo-oo!"

It was the alarum in his tail-pocket. The bull looked up, gazed wildly at the umbrella, snorted, lashed out with his tail, and started in pursuit. Quick as thought, Mr. Fogo dropped his screen, and, with a startled glance around, dashed at full speed for the ridge, the infernal machine still dinning behind him.

Luckily, the bull's onset was directed at the umbrella. There was a thundering of hoofs, a dull roar, and the poor man, as he gained the summit and cast a frantic look behind, saw a vision of jagged silk and flying ribs. With a groan he tore forwards.

There was a hedge about fifty yards away, and for this he made with panting sides and tottering knees. If he could only stop that alarum! But the relentless noise continued, and now he could hear the bull in fresh pursuit. However, the umbrella had diverted the attack. After a few seconds of agony Mr. Fogo gained the hedge, tore up it, turned, saw the brute appear above the ridge with a wreck of silk and steel upon his horns, and with a sob of thankfulness dropped over into the next field.

But alas! in doing so Mr. Fogo performed the common feat of leaping out of the frying-pan into the fire. For it happened that on the other side a tramp was engaged in his legitimate occupation of sleeping under a hedge, and on his extended body our hero rudely descended.

"Hi!" said the tramp, "where be you a-comin' to?"

Mr. Fogo picked himself up and felt for his spectacles; they had tumbled off in his flight, and without them his face presented a curiously naked appearance. The alarum in his pocket had stopped suddenly with the jerk of his descent.

"I beg your pardon," he mildly apologised, "but a bull in the next field—"

"That's no cause for selectin' a gentl'm'n's stomach to tumble 'pon, growled the tramp.

"I beg your pardon, I'm sure," repeated Mr. Fogo; "you may be sure that had time for selection been allowed me—"

"Look 'ere," said the tramp with sudden ferocity, "will you fight?"

"Look 'ere," said the tramp ... "will you fight?"

Mr. Fogo retreated a step.

"Really—"

"Come, look sharp! You won't? Then I demands 'arf-a-crown."

With this the ruffian began to tuck up his ragged cuffs, and was grimly advancing. Mr. Fogo leapt back another pace.

"*Cl'k—Whir-r-r-r-roo-oo-oo!*"

This time the alarum was his salvation. The tramp pulled up, gave a hasty terrified stare, and with a cry of "The Devil!" made off across the field as fast as his legs would carry him. Overcome with the emotions of the last few minutes Mr. Fogo sat suddenly down, and the alarum ceased.

When he recovered he found himself in an awkward predicament. He knew of but one way homewards, and that was guarded by the bull; moreover, if he attempted to find another road he was hampered by the loss of his spectacles, without which he could not see a yard before his nose.

However, anything was better than facing the bull again; so he arose, picked the brambles out of his clothing, and started cautiously across the field.

As luck would have it he found a gate; but another field followed, and a third, into which he had to climb by the hedge. And here he suffered from a tendency known to all mountaineers who have lost their way in a mist; unconsciously he began to trend away towards the left, and as this led him further and further from home, his plight became every moment more desperate.

At last he struck into a narrow lane, just as the sun sank. He halted for a moment to consider his direction.

"Pat—pat—pat."

He looked up. A little girl in an immense sun-bonnet was toddling up the lane towards him. She swung a satchel in her left hand, and at sight of the stranger paused with her unoccupied forefinger in mouth.

Mr. Fogo advanced straight up to her, stooped with his hands on his knees, and peered into her face. This behaviour, though necessitated by his shortness of sight, worked the most paralysing effect on the child.

"Little girl, can you tell me the way to Kit's House?"

There was no answer. Mr. Fogo peered more closely.

"Little girl, can you tell me the way to Kit's House?"

Still there was no answer.

"Little girl—"

"*Cl'k—whir-r-r-r-roo-oo* !"

The effect of the alarum was instantaneous.

"Boo-hoo!" yelled the little girl, and broke into a paroxysm of weeping.

"Little girl—"

"Boo-hoo! Take me home. I want mammy!"

"Dear me," cried Mr. Fogo wildly, "this is the most appalling situation in which I have ever been placed." He thought of running away, but his humanity forbade it. At length the alarum ran down; but the child continued to scream—

"I want mammy! Take me home!"

"Hush! hush! She shall go to mammy—ickle tootsey shall go to mammy. Did-ums want-ums mammy?" shouted Mr. Fogo, with an idiotic effort to soothe.

But it was useless. The screams merely increased in volume. Mr. Fogo, leaning against the hedge, mopped his brow and looked helplessly around.

"Boo-hoo! I want mammy!"

"What on earth is to be done?"

There was a sudden sound of light footsteps, and then, to his immense relief, Tamsin Dearlove stood before him. She looked as fresh and neat as ever and carried a small basket on her arm.

"Whatever is the matter? Why, 'tis little Susie Clemow! What's the matter, Susie?" She set down her basket and ran to the child, who immediately ceased to yell.

"There now, that's better. Did the big strange gentleman try to frighten her? Poor little maid!"

"I assure you," said Mr. Fogo, "I tried to do nothing of the kind."

Tamsin paid no attention.

"There now, we're as good as gold again, and can run along home. Give me a kiss first, that's a dear."

The little maid, still sobbing fitfully, gave the kiss, picked up her satchel, and toddled off, leaving Tamsin and Mr. Fogo face to face.

"Why did you frighten her?" the girl asked severely. There was an angry flush on her cheek.

"I did not intentionally. It was the alarum. First of all I was chased by a bull, and then—" Mr. Fogo told his story incoherently. The angry red left Tamsin's cheek, and a look of disdain succeeded.

"And you," she said very slowly, when he had finished, "think you are able to despise womankind."

It was Mr. Fogo's turn to grow red.

"And to put up a board," she continued, "with that silly Notice upon it—you and that great baby Caleb Trotter—setting all women at naught, when you never ought to be beyond tether of their apron-strings. Why, only this morning you'd have caught a sun-stroke if I hadn't spread your umbrella over you."

"Did you do that?"

"And who else do you suppose? A man, perhaps? Why, there isn't a man in the world would have had the sense—'less it was Peter or Paul," she added, with a sudden softening of voice, "and they're women in everything but strength. And now," she went on, "as I am going that way, I suppose you'll want me to see you home. Will you walk in front or behind, for doubtless you're above walking beside a woman?"

"I think you are treating me very hardly."

"Maybe I am, and maybe I meant to. Maybe you didn't know that that Notice of yours might hurt people's feelings. Don't think I mean mine," she explained quickly and defiantly, "but Peter's and Paul's."

There was a pause as they walked along together.

"The board shall come down," said he; "and now may I carry your basket?"

"My basket? Do you think I'd trust a man to carry eggs?" She laughed, but with a trace of forgiveness.

He did not answer, but seemed to have fallen into a fit of troubled contemplation. They walked on in silence.

Presently she halted.

"I doubt you've had trouble in your time, and I've hurt your feelings and spoken as I oughtn't to have spoken to my betters; but I've seen that Peter and Paul were hurt in mind, and that made me say more than I meant. Yonder's your way down to Kit's House. Good-night, sir."

Mr. Fogo would have held out his hand, but she was gone quickly down the road. He stood for a minute looking after her; then turned and walked quickly down the path to Kit's House.

Caleb met him at the door.

"So you'm back, an' I hopes you enj'yed your walk, as Sal said when her man comed home from France. I was just a-comin' to luk for 'ee. Where's your easy-all and your umbrella?"

Mr. Fogo told his story.

"H'm!" said Caleb, "an' Tamsin saw 'ee home?"

"Yes; and by the way, Caleb, you may as well take down that notice to-morrow."

"H'm!" muttered Caleb again. "You're quite sure thicky coddysel won't do?"

"Quite."

"Very well, sir," said Caleb, and began to busy himself with the evening meal. But he looked curiously at his master more than once during the evening. Mr. Fogo spent most of his time in a brown study, smoking and gazing abstractedly into the fire. Caleb also smoked (it was one of his privileges), and finally, with an anxious glance, and two or three hard puffs at his pipe, broke the silence—

"The bull es a useful animal, an' when dead supplies us wi' rump-steaks an' shoe-horns, as the Sunday-school book says: but for all that there's suthin' *lackin'* to a bull. 'Tain't conviction: you niver seed a bull yet as wasn' chuck-full o' conviction, an' didn' act up to hes rights, such as they be. An' 'tain't consistency: you drill a notion into a bull's head an' fix et, an' he'll save et up, may be for six year, an' then rap et out on 'ee till you'm fairly sick for your own gad-about ways. 'Tes logic he wants, I reckon—jest logic. A bull, sir, es no more'n a mass o' blind onreas'ning prejudice from horn to tail. Take hes sense o' colour: he can't abide red. Ef you press the matter, there ain't no more reas'n for this than that hes father afore him cudn' abide et; but how does he act? 'Hulloa!' says he, 'there's a party in red, an' I don't care a tinker's cuss whether 'tes a mail-cart or a milisha-man: I'm bound to stop this 'ere taste for red ef I dies nex' minnit.' And at et he goes accordin'. Ef he seed the Scarlet Woman about in his part o' the country, he'd lay by an' h'ist her, an' you'd say, 'Well done!' an' I don't say you'd be wrong. But jest you stop an' ax hes motives, an' you'll find 'taint religion. Lor' bless 'ee, sir, a bull's got no more use for religion than a toad for side-pockets. 'Tes obstinacy—that's what 'tes. You tells me a jackass es obstinate. Well, an' that's true in a way; and so's a hog. Ef you wants quiet contrariness, a jackass or a hog'll both *sit out* a bull; an' tho' you may cuss the pair till you sweats like a fuz'-bush on a dewy mornin', 'tes like heavin' bricks into a bott'mless pit. But a bull ups an' lets 'ee know; there aint no loiterin' round an' arrangin' yer subjec' under heads when *he's* about. You don't get no pulpit; an', what's more, you don't stop to touch your hat when you makes your congees. 'Tes just pull hot-foot, and thank the Lord for hedges; 'cos he's so full o' his own notions as a Temp'rance speaker, an' bound to convence 'ee, ef he rams daylight in 'ee to do et. That's a bull. An' here's anuther p'int; he lays head to ground when hes beliefs be crossed, an' you may so well whissle as try the power o' the human eye—talkin' o' which puts me i' mind o' some curious fac's as happ'n'd up to Penhellick wan time, along o' this same power o' the human eye. Maybe you'd like to hear the yarn."

"Eh?" Mr. Fogo roused himself from his abstraction. "Yes, certainly, I should like to hear it."

Caleb knocked his pipe meditatively against the bars of the grate; filled it again and lit it; took an energetic pull or two, and then, after another hard look at his master across the clouds of smoke, began without more ado.

CHAPTER XI.

OF A WESLEYAN MINISTER THAT WOULD IMPROVE UPON
NATURE, AND THEREBY TRAINED A ROOK TO GOOD
PRINCIPLES.

"Well, sir, et all happen'd when I lived up to Penhellick, an' worked long wi' Varmer Mennear. Ould Lawyer Mennear, as he was a-nicknamed—a little cribbage-faced man, wi' a dandy-go-russet wig, an' on'y wan eye: leastways, he hadn' but wan fust along when I knowed 'n. That's what the yarn's about, tho'; so us'll go slow, ef you plaise, an' hush a bit, as Mary Beswetherick said to th' ingine-driver.

"Now, Lawyer Mennear was a circuit-preacher, o' the Wesleyan Methody persuash'n, tho' he'd a-got to cross-pupposes wi' the rest o' the brethren an' runned a sect all to hissel', which he called th' United Free Church o' 'Rig'nal Seceders. They was called 'Rig'nal Seceders for short, an' th' ould man had a toler'ble dacent followin', bein' a fust-class mover o' souls an' powerful hot agen th' unregenrit, which didn' prevent hes bein' a miserable ould varmint, an' so deep as Garrick in hes ord'nary dealin's. Aw, he was a reg'lar split-fig, an' 'ud go where the devil can't, an' that's atween the oak an' the rind."

"I see," said Mr. Fogo.

"Iss, sir. Why, the very fust day I tuk sarvice—I was a tiny tacker then—he says to me, 'Caleb, my boy, you'm lookin' all skin an' bones for the present, but there's no knawin' what Penhellick beef and pudden may do for 'ee yet, ef 'tes eaten wi' a thankful heart. Hows'ever, 'bout the work. I wants you to take the dree jackasses an' go to beach for ore-weed, an' as I likes to gie a good boy like you a vew privileges, you be busy an' carry so many seams [1] as you can, an' I'll gie drappence for ivery seam more'n twenty.'

"Well, sir, I worked like a Trojan, an' ha'f killed they jackasses; an' I tell 'ee 'twas busy all to carry dree-an'-twenty seam. In the eveling, arter work, I went to Lawyer Mennear an' axed 'n 'bout the nine-pence—I niver got ninepence so hard in all my born days. When he paid me, he looked so sly, an' says he—

"' You'm a nation clever boy, you be, an' I doan't gridge 'ee the money. But now I sees what you *can* do, of cou'se I shall 'spect 'ee to carry dree-an'-twenty seam ivery day, reg'lar: for the workman,' says he, 'es worthy of hes hire.'

"'Darn et!' thought I to mysel', 'this won't do;' an' I niver seed azackly the beef an' pudden th' ould man talked about. Hows'ever, I stayed wi' the psalmas-'untin' ould cadger, tho' et made me 'most 'mazed at times to hear the way he'd carry on down at the Meetin' House 'bout the sen o' greed an' the like, an' all the time lookin' round to see who owed 'n a happeny. 'My brethren,' he'd call out, 'my pore senful flock, ef you clings to your flocks an' herds, an' tents an' dyed apparel, like onto Korah shall you be, an' like onto Dathan an' Abiram, so sure as I be sole agent for Carnaby's Bone Manure in this 'ere destrict.' 'Tes true, sir. An' then he'd rap out the hemn, 'Common metre, my brethren, an' Sister Tresidder'll gie the pitch—"

> 'Whativer, Lord, us lends to Thee
> Repaid a thousan'fold'll be,
> Then gladly will us gie to Thee.'

"An' I reckon that was 'bout the size o't. Aw, he was an anointed ould rascal.

"All the same, Lawyer Mennear was reckon'd a powerful wrastler en the sperrit by the rest o' the Church-Membership; on'y there was wan thing as went agen 'un, an' that was he hadn' but wan eye; tho' Maria Chirgwin, as was known to have had experience, an' was brought under conviction by th' ould man, told me that et made 'n luk the more terrifyin' —"

"Like Polyphemus," put in Mr. Fogo.

"Polly which?"

"Never mind."

"I disknowledged the surname. But niver mind, as you say, sir; feelin's es feelin's, an' th' ould Mennear's wan eye went mortal agen 'un. Not but what he wudn' turn et to account now an' then. 'Tummas doubted,' he said wan day, 'an' how was he convenced? Why, by oracular demonstrashun—'"

"Ocular, Caleb."

"Right you are, sir, an' thankye for the correcshun, as the boy said to the pupil-teacher; 'by oc-u-lar demonstrashun,' says he. 'P'raps you dunno what ocular demonstrashun es, my brethren. Well, I'll tell 'ee. That's a wall, ain't et? An' I'm a preacher, arn't I? An' you be worms, bain't 'ee? Why, I can see that much tho' I *han't* but wan eye. An' that's ocular demonstrashun.'

"But, as I was sayin', wan eye *es* a wisht business, howsomever you may turn et up'ards an' call et your thorn i' the flesh, an' the likes; an' more'n a few o' the 'Rig'nal Seceders fell away from th' ould man's Meetin' House, and became backsliders dro' fear o' being overlooked an' ill-wished, so they said. I reckon 'twas all quignogs, but et *did* luk plaguey like th' evil eye, an' that there's no denyin'.

"Well, sir, matters went on i' this way for a brave time, an' the 'tendance got less, till Lawyer Mennear wos fairly at hes wits' end. He talked a' weak-kneed brethren, an' 'puttin' your han's to the plough,' an' dreshed the pilm [2] out o' cush'n afore 'un, an' kicked up a purty dido, till you cou'd hear the randivoose o' Sunday mornin's 'way over t'other side o' Carne hill; but 'twarn't no manner o' good. An' as for the childer at the Sunday-school—th' ould rapscallion laid powerful store by hes Sunday-school—'twas 'bear a hand ivery wan' to get mun to face that eye: an' you mou't clane their faces an' grease their hair as you wou'd, the mothers told me, an' see mun off 'pon the road to Meetin' House; but turn your back, an' they'd be mitchin' [3] in a brace o' shakes an' 'way to go for

Coombe beach, an' playin' hidey-peep in their clane pinnyfores 'mong the rocks.

"Aw, 'twas shee-vo! 'mong the Church Members, an' no mistake; an' how 'twud ha' come round, there's no telling, ef et hadn' a-been for what Lawyer Mennear called a vouchsafement o' marcy. An' the way thicky vouchsafement comed about was this:

"Th' ould man was up to Plymouth wan day 'bout some shares he'd a-tuk in a tradin' schooner; for he'd a finger in most pies. Nuthin' i' the way o' bus'ness comed amiss to'n. Like Nicholas Kemp, he'd occashun for all."

"Who was Nicholas Kemp?" inquired Mr. Fogo.

"On'y a figger o' speech, sir. Well, ould Mennear had a-done bus'ness, an' was strollin' up Union Street 'long wi' his missus— Aunt Deb'rah Mennear, as her name was—a fine, bowerly woman, but a bit ha'f-baked in her wits; put in wi' the bread, as they say, an' tuk out wi' the cakes—when he fetches up 'pon a sudden afore a shop-windey. There was crutches inside, an' jury-legs fash'ned out o' cork, an' plaster heads drawn out in maps wi' county-towns marked in, an' bumps to show why diff'rent folks broke diff'rent Commandments, an' rows o' teeth a-grizzlin', an' blue spectacles, an' splints enough to camp-shed a thirty-acred field, an' ear-trumpets an' malignant growths—"

"Malignant growths?"

"Iss, sir—in speerits o' wine. But what tuk th' ould man's notice were a trayful o' glass eyes put out for sale i' the windey, an' lookin' so nat'ral as life—blue eyes, brown eyes, eyes as black as a sloan, [4] an' others, they told me, as went diff'rent colours 'cordin' as you looked at mun. Anyway, ould Mennear pulled up short an' clinched Deb'rah by the elbow.

"'Like onto the fishpools in Heshbon!' says he; an' wi' that he bounces into the shop.

"'How much for them eyes?' he axes.

"'Do 'ee want the lot?' says the chap in the shop, a reg'lar little dandy-sprat, an' so pert as a jay-pie in June. "'Cos us makes a reducshun on takin' a quantity,' says he.

"'Wan'll do for me,' says Lawyer Mennear.

"'They be two pund-ten apiece,' says the whipper-snapper, 'an' ten shillin' for fixin'.'

"Well, sir, you may fancy th' ould man's face when he heerd the price. He sot down, like as ef the wind was tuk out of hes sails, an' says he—'I'll gie thirty shillin.'

"The shopman wudn' ha' this; so at et they went, higglin' an' hagglin' on til 'twas agreed at las' he shud ha' the eye for two pund-five, fixin's included. 'Twas like drawin' blood from a stone; but th' ould man had done a stroke of bus'ness that day, so in th' end he pulls out hes bag an' tells out the money 'pon the counter.

"'An' now,' says the whipper-snapper, 'which'll 'ee ha'? Grey's the colour, I reckons, ef you wants a match.'

"'Drat the colour!' says ould Mennear, 'I've a-paid my price, an' I'll ha' the biggest, ef et be bassomy-red.' [5]

"Well, the shopman laffs, o' cou'se, but lets 'n ha' hes own way; an' th' ould man picked out the biggest—bright blue et was, suthin' the colour of a hedgy-sparrer's egg, an' shiny-clear like a glass-alley. They was a brave long while gettin' et fixed, 'cos 'twas so big. Ef he'd a-been content an' took a smaller wan, he'd ha' done better: but he was bound to be over-reachin', was th' ould varmint, an' so he comed to grief, as you shall hear. There's many folks i' this world be knowin' as Kate Mullet."

"I never heard of that lady," said Mr. Fogo.

"There's not much to know, sir, 'cept that they say her was hanged for a fool. Hows'ever, to shorten the yarn, ould Mennear got hes eye fixed at las', an' went home wi' Aunt Deb'rah so pleased as Punch.

"Nex' Sunday 'twas Hamlet's Ghost 'mong the 'Rig'nal Seceders, an' no mistake! Some o' the female members fell to screamin' so soon as iver they clapped eyes on th' ould man, an' Sister Trudgeon was tuk wi' a fit, an' had to be carr'd out wi' two deacons to her head an' two to her heels, an' kickin' so that Deacon Hoskins cudn' master hes vittles for up a fortni't, he was that hurted internally. An' the wust was, that what wi' the rumpus an' her singin' out 'Pillaloo!' an' how the devil was amongst mun, havin' great wrath, the Lawyer's sarmon about a 'wecked an' 'dulterous generation seekin' arter a sign' was clean sp'iled. Arter the sarvice, too, there was a deal of discussin'. Some said 'twas senful to interfere wi' Natur' i' that way, an' wrong in a purfessin' Christian like Mennear; an' all agreed the new eye gave 'n a janjansy [6] kind o' look, 'as ef,' said Deacon Hoskins, 'he was blinchin' [7] fifty ways for Grace.' There was some talk, too, about axin' the old man to resign; but nuthin' came o't. An' arter a time, when the congregashun got a bit reconciled, folks began to allow the new eye improved Mennear's pulpit manner, an' guessed that, arter all, et mou't be a powerful engine for effectual salvashun. Et had a *dead* appearance, ef you understands me, sir, and yet a sort o' gashly wakefulness, like a thing onhuman, 'cos o' cou'se et niver winked; th' ould man cudn' ha' winked, not for a fi'-pund note, for the thing was that big et strained his eyelid like a drum. 'Sides which, et had a way o' keepin' order 'mong the worshippers that you cudn' believe onless you seed it; for, let alone the colour o't, you niver knawed whether 'twas fixed on you or ten pews off, but somehow felt dead-sure 'twas you all the time, an' cudn' ha' moved, not if you had a blue-tailed fly inside the back o' your collar.

"Well, sir, nat'rally the Meetin' House began to fill agen, at fust out o' curiosity, but by-'m-by the list of Admitted Members began to fill up. Folk cudn' hold out when th' ould Lawyer ramped on 'bout t' other world an' there was that eye fixin' mun an' lookin' as though et had *been there*. I needn' tell 'ee th' ould man wore et ivery Sunday: 'deed, he wore et most days, but tuk et out o' nights, I've heerd, for 'twudn' shut when he slep', but used to scare ould Deb'rah Mennear fairly out of her sken o' moonshiny nights, when the light comed in 'pon et. An' even when her got 'n to lave et off, her used allays to put a tay-cup 'pon top o't afore closin' an eye.

"So et went on, sir, till wan Sunday mornin', when the Lawyer was fairly warmin' to hes work over the weckedness o' backsliders an' the wrath to come, he whacks the cush'n more'n ord'nary vi'lent, an' I reckon that made the eye work loose. Anyway, out et drops, and clatters down along the floor o' the Meetin' House.

"Now Deacon Hoskins i' them days had charge o' the Sunday-school boys. He was a short-sighted man, the Deacon, tho' that were hes misfortun'; but he had faults as well, an' wan o' these was a powerful knack o' droppin' off to sleep durin' sarmon-time. Hows'ever, he managed very tidily, for he knawed he was bound to wake hissel' so soon as he began to snore, an' then he'd start up sudden an' fetch the nighest boy a rousin' whistcuff 'pon the side o' the head to cover the noise he'd made, an' cry out, 'I've a-caught 'ee agen, ha' I? I'll tache 'ee to interrup' the word o' Grace wi' your gammut [8] an' may-games!'—an' he'd look round like as ef he'd say, 'Sorry to interrup', brethren, but desceplin' es desceplin'!' Many's the time I've a-seed 'n do this, an' you may take my word, sir, 'twas so good as a play!"

Now this morning Deacon Hoskins was takin' forty winks as ushul, when the clatter made by th' ould Mennear's eye makes 'n set up, wide-awake an' starin'. This time, jedgin' by the noise, he tuk a consait that the boys had been a-playin' marbles sure 'nuff; so he takes two at haphazard, knacks their heads together, an' then looks about. Fust thing he sees es th' eye lying out 'pon the aisle an' lookin' for all the world like a big shiny glass-alley.

"I told 'ee, sir, the Deacon were short o' sight. He hadn' a doubt by this time the boys had been foolin' about wi' marbles, so he reaches out, grabs the eye, an' slips et into hes trowsy-pocket; an' then he takes a glance round, so much as to say, 'I reckon the owner of this 'ere glass-alley'll ha' to wait afore he sees 'n agen.'

"In cou'se, the rest o' the brethren knawed what had happened, an' wan or two fell to titterin' a bit; but altogether there was a kind o' breathlessness for a moment or so, an' then th' ould Mennear sings out from the pulpit—

"'Brother Hoskins, I'll trouble you to kindly pass up that eye.'

"Deacon Hoskins stared a bit, but was too short o' sight to see what the matter was.

"'Eh?' says he.

"'Hand up that eye, ef you plaise.'

"'What eye?' says the Deacon.

"Th' ould Mennear stamped and seemed fit to swear.

"'Why, *my* eye, you nation bufflehead!' The Lawyer didn't mind much what he said when hes back was up; an' arter all 'twere, in a kind o' way, 'scuseable.

"'Look 'ere,' answers back the Deacon, 'ef you've drapped your eye, an' be that fond o' the cheap-jack thing that you can't get on wi'out et, send round Deacon Spettigue to hunt, an' not a man as can't see sax inches afore hes nose. Et's out o' reas'n,' he said, 'an' you ort to know better.'

"In cou'se, tho', when he found out hes mistake an' lugged the thing out o' hes pocket, there was Bedlam let loose, for up five minnits, ivery mother's son chitterin' an' laffin, an' the Deacon lookin' like a pig in a fit. He desarted the Seceders that very week, an' niver darken'd the Meetin' House door agen to the day o' hes death.

"Well, the fuss got calmed over, but somehow the Lawyer cudn' niver trust hes eye as he used to. He said 'twarn't fully dependable; an', sure 'nuff, within a month et slipped out agen, and th' ould man was forced to go to Plymouth an' buy another, a bit smaller. So he lost by his mean ways arter all. He tried to trade back th' ould eye, but the shopman wudn'; so he brought et home in hes pocket, and laid it by in the chaney cupboard, 'long wi' the cloam, [9] an' there et bided.

"An' now, sir, I'm a-comin' to the most curiosest part o' my yarn: an' you can believe or no, as you thinks fit, but I'll tell 'ee jest what I knows an' no more.

"Some two year arter, Lawyer Mennear tuk a corner out o' the twenty-acred field—a little patch to the right o' the gate as you went in—an' planted et wi' green peas. Six rows he planted, an' beautiful peas, too, on'y the birds wudn' let mun ha' a chance. Well, at las' th' ould man got mad, an' stuck me 'pon top o' the hedge wi' a clapper to scare the birds away; 'sides which, to make sure, he rigged up a scarecrow. 'Twas a lovely scarecrow: two cross-sticks an' the varmer's own coat—'twas the coat he'd a-got married in forty year afore. He gied et to me when the scarecrow had done wi' et, an' the tails were so long as an Act o' Parlyment. 'Top o' this was a whackin' big turmut by way o' face, wi' a red scarf round the neck—from Aunt Deb'rah's petticoat—an' wan o' th' ould man's left-off wigs 'pon the crown, an' a high-poll hat, a bit rusted wi' Sunday obsarvance, to finish. Did I say 'to finish'?

"Well, then, I said wrong. 'Cos jest when I'd a-rigged 'n up, down comes Aunt Deb'rah an' cries out, 'Aw, Caleb, here be suthin' more! Do 'ee fix et in, that's a dear; an' ef et don't scare away any bird as iver flied, then,' says she, 'I'm wuss nor any bird'; an' wi' that she opens her hand an' gies me the Lawyer's cast-off eye.

"So I outs wi' my pocket-knife an' digs a hole in the turmat face, an' inside o' ten minnits there was the scarecrow finished off. Aw, sir, 'twas a beautiful scarecrow; an' when us stuck et up, I tell 'ee that from the kitchen windeys, three hundred yards away, et seemed like life itsel'.

"Well, sir, fust day 'twas stuck there, I sot beside the hedge, round the corner, watchin', and while I sot two queerish things happen'd—

tho' the fust warn't so queer nuther, but jest human natur', when you comes to consider et. 'Twas this. I hadn' been there an hour afore *two score an' dree wimmen*—I knows, 'cos I kep' count—came, wan arter anuther, down to the gate to make sheep's eyes at that scarecrow, havin' heerd as there was a well-dressed lad down among the peas. An' that's true, ef I swears et 'pon the Book."

"Ah!" was Mr. Fogo's only comment.

"Iss, sir; an' well you may say so. But the nex' thing I noticed was a sight queerer. In fac' I dunno but et's the queerest go I iver heard tell 'bout. But you may jedge for yoursel'.

"I'd been a-settin' there for the best part o' two hour, an' keepin' count o' how wan bird arter another comed up for they peas, an' turned tail at sight o' the scarecrow. For et didn' seem like no ord'nary scarecrow, sir, wi' that eye a-glintin' in the sunshine. I cou'd see 't from where I sot—an' so the birds thought. Well, wan arter another, they steps up an' flies off as ef hurried for time, when by-'m-by 'long comes an ould rook.

"He jest sa'ntered up quite leisurable, did this rook, an' lit 'pon a pea-stick to take a blinch round. Nat'rally he cotches sight o' the scarecrow, an' nat'rally I looked for 'n to turn tail, like the rest. But no, sir.

"Where he was, the scarecrow's back was t'wards 'un, an' th' ould bird jest looks et up an' down, an' this way an' that, an' cocks his head 'pon wan side, an' looks agen an' chuckles, for all the world as ef to say, 'Et looks like a man, an' 'tis fixed like a man; but dash my wig! ef 'tain't a scarecrow an' no more, I ain't fit to live in an age o' imitashuns.'

"Well, he jest sot an' sot, an' arter a while he began for to taste the flavour o' the joke, an' then he lay back an' laffed, did that bird, till he was fit to sweat. I reckoned I'd a-heerd birds laff afore this, but I made an error. My 'ivens, sir! but he jest clinched on to that pea-stick, an' shook the enj'yment out of hissel' like a conjurer shellin'

109

cannon-balls from a hat. An' then he'd stop a bit, an' then fall to hootin' agen, till I was forced to laff too, way back behind the hedge, for cumpanny. An' ivery time he noted a fresh bit o' likelihood in the scarecrow he'd go off in a fresh fit. I thought he'd niver ha' done.

"But in a while he hushed, an' waited a bit to calm hes nerves, an' stepped down off the pea-stick. Thinks I, 'What es he up to now?' An' I stood up to see, but quiet-like, so's I shudn' scare 'n.

"I hadn' long to wait. He jest steps up behind the scarecrow, makes a leg, so grave as you plaise, an' commences for to dance round 'un— fust 'pon wan leg, then 'pon t'other—like as ef 'twas a haythen dancin' round a graven image. But the flauntin' ins'lence o't, sir! The brazen, fleerin' abusefulness! Not a feather, ef you'll believe me, but fairly leaked wi' ribaldry—jest *leaked*.

"Th' ould bird had got ha'f-way round, a-mincin' an' japin', an' throwin' out hes legs this way an' that an' gettin' more boldacious an' ondacent wi' ivery step, when he cocks his head askew for a second, jest to see how the pore image was a-takin' o't, an' that moment he catches the scarecrow's eye.

"Aw, sir, to see the change as comed over that bird! The forthiness [10] went out o'n for all the world like wind out 'n a pricked bladder; an' I reckon nex' minnit there warn't no meaner, sicklier-lookin' critter atween this an' Johnny Groats' than that ould rook. There was a kind o' shever ran through 'n, an' hes feathers went ruffly-like, an' hes legs bowed in, an' he jes' lay flat to groun' and goggled an' glazed up at that eye like a dyin' duck in a thunderstorm. 'Twas a rich sight, sir; an' how I contrived not to bust mysel' wi' laffin', es more'n I can tell 'ee to this day.

"So he lay for up ten minnits, an' then he staggered up 'pon hes feet an' sneaked out o' them peas like a chuck-sheep dog, an' the repent'nce a-tricklin' out 'n ivery pore. He passed me by that close I cou'd ha' knacked 'n over wi' a stick, but he didn' see me more'n ef I'd a'been a pisky-man. [11] All hes notiss, I reckon, were for that gashly eye; an' he looked back ivery now and agen, like as ef he'd

110

say, 'I be but worms; an', wuss nor that, I've a-been a scoffin', lyin', Sabbath-breakin' ould worms; but do 'ee let me off this wance, an' I'll strive an' wrastle,' he seemed to say, 'an' do purty well all a rook can to be gathered to the fold.' An' wi' that he slinks over th' hedge an' out o' sight.

"Well, sir, I didn' see 'n agen nex' day, nor for many days arter; but on Sunday-week, as et mou't be, i' the mornin' I'd a-took French lave an' absented mysel' from Meetin' House, an' were quietly smokin' my pipe up in the town-place, [12] when I hears a chitterin' an' a chatterin' like as 'twere a little way off; an' lookin' down t'wards the twenty-acred field, I seed 'twere black wi' rooks—fairly black, sir— black as the top o' your hat. Thinks I, 'I reckon here's some new caper,' an' I loafes down to see the fun.

"I stales down the lane, an' looks over the gate, an' when I takes in, at las', what 'tes all about, my!—you mou't ha' knacked me down wi' a feather! 'Twas a prayer-meetin' them rooks was a-holdin', sir, as I'm a senner. The peas was fairly hid wi' the crowd, an' 'twas that thick I counted sax 'pon wan pea-stick. An' in the middle, jes' onder the scarecrow, stood up th' ould rook I'd a-seen afore, an' told hes experiences. He ramped, an' raved, an' mopped, an' mowed, an' kep' a-noddin' his head t'wards the scarecrow, to show how hes salvashun was worked; an' all the time the rest o' the rooks sat still as mice. On'y when he pulls up to breathe a bit, they lets out an' squalls, as ef to say, 'Amen. 'Tes workin'—'tes workin'! Pray strong, brother!' an' at et he'd go agen, same as he *must*. An' at las', when 'twas 'hold breath or bust' wi' 'un, he ups an' starts a hemn, an' they all jines in, till you mou't hear the caprouse [13] two mile off. That were the finish, too; for arter the row died away, there was a minnit or so o' silent prayer, an' then the whole gang gets up off they pea-sticks an' sails away for Squire Tresawsen's rookery, t'other side o' the hill.

"Well, in cou'se I tells the tale, an' was called a liard for my pains. But the same thing happen'd nex' Sunday, an' the Sunday arter—an' not a pea stolen all the time—an' a good few people comed down behind the hedge to see, an' owned up as I were right. Et got to be the talk o' the country; an' how 'twud ha' ended, goodness on'y knaws, ef I hadn' a-spi'led the sport mysel'. An' how I did so, you shall hear.

"Wan day I tuk a consait as 'twud be a game to take away the scarecrow's eye an' see what happen'd. So, late 'pon a Sat'rday night, down I goes an' digs out the eye wi' my jack-knife, an' lays et careful down 'pon the ground beside et, an' so off to bed.

"Nex' mornin' I were down waitin' some time afore the rooks was due, an' by-'m-by, about 'leven in the forenoon, 'long they comes by the score, an' takes the sittin's 'pon the pea-sticks. They was barely settled, when out steps my ould rook an' walks up to the scarecrow to lead off same as ushul.

"He gives a shake o' the head to set hes jawin'-tacks loose, casts a glance up'ards t'wards the eye, jes' to fetch inspirashun, an' starts back like as ef shot. You cou'd see the 'stonishment *clinch* 'n, an' the look o' righteousness melted off hes face like snow in an oven. For that bird had *gifts*, sir; an' wan o' these was a power o' fashul expresshun. Well, back he starts, an', with the same, cotches sight o' the eye lyin' 'pon the ground an' starin' up all heav'nly-blue an' smilin'.

"There was a pause arter this, jes' about so long as you cou'd count twenty; an' the rest o' the congregashun began to fidget an' whisper round that suthin' was up, when all 'pon a sudden my ould rook straightens hissel' up an' begins to cuss and to swear. What's that you say, sir? Rooks don't swear? Don't tell me. Blasphemin'? Why, in two minnits the air was stiff wi' blasphemy—you might ha' cut et wi' a knife. An' oaths? Why, you cou'd *feel* the oaths. An' there he sot an' cussed, an' cussed an' sot, an' let the hatefulness run out like watter from a pump.

"In cou'se, 'twarnt long afore the rest gather'd round to larn what the mess was, an' then there was Chevychace. They handed round the eye, an' looked at et this way an' that, an' 'splained what had happen'd wan to t'other; an' then they hushed an' stood quiet while their dasayved brother cussed hissel' out. Not a smile 'mongst the lot, sir; not a wink, as I be a truthful man.

"At las' he'd a-done, an' not too soon for hes lungs; an' then the lot sat down an' consedered et out, an' still not a word for minnits togither. But all to wanst up starts a youngish-lookin' rook, an' makes a speech.

"'Twarn't a long speech, sir, an' nat'rally I didn't understand a word: but I cotched his drift in a minnit, tho'. For they rooks started up, walked back to their seats, an' what do 'ee think they did?"

"I couldn't pretend to guess," said Mr. Fogo.

"They jes' started that sarvice agan, sir, an' paradised et from start to finish. They mixed up ow jests wi' the prayers, an' flung in fancy yarns wi' their experiences, an' made a mock at th' exhortashun; an' what they sung in place o' the hemn, I don't know; but I do knaw this much—et warn't fit for a woman to list'n to.

"Well, I laffed—I was forced to laff—but arter a while et grew a bit too strong, an' I runned up to th' house to fetch down a few folks to look. I warn't away 'bove ten minnits; but when I comed back there warn't no rook to be seen, nor no eye nuther. They'd a-carr'd et off to Squire Tresawsen's rookery, an' et's niver been seen fro' that day to this."

There was silence for a few moments as Caleb finished his story and lit another pipe. Finally Mr. Fogo roused him to ask—

"What became of your master, Caleb?"

"Dead, sir—dead," answered Caleb, staring into the embers of the fire. "He lived to a powerful age, tho' albeit a bit totelin' [14] in hes latter days. But for all that he mou't ha' been like Tantra-bobus— lived till he died, or at least been a centurion—"

113

"A what?"

"Centurion, sir; otherwise a hundred years old. But he went round land [15] at las', an' was foun' dead in hes bed—o' heart-break, they did say, 'long o' his gran'-darter Joanna runnin' away wi' an army cap'n.'"

"Ah!" said Mr. Fogo, pensively, "she was a woman, was she not?"

"To be sure, sir; what elst?—a female woman, an' so baptised."

There was a moment's silence; then Caleb resumed—

"But contrari-wise, sir, the army cap'n was a man."

"Ah! yes, of course; let us be just—the army captain was a man. Caleb," said Mr. Fogo, with a sudden change from his pensive manner, "has it ever occurred to you to guess why I—not yet an old man, Caleb—am living in this solitude?"

"Beggin' your pard'n, sir, an' makin' so free as to guess, but were it a woman by any chance?"

"Yes," said his master, rising hurriedly and lighting his candle, "it was a woman, Caleb—it was a woman. You won't forget that Notice to-morrow morning, will you?—the first thing, if you please, Caleb."

[1] A cart-load.
[2] Dust.
[3] Playing truant.
[4] Sloe.
[5] Heather-coloured.
[6] Two-faced. Qy. from Janus?
[7] Prying, looking about.
[8] Nonsense.
[9] Crockery. Drinking in Troy is euphemistically called "emptyin' cloam."
[10] Boldness, forwardness.

[11] A fairy.
[12] Farm-yard.
[13] Noise, tumult.
[14] Demented, imbecile.
[15] Died.

CHAPTER XII.

OF DETERIORATION; AND A WHEELBARROW
THAT CONTAINED UNEXPECTED THINGS.

Great events meanwhile were happening in Troy. On the eighth morning of his eclipse Admiral Buzza was startled by a brisk step upon the stairs; the devil's tattoo was neatly struck upon his bedroom door, and the head of Mr. Goodwyn-Sandys looked in.

"Ah! Admiral, here you are; like What's-his-name in the ruins of Thingummy. You'll pardon me coming up, but my wife is downstairs with Mrs. Buzza, and I was told I should find you here. Don't rise— 'no dress,' as they say. May I smoke? Thanks. And how are you by this time? I heard something of your mishap, but not the rights of it. I'll sit down, and you can tell me all about it."

Here was affability indeed. The Admiral conquered his first impulse of diving beneath the bed-clothes, and, lying back, recounted his misadventure at some length. The Honourable Frederic listened and smoked with perfect gravity. At the close he said—

"Very dirty treatment, 'pon my word; though I'm not sure I don't sympathise with the fellow in warning off the women. But why stay in bed?"

"There are feelings," —began the Admiral.

"Ah! to be sure—injured feelings—ungrateful country—blow, blow, thou winter wind, &c. So you take to bed, like the Roman gentleman who went too; forget the place. Gets rid of the women, too; nuisance—women—when you're upset; nonsense, that about pain and anguish playing the deuce, and a ministering angel thou— tommy-rot, I call it. Can't be bothered, now, in bed—turn round and snore; wife has hysterics—snore louder. Capital! I've a mind to try the same plan when Geraldine is fussing and fuming. These infernal women—"

I am sorry to say that the Admiral, instead of defending Mrs. Buzza, began to exculpate Mrs. Goodwyn-Sandys.

"But your wife is so charming, so—"

"Of course, my dear sir; so is Mrs. Buzza."

"She was termed the 'Belle of Portsmouth' at the Ball where I proposed to her," remarked the Admiral, with some complacency.

"To be sure; trust a sailor to catch the pretty girls—eh?"

The Admiral chuckled feebly.

"But these women—"

"Ah! yes; these women—"

"Bachelor life was pleasant—eh, Admiral?"

"Ah!"

The two men looked at each other. A smile spread over either countenance. I regret to say the Admiral winked, and then chuckled again.

"Admiral, you must get up."

The Admiral stared interrogatively; his visitor pursued, with some inconsequence—"By the way, is there a club here?"

"There's the 'Jolly Trojans' down at the 'Man-o'-War'; they meet on Tuesdays, Thursdays, and—"

"Low lot, I suppose?"

"Well, yes," admitted the Admiral; "a certain amount of good fellowship prevails, I understand; but low, of course—distinctly low."

The Honourable Frederic tapped his boot reflectively with his malacca.

"Admiral," he said at last, "you ought to found a Club here."

"Bless my heart! I never thought of it."

"It is your duty."

"You think so?"

"Sure of it."

"I will get up," said the Admiral decisively. He started out of bed, and looked around for his clothes.

"Nice place, the country," pursued the Honourable Frederic thoughtfully; "fresh eggs, and grass to clean your pipe with—but apt to be dull. Now, a pleasant little society; cards, billiards, and social *reunions*—select, of course—"

"Of course. Do you happen to be sitting on my trousers?"

"Eh? No, I believe—no. Let me see—limited loo and a modest pool of an evening. Hullo! what's the matter?"

The Admiral had rushed to the door.

"Emily!" he bawled down the stairs.

"Well, I'll be going. Can't find your trousers? Admiral, it's the last straw. But we'll be revenged, Admiral. We'll found a Club; and, by George, sir, we'll call it 'The Inexpressibles'! Ta-ta for the present," and Mr. Goodwyn-Sandys retired.

But what was being discussed below when the Admiral's voice disturbed his wife? Alas! you shall hear.

"These men," Mrs. Goodwyn-Sandys was saying, "are all alike. But, my dear, why not disregard his absurd humours? I have revolted from Frederic long ago."

"You don't say so!"

"It is a fact. Take my advice and do the same. It needs courage at first, but they are all cowards—oh, such cowards, my dear! Revolt. Cry 'Havoc!' and let slip—"

"My dear, I should faint."

"Oh, poor soul! Reflect! How pretty the domestic virtues are, but how impossible! Besides, how unfashionable!"

Mrs. Buzza reflected.

"I will!" she exclaimed at last. Just then her husband's voice detonated in the room above. She arose, trembling like a leaf. "Be firm," said her adviser.

"I will."

"Sit down again. It will do him no harm to wait."

Mrs. Buzza obeyed, still trembling.

It was at this moment that the Honourable Frederic re-entered the room, and looked around with a slow smile.

"Nellie," he observed, when they were outside the house, "you're a vastly clever woman, my love."

"How's the Admiral?" was the reply.

"He nibbles, my angel; he bites."

"I heard him barkin'. An' how long will Brady be givin' us?"

"Two months, my treasure."

Mrs. Goodwyn-Sandys reflected for a moment, and then made the following extraordinary reply—

"Be aisy, me dear. In six weeks I'll be ready to elope from yez."

What passed between the Admiral and Mrs. Buzza when they were left together was never fully known. But it was quickly whispered that in No. 2, Alma Villas, the worm had turned. Oddly enough, the spread of conjugal estrangement did not end here. It began to be rumoured that Lawyer Pellow and his wife had "differences "; that Mr. and Mrs. Simpson dined at different hours; and that the elder Miss Strip had broken off a very suitable match with a young ship's chandler, on the ground that ship's candles were not "genteel." It was about this time, too, that Mrs. Wapshot, at the confectionery shop, refused to walk with Mr. Wapshot on the Rope-walk after Sunday evening service, because domestic bliss was "horrid vulgar"; and Mrs. Goodwyn-Sandys' dictum that "one admirer, at least, was no more than a married woman's due," only failed of acceptance because the supply of admirers in Troy fell short of the demand. She had herself annexed Samuel Buzza and Mr. Moggridge.

Meanwhile the Admiral was not idle; and had anything been needed to whet his desire for a Club, it would have been found in a dreadful event that happened shortly afterwards.

It was May-morning, and the Admiral was planted in the sunshine outside No. 2, Alma Villas, loudly discussing the question of the hour with Mr. Goodwyn-Sandys, Lawyer Pellow, and the little Doctor.

"No, we can't have him," he was roundly declaring; "the Club must be select, or it is useless to discuss it further."

"Must draw the line somewhere," murmured the Honourable Frederic.

"Quite so; at this rate we shall be admitting all the 'Jolly Trojans.'"

Just then an enormous wheelbarrow was observed approaching, seemingly by supernatural means, for no driver could be seen. The barrow was piled to a great height, and staggered drunkenly from side to side of the road; but the load, whatever it was, lay hidden beneath a large white cloth.

"H'm!" said the little Doctor dubiously. "Well, of course, you know best, but I should have thought that as an old inhabitant of Troy—"

"Pooh, my dear fellow," snapped the Admiral, "it is natural that the feelings of a few will be hurt; but if once we begin to elect the 'Jolly Trojans'—"

The barrow had drawn near meanwhile, and now halted at the Admiral's feet. From behind it stepped into view an exceeding small boy, attired mainly in a gigantic pair of corduroys that reached to the armpits, and were secured with string around the shoulders. His face was a mask of woe, and he staunched his tears on a very grimy shirt-sleeve as he stood and gazed mutely into the Admiral's face.

"Go away, boy!" said Admiral Buzza severely.

The boy sobbed loudly, but made no sign of moving.

"Go away, I tell you!"

"'Tes for you, sir."

"For me? What does the boy mean?"

"Iss, sir. Missusses orders that I was to bring et to Adm'ral Buzza's; an' ef I don't pay out Billy Higgs for this nex' time I meets wi' 'un—"

"The child's daft!" roared the Admiral. "D—— the boy! what has Billy Higgs to do with me?"

"Poured a teacupful o' water down the nape o' my breeches when I'd got ha'f-way up the hill an' cudn' set the barrow down to fight 'un—the coward! Boo-hoo!" and tears flowed again at the recollection.

"What is it?"

"Cake, sir."

"Cake!"

"Iss, sir—cake."

The youth stifled a sob, and removed the white cover from the wheelbarrow.

"Bless my soul!" gasped the Admiral, "there must be some mistake."

"It certainly seems to be cake," observed the Honourable Frederic, examining the load through his eye-glass; "and very good cake, too, by the smell."

He was right. High on the barrow, and symmetrically piled, rested five-and-twenty huge cakes—yellow cakes such as all Trojans love—each large as a mill-stone, tinctured with saffron, plentifully stowed with currants, and crisp with brown crust, steaming to heaven, and wooing the nostrils of the gods.

"Bless my soul!" repeated the Admiral, "but I never ordered this."

"It certainly seems to be cake," observed the Honourable Frederic.

Each member of the group in turn advanced, inspected the cake, sniffed the savour, pronounced it excellent, and looked from the Admiral to the boy for explanation.

"Mrs. Dymond down to the 'Man-'o-War' sent et, sir, wi' her compliments to Maaster Sam, an' hopin' as he'll find et plum i' the bakin' as it leaves her at present, an' the currants all a-picked careful, knowin' as he'd a sweet tooth."

"Sam! Do you mean to tell me that Sam—that my son—ordered *this*? Upon my word, of all—"

"Didn' azackly order et, sir. Won et fair an' square. Bill Odgers comed nex' wi' seven-an'-ninety gallon. But Master Sam topped the lot by a dozen gallon aisy."

"Gallons! What the devil is the boy talking bout?"

"Beer, sir—beer; fust prize for top score o' beer drunk down to the 'Man-o'-War' sence fust o' November last. He's a wunner for beer, es Maaster Sam," pursued the relentless urchin, who by this time had forgotten his tears. "Hunderd an' nine gallons, sir, an' Bill Odgers so jallous as fire—says he'd ha' won et same as he did last time, on'y Maaster Sam's got the longer purse—offered to fight 'un, an' the wuss man to pay for both nex' time."

Mr. Goodwyn-Sandys turned aside to conceal a smile. Lawyer Pellow rubbed his chin. The Admiral stamped.

"Take it away!"

"Where be I to take it to, plaise, sir?"

"Take it away—anywhere; take it to the devil!"

But worse remained for the little man. During this conversation there had come unperceived up the road a gentleman of mild appearance, dressed in black, and carrying under his arm a large parcel wrapped about with whitey-brown paper.

The new-comer, who was indeed our friend Mr. Fogo, now advanced towards the Admiral with a bow.

"Admiral Buzza, I believe?"

The Admiral turned and faced the speaker; his jaw fell like a signal flag; but he drew himself up with fine self-repression.

"Sir, I am Admiral Buzza."

"I have come," said Mr. Fogo, quietly pulling the pins out of his parcel, "to restore what I believe is your property (Will somebody oblige me by holding this pin? Thank you), and at the same time to apologise for the circumstances under which it came into my hands.

(Dear me, what a number of pins, to be sure!) I have done what lay in my power with a clothes-brush and emery-powder to restore it to its pristine brilliance. The treatment (That is the last, I think) has not, I am bound to admit, answered my expectations; its result, however, is as you see."

Here Mr. Fogo withdrew the wrapper and with a pleasant smile held out—a cocked hat.

The Admiral, purple with fury, bounced back like a shot on a red-hot shovel; stared; tried to speak, but could not; gulped; tried again; and finally, shaking his fist in Mr. Fogo's face, flung into the house and slammed the front door.

The cause of this transport turned a pair of bewildered spectacles on the others, and found them convulsed with unseemly mirth. He singled out the Honourable Frederic, and addressed himself to that gentleman.

"I have not the pleasure to be acquainted with you, sir; but if you can supply me with any reason for this display of temper, believe me—"

"My name is Goodwyn-Sandys, sir, at your—"

"What!"

Mr. Fogo dropped the cocked hat and sat down suddenly among the cakes.

"Are you," he gasped—"are you Mr. Goodwyn-Sandys—the Honourable Frederic Augustus Hythe Good—? Heavens!"

"No, sir," said the Honourable Frederic, who had grown a thought pale. "Good *wyn*, sir—Goodwyn-Sandys. What then?"

"I never saw your face before," murmured Mr. Fogo faintly.

125

"That, sir, if a misfortune, is one which you share with a number of your fellow-men. And permit me to tell you, sir," continued Mr. Goodwyn-Sandys, with unaccountable change of mood, "that I consider your treatment of my friend Admiral Buzza unworthy of a gentleman, sir—unworthy of a gentleman. Come, Doctor; come, Pellow—I want a word or two more with you about this Club."

And Mr. Goodwyn-Sandys ruffled away, followed by his two slightly puzzled companions.

For the space of two minutes Mr. Fogo gazed up the road after them. Then he sighed, took off his spectacles, and wiped them carefully.

"So *that*," he said slowly, "is the man she married."

"Iss, sir."

Mr. Fogo started, turned round on the barrow, and beheld the urchin from the "Man-o'-War."

"Little boy," he said sternly, "your conduct is unworthy of a—I mean, what are you doing here?"

"You've a-been an' squashed a cake," said the boy.

Mr. Fogo gave him a shilling, and hurried away down the road; but stopped once or twice on his homeward way to repeat to himself—

"So *that*—is the man—she married."

It took Admiral Buzza several days to recover his composure; but when he did, the project of the new Club grew with the conjugal disintegration of Troy, and at a rate of progress scarcely inferior. Within a week or two a house was hired in Nelson Row, a brass-plate bearing the words "Trojan Club" affixed to the door, and Admiral Buzza installed in the Presidential Chair. The Presidential Chair occupied the right-hand side of the reading-room window, which overlooked the harbour; and the Presidential duties consisted mainly in conning the morning papers and discussing their contents with Mr. Goodwyn-Sandys, who usually sat, with a glass of whiskey and the Club telescope, on the left-hand side of the window. Indeed, it would be hard to say to which of the two, the whiskey or the telescope, the Honourable Frederic more sedulously devoted himself: it is certain, at least, that under the Admiral's instruction he soon developed a most amazing familiarity with nautical terms, was a mine of information (almost as soon as the Club invested in a Yacht Register) on the subject of Lord Sinkport's yacht, the auxiliary screw *Niobe*, and swept the horizon with a persistence that made his fellow-members stare.

But the most noticeable feature in this nautical craze was the disproportionate attention which the Honourable Frederic lavished on barques. It was the first rig that he learnt to distinguish, and his early interest developed before long into something like a passion.

One morning, for instance, Sam Buzza lounged into the reading-room and observed —

"I say, have you seen that American barque that came in last night — the *Maritana?*"

"What name?" asked Mr. Goodwyn-Sandys, looking up suddenly.

"The *Maritana*, or the *Mariana*, or *Mary Ann*, or something of the — Hullo! what's wrong?"

But the Honourable Frederic had caught up his hat and fled. Half an hour afterwards, when he returned, his usual calm self, the little Doctor took occasion to remark, "Upon my word, you might be a detective, you keep such a look-out on the harbour" — a remark which caused Mr. Goodwyn-Sandys to laugh so consumedly that the Doctor, without exactly seeing the point, began to think he had perpetrated quite a considerable joke.

But let no one imagine that the disruption of Trojan morals avoided heart-burning or escaped criticism. For the line which Mr. Goodwyn-

Sandys declared must be drawn somewhere was found not only to bisect the domestic hearth, but to lead to a surprising number of social problems. It fell across the parallels of our small society, and demonstrated that Mrs. A and Mrs. B could never meet; that one room could not contain the two unequal families X and Y; and that while one rested on the basis of trade, and the other on professional skill, it was unreasonable to expect the apex Mrs. Y to coincide with the apex Mrs. X. Finally the New Geometry culminated in a triumphant process, which proved that while Mrs. Simpson was allowed to imbibe tea and scandal in the company of the great, her husband must sip his gin and water in solitude at home.

We had always been select in Troy; but then, In the old days, *all* Troy had been included in the term. When Mr. Simpson had spoken of the "Jack of Oaks" (meaning the Knave of Clubs), or had said "fainaiguing" (where others said "revoking"), we had pretended not to notice it, until at length we actually did not. So that a human as well as a philological interest attaches to the date when fashion narrowed the meaning of *Cumeelfo* to exclude the Jack of Oaks, and sent Mr. Simpson home to his gin and water.

The change was discussed with some asperity in the bar-parlour of the "Man-o'-War."

"The hupper classes in Troy es bloomin' fine nowadays," remarked Rechab Geddye (locally known as Rekkub) over his beer on the night when the resignations of Mr. Buzza Junior and Mr. Moggridge had been received by the "Jolly Trojans."

"Ef they gets the leastest bit finer, us shan't be able to see mun," answered Bill Odgers, who was reckoned a wit. "I have heerd tell as Trojans was cousins an' hail-fellow-well-met all the world over; but the hayleet o' this place es a-gettin' a bit above itsel'."

"That's a true word, Bill," interposed Mrs. Dymond from the bar; "an' to say 'Gie us this day our daily bread,' an' then turn up a nose at good saffron cake es flyin' i' the face o' Pruvvidence, an' no less."

"I niver knawed good to come o' titled gentry yet," said Bill.

"You doan't say that?" exclaimed Rekkub, who was an admirer of Bill's Radical views.

"I do, tho'. Look at King Richard—him i' the play-actin'. I reckon he was wan o' the hupper ten ef anybody. An' what does he do? Why, throttles a pair o' babbies, puts a gen'l'm'n he'd a gridge agen into a cask o' wine—which were the spoliation o' both—murders 'most ivery wan he claps eyes on, an' then when he've a-got the jumps an' sees the sperrits an' blue fire, goes off an' offers to swap hes whole bloomin' kingdom for a hoss—a hoss, mind you, he hadn' seen, let alone not bein' in a state o' mind to jedge hoss-flesh. What's true o' kings I reckon es true o' Hon'rubbles; they'm all reared up to the same high notions, an' I reckon us'll find et out afore long. I niver seed no good in makin' Troy fash'nubble mysel'."

CHAPTER XIII.

THE SIGNIFICANCE OF POMEROY'S CAT; AND HOW THE MEN
AND WOMEN OF TROY ENSUED AFTER PLEASURE IN BOATS.

The historian of Troy here feels at liberty to pass over six weeks with
but scanty record. During that time the Bankshire rose bloomed over
Kit's House, peered in at the windows, and found Mr. Fogo for the
most part busied in peaceful carpentry, though with a mysterious
trouble in his breast that at times drove him afield on venturous
perambulations, or to his boat to work off by rowing his too-
meditative fit. From these excursions he would return tired in body
but in heart eased, and resume his humdrum life tranquilly enough;
though Caleb was growing uneasy, and felt it necessary, more than
once, to retire apart and "have et out," as he put it, with his
conscience.

"Question es," he would repeat, "whether I be justyfied in meddlin'
wi' the Cou'se o' Natur'—'speshully when the Cou'se o' Natur' es
sich as I approves. An' s'posin' I bain't, furder question es, whether I
be right in receivin' wan pound a week an' a new set o' small-
clothes."

This nice point in casuistry was settled for the time by his waiving
claim to the small-clothes, and inserting in his old pair a patch of
blue seacloth that contrasted extravagantly with the veteran stuff—
so extravagantly as to compel Mr. Fogo's attention.

"Does it never strike you," he asked one day as Caleb was stooping
over the wood-pile, "that the repairs in your trousers, Caleb, are a
trifle emphatic? *Purpureus, late qui splendeat*—h'm, h'm— *adsuitur
pannus*. I mean, in the seat of your—"

"Conscience, sir," said Caleb abruptly. "Some ties a bit o' string
round the finger to help the mem'ry. I does et this way."

"Well, well, I should have thought it more apt to assist the memory of others. Still, of course, you know best."

And Mr. Fogo resumed his work, and thought no more about it; but Caleb alternated between moods of pensiveness and fussy energy for some days after.

In Troy, summer was leading on a train of events not to be classed among periodic phenomena. It stands on record, for instance—

That Loo began to be played at the Club, and the Admiral's weekly accounts to grow less satisfactory than in the days when he and Mrs. Buzza were steadfast opponents at Whist.

That Mrs. Simpson discovered her great uncle to have been a baronet on this earth.

That Mrs. Payne had prefixed "Ellicome" to her surname, and spoke of "*the* Ellicome-Paynes, you know."

That Mr. Moggridge had been heard to speak of Sam Buzza as a "low fellow."

That Sam had retorted by terming the poet a "conceited ass."

And—

That Admiral Buzza intended a Picnic.

To measure the importance of this last item, you must know that a Trojan picnic is no ordinary function. To begin with, it is essentially patriotic—devoted, in fact, to the cult of the Troy river, in honour of which it forms a kind of solemn procession. Undeviating tradition has fixed its goal at a sacred rock, haunted of heron and kingfisher, and wrapped around with woodland, beside a creek so tortuous as to simulate a series of enchanted lakes. Here the self-respecting Trojan, as his boat cleaves the solitude, will ask his fellows earnestly and at regular intervals whether they ever beheld anything more lovely; and they, in duty bound and absolute truthfulness, will answer that they never did.

It follows that a Trojan picnic depends for its success to quite a peculiar degree upon the weather. But on the day of the Admiral's merry-making, this was, beyond cavil, kind. Four boats started from the Town Quay; four boats—alas!—could by this time contain the *cumeelfo* of Troy; for everybody who was anybody had been invited, and nobody (with the exception of the Honourable Frederic, who could not leave his telescope) had refused. Sam Buzza did not start with the rest, but was to follow later; and in his absence Mr. Moggridge paid impressive court to Mrs. Goodwyn-Sandys, though uneasily, for Sophia's saddened eyes were upon him.

Yet everybody seemed in the best of spirits and tempers. The Admiral, after bestowing his wife in another boat, and glaring vindictively at Kit's House, where the figure of Mr. Fogo was visible on the beach, grew exceedingly jocose, and cracked his most admired jokes, including his famous dialogue with the echo just beyond Kit's House—a performance which Miss Limpenny declared she had seldom heard him give with such spirit. She herself, spurred to emulation, told her favourite story, which began, "In the Great Exhibition of Eighteen Hundred and Fifty-one, when her Majesty— long may she reign!—partook of a public luncheon—" and contained a most diverting incident about a cherry-pie. And always, at decent intervals, she would exclaim—

"Did you ever see anything more lovely?"

To which the Admiral as religiously would reply—

"Really, I never did."

Indeed the scene was, as Mrs. Goodwyn-Sandys, in another boat, observed, "Like a poet's dream"—a remark at which Mr. Moggridge blushed very much. I wish I could linger and describe with amorous precision the bright talk, the glories of the day, each bend and vista of the river which I have loved from childhood; but amid the stress of events now crowding with epic vehemence on Troy, the Muse must hasten. Fain would she dally over the disembarkation, the feast, the manner in which Admiral Buzza carved the chicken-pie, and his humorous allusion to the merry thought; or dwell upon the salad compounded by Mr. Moggridge, the spider that was found in it, and the conundrum composed upon that singular occurrence; or loiter to tell how Miss Lavinia upset the claret cup over the Vicar's coat-tails, and, in her confusion, said it "did not signify," which was very amusing. On this, and more, would she blithely discourse, did not sterner themes invite her.

It happened that on this particular morning Mr. Fogo had been restless beyond his wont. For a full hour he had wandered on the beach, as Caleb expressed it, "Back'ards an' forrards, like Boscas'le Fair." He had taken up mallet and chisel; had set them down at the end of half an hour for his paintbox, and ruined a well-meaning sketch of the previous day; had deserted this in turn for another ramble on the beach, and finally returned, with a helpless look, to Caleb, who sat whistling and splicing a rope upon the little quay.

"Hurried in mind, sir, like Pomeroy's cat," suggested he sympathetically.

"I have no acquaintance with the animal you mention," said his master.

"I reckon 'twas she as got killed by care, sir. I niver knawed mysel' but wan animal as got downright put-goin' i' that way, an' that were a hen."

"A hen?"

"Iss, sir. Et happen'd up to Penhellick, the las' year I stayed 'long wi' Lawyer Mennear. 'Twas a reg'lar fool-body, this hen—a black Minorcy she were; but no egg iver laid were fuller o' meat than she o' good-feelin'; an' prenciple! she'd enuff prenciple to stock a prayer-meetin'. But high prenciple in a buffllehead's like a fish-bone i' the throat—useful, but out o' place.

"Well, sir, th' ould Mennear wan day bought a baker's dozen of porc'lain eggs over to Summercourt Fair: beautiful eggs they were, an' you cudn' tell mun from real, 'cept by the weight. The very nex' day, findin' as hes Minorcy were layin' for a brood i' the loft above the cowshed, he takes up the true egg while the old fowl were away an' sets a porc'lain egg in place of et. In cou'se, back comes the hen, an' bein' a daft body, as I told 'ee, an' not used to these 'ere refinements o' civilizashun, niver doubts but 'tes the same as she laid. 'Twarn't long afore her'd a-laid sax more, and then her sets to work to hatch mun out.

"Nat'rally, arter a while the brood was all hatched out, 'ceptin', o' cou'se, the porc'lain egg. The mother didn't take no suspishun but 'twere all right, on'y a bit stubborn. So her sot down for two days more, an' did all a hen cud do to hatch that chick. No good; 'twudn' budge. You niver seed a fowl that hurted in mind; but niver a thought o' givin' in. No, sir. 'Twasn' her way. Her jes' cocked her head aslant, tuk a long stare at the cussed thing, an' said, so plain as looks cud say, 'Well, I've a-laid this egg, an' I reckon I've a-got to hatch et; an' ef et takes me to th' aluminium, I'll see et out.'"

"The millennium," corrected Mr. Fogo, who was much interested.

"Not bein' over-eddicated, sir," said Caleb, with unconscious severity, "that old hen, I reckon, said 'aluminium.' But niver mind. Her sot, an' sot, an' kept on settin', an' neglected the rest o' they chicks for what seemingly to her was the call o' duty, till wan' by wan they all died. 'Twas pitiful, sir; an' the wust was to see her lay so much store by that egg. Th' ould Mennear was for takin' et away; but 'twud ha' broke her heart. As 'twas, what wi' anxi'ty an' too little food, her wore to a shadow. I seed her was boun' to die, anyway; an' wan arternoon, as I was in the cowshed, I heerd a weakly sort o' cluckin' overhead, an' went up to look. 'Twas too late, sir. Th' ould hen was lying beside th' egg, glazin' at et in a filmy sort o' way, an' breathin' terrable hard. When I comes, she gi'es a look same as to say, 'I reckon I've a-got to go. I've a-been a mother to that there egg; an' I'd ha' liked to see't through afore I went. But, seemingly, 'twarn't ordained.' An' wi' that there was a kind o' flutter, an' when

I turned her over I seed her troubles were done. Thet fowl, sir, had *passed*."

"You tell the story with such sympathy, Caleb, that I appeal to you the more readily for advice. I find it hard to concentrate my attention this morning."

"Ef I mou't make free to shake 'ee agen—"

"I should prefer any other cure."

"Very well, sir. I *have* heerd, from trippers as comes to Troy, to spend the day an' get drunk in anuther parish for vari'ty's sake, as a pennorth o' say es uncommon refreshin'."

"A pennyworth of sea?"

"That's so, sir. Twelve in a boat, an' a copper a head to the boatman to row so far as there an' back, which es cheap an' empt'in' at the price, as a chap told me."

"You advise me to take a row?"

"Iss, sir; on'y I reckon you'd best go up the river, ef you'm goin' alone. Though whether you prefers the resk o' meetin' Adm'ral Buzza to bein' turned topsy-versy outside the harbour-mouth, es a question I leaves to you. 'Tes a matter o' taste, as Mounseer said by the yaller frog."

Mr. Fogo decided to risk an encounter with the Admiral. In a few minutes he was afloat, and briskly rowing in the wake of the picnic-party.

But black Care, that clambers aboard the sea-going galley, did not disdain a seat in the stern of Mr. Fogo's boat. She sat her down there, and would not budge for all his pulling. Neither could the smile of the clear sky woo her thence, nor the voices of the day; but as on ship-board she must still be talking to the man at the wheel, and on horseback importunately whispering to the rider from her pillion, so now she besieged the ear of Mr. Fogo, to whom her very sex was hateful.

Further and further he rowed in vain attempt to shake off this incubus; passed at some distance the rock where the picnickers had spread their meal (luckily, the Admiral's back was turned to the river), doubled the next bend, ran his boat ashore on a little patch of shingle overarched with trees, and, stepping out, sat down to smoke a pipe.

Secure from observation, he could hear the laughter of the picnickers borne melodiously through the trees; and either this or the tobacco chased his companion from his side; for his brow cleared, the puffs of smoke came more calmly, and before the pipe was smoked out, Mr. Fogo had sunk into a most agreeable fit of abstraction.

He was rudely aroused by the sound of voices close at hand. Indeed, the speakers were but a few yards off, on the bank above him.

Now Mr. Fogo was the last man to desire to overhear a conversation. But the first word echoed so aptly his late musings, and struck his memory, too, with so deep a pang, that before he recovered it was too late.

"Geraldine!"

"Oh! why is it?" — (it was a woman's voice that asked the question, though not the voice that Mr. Fogo had half expected to hear, and his very relief brought a shudder with it) — "oh! why is it that a man and a woman cannot talk together except in lies? You ask if I am unhappy. Say what you mean. Do I hate my husband? Well, then — yes!"

"My dear Mrs. —"

"Is that frank enough? Oh! yes, I have lied so consistently throughout my married life that I tell the truth now out of pure weariness. I detest him: sometimes I feel that I must kill either Fred or myself, and end it all."

"Bless my soul!" murmured Mr. Fogo, cowering more closely. "This country teems with extraordinary people!"

He held his breath as the deeper voice answered—

"Had I thought—"

"Stop! I know what you would say, and it is untrue. Be frank as I am. You had half-guessed my secret, and were bound to convince yourself: and why? Shall I tell you, or will you copy my candour and speak for yourself?"

Dead silence followed this question. After some seconds the woman's voice resumed—

"Ah! all men are cowards. Well, I will tell you. Your question implied yet another, and it was, Do I, hating my husband, love you?"

"Geraldine!"

"Do you still wish that question answered? I will do you that favour also: Listen: for the life of me—I don't know."

And the speaker laughed—a laugh full of amused tolerance, as though her confession had left her a careless spectator of its results. Mr. Fogo shuddered.

"In heaven's name, Geraldine, don't mock me!"

"But it is true. How *should* I know? You have talked to me, read me your verses—and, indeed, I think them very beautiful. You have with comparative propriety, because in verse, invited me to fly with thee to a desolate isle in the Southern Sea—wherever that is—and forgetting my shame and likewise blame, while you do the same with name and fame and its laurel-leaf, go to moral grief on a coral reef—"

"Geraldine, you are torturing me."

"Do I not quote correctly? My point is this:—A woman will listen to talk, but she admires action. Prove that you are ready, not to fly to a coral reef, but to do me one small service, and you may have another answer."

"Name it."

Mr. Fogo, peering through the bushes as one fascinated, saw an extremely beautiful woman confronting an extremely pale youth, and fancied also that he saw a curious flash of contempt pass over the woman's features as she answered—

"Really unless you kill the Admiral next time he makes a pun, I do not know that just now I need such a service. By to-morrow, though, or the next day, I may think of one. Until then"—she held out her hand—"wait patiently, and be kind to Sophia."

Mr. Moggridge started as though stung by a snake; but, recollecting himself, imprinted a kiss upon the proffered fingers. Again Mrs. Goodwyn-Sandys laughed with unaffected mirth, and again the hidden witness saw that curious gleam of scorn—only now, as the young man bent his head, it was not dissembled.

They were gone. Mr. Fogo sank back against the bushes, drew a long breath, and passed his hand nervously over his eyes; but though the scene had passed as a dream, the laugh still rang in his ears.

"It is a judgment on me!" muttered the poor man—"a judgment! They are all alike."

Curiously enough, his next reflection appeared to contradict this view of the sex.

"An extraordinary woman! But every fresh person I meet in this place is more eccentric than the last. Let me see," he continued, checking off the list on his fingers; "there's Caleb, and that astounding Admiral, and the Twins, and Tamsin—"

Mr. Fogo stared very hard at the water for some seconds.

"And Tamsin," he repeated slowly. "Hullo! my feet seem to be in the water—and, bless my soul! what has become of the boat?"

He might well ask. The tide had been steadily rising as he crouched under the banks, and was now lapping his boots. Worse than this, it had floated off the boat, which he had carelessly forgotten to secure, and drifted it up the river, at first under cover of the trees, afterwards more ostentatiously into mid-channel.

Mr. Fogo rushed up the patch of shingle until brought to a standstill by its sudden declension into deep water. There was no help for it. Not a soul was in sight. He divested himself rapidly of his clothes, piled them in a neat little heap beyond reach of the tide, and then with considerable spirit plunged into the flood and struck out in pursuit of the truant.

CHAPTER XIV.

OF A LADY OF SENSIBILITY THAT, BEING AWKWARDLY
PLACED, MIGHT EASILY HAVE SET MATTERS RIGHT, BUT DID
NOT: WITH MUCH BESIDE.

It is hardly necessary by this time to inform my readers that Miss
Priscilla Limpenny was a lady of sensibility. We have already seen
her obey the impulse of the heart rather than the cool dictates of
judgment: her admiration of natural beauty she has herself confessed
more than once during the voyage up the river. But lest more than a
due share of this admiration should be set down to patriotism, I wish
to put it on record that she possessed to an uncommon degree an
appreciative sense of the poetic side of Nature. She was familiar with
the works of Mrs. Hemans and L. E. L., and had got by heart most of
the effusions in "Affection's Keepsake" and "Friendship's Offering."
Nay, she had been, in her early youth, suspected, more than vaguely,
of contributing fugitive verse to a periodical known as the *Household
Packet*. She had even, many years ago, met the Poet Wordsworth "at
the dinner-table," as she expressed it, "of a common friend," and
was never tired of relating how the great man had spoken of the
prunes as "pruins," and said "Would you obleege me with the salt?"

With such qualifications for communion with nature it is not
wonderful that, on this particular afternoon, Miss Limpenny should
have wandered pensively along the river's bank, and surrendered
herself to its romantic charm. Possessed by the spirit of the place and
hour, she even caught herself straying by the extreme brink, and
repeating those touching lines from "Affection's Keepsake":—

"The eye roams widely o'er glad Nature's face,
    To mark each varied and delightful scene;
The simple and magnificent we trace,
    While loveliness and brightness intervene;
Oh! everywhere is something found to—"

At this point Miss Limpenny's gaze lost its dreamy expansiveness, and grew rigid with horror. Immediately before her feet, and indelicately confronting her, lay a suit of man's clothing.

It is a curious fact, though one we need not linger to discuss, that while clothes are the very symbol and first demand of decency, few things become so flagrantly immodest when viewed in themselves and apart from use. The crimson rushed to Miss Limpenny's cheek. She uttered a cry and looked around.

Inexorable fate, whose compulsion directed that gaze! If raiment apart from its wearer be unseemly, how much more—

About thirty yards from her, wading down the stream, and tugging the painter of his recovered boat, advanced Mr. Fogo.

To add a final touch of horror, that gentleman, finding that the damp on his spectacles completely dimmed his vision, had deposited them in the boat, and was therefore blind to the approaching catastrophe. Unconscious even of observation, he advanced nearer and nearer.

Miss Limpenny's emotion found vent in a squeal.

Mr. Fogo, heard, halted, and gazed blankly around.

"How singular!" he murmured. "I could have sworn I heard a cry."

He made another step. The sound was repeated, more shrilly.

"Again! And, dear me, it sounds human—as of some fellow-creature in distress."

"Go away! Go away at once!"

"Eh? Bless my soul, what can it be?" Mr. Fogo stared in the direction whence the voice proceeded, but of course without seeing anything.

"I beg your pardon?" he observed mildly.

"Go away!"

"If you will allow me—" he began, courteously addressing vacancy.

"Monster!"

The awful truth began to dawn upon him, and was followed by a hasty impulse to dive.

"If," he stammered, "I am right in supposing myself to address a lady—"

"Don't talk to me, but go away."

"I was about to ask permission to resume my spectacles, which I have unfortunately laid aside."

"No, no. That would be worse. Oh! go away at once."

"Pardon me, madam. I am aware that spectacles are insufficient as a—I mean, I did not propose to consider them in the light of a costume, but as an assistance to my sight, without which—"

"Oh! I shall faint."

"Without which it will be impossible for me to extricate myself from this extremely unfortunate situation. I am notoriously short-sighted, madam, and at this distance could not tell you from Adam—I should say, from Eve," continued Mr. Fogo, desperately reaching out for his spectacles and adjusting them.

By the imperfect glimpse which he obtained through the glasses (which were still damp) he was almost moved to adopt his first impulse of deserting the boat and diving. But even if he swam away the case would be no better, for this unreasonable female stood sentry beside his clothes.

"If I might make a suggestion, madam—"

But by this time Miss Limpenny had broken forth into a series of sobs and plaintive cries for protection. Alas! the rest of the picnic-party were deep within the woods, and out of hearing.

"Believe me, my dear madam—"

"I am not your dear madam."

"I have no other intention than to get out of this."

"Ah! he confesses it."

"I assure you—"

"Will no one protect me?" wailed the lady, wringing her hands and sobbing anew. But help was near, though from an unexpected quarter.

And Peter Dearlove pushed aside the bushes and descended to the shingle, closely followed by Paul. He was just in time, for Miss Limpenny, with a thankful little cry, staggered and fell fainting into his arms.

"Mercy 'pon us!" exclaimed Peter, seeing only the lady, and not at first the cause of her distress, "'tes Miss Limpenny."

"Well, I'm jiggered!" ejaculated Paul, "so 'tes."

The Twins bent over the lady, and looked at each other in dismay. To Mr. Fogo the tableau might have borne a ridiculous likeness to that scene in *Cymbeline* where Guiderius and Arviragus stoop over the unconscious Imogen. But Mr. Fogo, as he stood neck-high in water, was far beyond drawing any such comparison; and Peter, instead of adjuring Miss Limpenny to fear no more the heat o' the sun, accinged himself to the practical difficulty.

"Will no one protect me?" wailed the lady...

"Hulloa!" cried a voice on the bank above, "what be all this?"

"Did 'ee iver hear tell o' what's best to be done when a leddy's took like this?" he asked his brother.

"No," answered Paul; "Tamsin was niver took this way. But that there little book us used to study when her had the whoopin'-cough an' measles wud likely tell all about et; I wish 'twas here. Wait a bit. I remembers the 'Instructions for Discoverin' th' Appariently Drownded.' Do 'ee reckon Miss Limpenny here es 'appariently drownded'?"

"Why, no."

"I don't think so nuther. Ef she was," added Paul regretfully, "you'd have to be extry partic'lar not to roll her body 'pon casks. That was a great p'int."

"'Tes a long step round to fetch that book," sighed Peter.

"An' terrable long words i' th' index when you've got et. Stop, now: es et faintin', do 'ee think?"

"Well," answered Paul thoughtfully, "et *mou't* be faintin'."

"'Cos, ef so, the best way es to hold the sufferer upsi-down an' dash cold water over the face."

"That wud be takin' too much of a liberty, wudn' et, Paul?"

But at this point the blood came trickling back into Miss Limpenny's cheeks; the eyelids fluttered, opened; she gasped a little, looked up, and—

"Is he gone?" she asked in a weak whisper.

"Gone? Who, ma'am?"

"The monster."

"Light-headed yet," muttered Peter. But following Miss Limpenny's stare the brothers caught sight of Mr. Fogo simultaneously, and for the first time. Their mahogany faces grew sensibly paler.

"Well, this beats cock-fightin'!"

"Would you mind taking that lady away?" pleaded Mr. Fogo, through his chattering teeth; "I am very cold indeed, and wish to dress."

"Oh! that voice again," sobbed Miss Limpenny; "please tell him to go away."

Being nonplussed by these two appeals, Peter addressed his reply to his brother.

"I dunno, Paul, as we've a-got to the bottom o' this; but I reck'n Mr. Fogo's been a-lettin' hes principles take 'n too far. As for dislikin' womankind, 'tes in a way 'scuseable p'raps; but notices es wan thing, an' teasin' anuther."

"That's so, Peter. Ef 'tes a matter o' fash'n, tho', I dunno as we've any call to interfere, not knawin' what's what."

"Ef you plaise, sir," shouted Peter, "Paul an' me wants to know whether you be a-doin' et by way o' bein' fash'nubble?"

"I don't know what you mean. I only wish to be allowed to get at my clothes. I really am suffering considerably, being quite unused to these long immersions."

Peter looked around and caught sight of the neat pile of Mr. Fogo's attire lying underneath the bank. Light began to dawn on him; he turned to Miss Limpenny—

"You'll excuse me, ma'am, but was you present by any chance when—?"

"Heaven forbid!" she cried, and put her hands before her face.

"Then, beggin' your pard'n, but how did you come here?"

"I was wandering on the bank—and lost in thought—and came upon these—these articles. And then—oh! I cannot, I cannot."

"Furder question es," pursued Peter, with an interrogative glance at his brother, who nodded, "why not ha' gone away?"

"Dear me!" exclaimed Miss Limpenny, "I never thought of it!"

She gathered up her skirts, and disdaining the assistance of the gallant Paul, clambered up the bank, and with a formal bow left the Twins staring. As she remarked tearfully to Lavinia that evening, "What one requires in these cases is presence of mind, my dear," and she heaved a piteous little sigh.

"But consider," urged the sympathetic Lavinia, "your feelings at the moment. I am sure that under similar circumstances"—she shuddered— "I should have behaved in precisely the same way."

Mr. Fogo emerged in so benumbed a condition, his teeth chattered so loudly, and his nose had grown so appallingly blue, that the Twins, who had in delicacy at first retired to a little distance, were forced to return and help him into his clothes. Even then, however, he continued to shiver to such an extent that the pair, after consulting in whispers for some moments, took off their coats, wrapped him carefully about, set him in the stern of his boat, and, jumping in themselves, pushed off and rowed rapidly homewards.

Their patient endeavoured to express his thanks, but was gravely desired not to mention it. For ten minutes or so the Twins rowed in silence, at the end of this time Paul suddenly dropped the bow oar;

then, leaning forward, touched his brother on the shoulder and whispered one word—

"Shenachrum."

"Or Samson," said Peter.

"I think poorly o' Samson."

"Wi' hes hair on?"

"Wi' or wi'out, I don't lay no store by Samson."

"Very well, then—Shenachrum."

The rowing was resumed, and Mr. Fogo left to speculate on these dark sayings. But as the boat drew near the column of blue smoke that, rising from the hazels on the left bank, marked the whereabouts of the Dearloves' cottage, he grew aware of a picture that, perhaps by mere charm of composition, set his pulse extravagantly beating.

At the gate above the low cliff, her frock of pink print distinct against the hazels, stood Tamsin Dearlove, and looked up the river.

She was bare-headed; and the level rays of evening powdered her dark tresses with gold, and touched the trees behind into bronze. One hand shielded her eyes; the other rested on the half-open gate, and swayed it softly to and fro upon its hinge. As she stood thus, some happy touch of opportunity, some trick of circumstance or grouping, must, I think, have helped Mr. Fogo to a conclusion he had been seeking for weeks. It is certain that though he has since had abundant opportunities of studying Tamsin, and noting that untaught grace of body in which many still find the secret of her charm, to his last day she will always be for him the woman who stood, this summer evening, beside the gate and looked up the river.

And yet, as the boat drew near, the pleasantest feature in the picture was the smile with which she welcomed her brothers, though it contained some wonder to see them in Mr. Fogo's boat, and gave place to quick alarm as she remarked the extreme blueness of that gentleman's nose and the extreme pallor of his other features.

"Tamsin, my dear, es the cloth laid?"

"Yes, Peter, and the kettle ready to boil."

"We was thinkin' as Shenachrum would be suitin' Mr. Fogo better. He've met wi' an accident."

"Again?" There was something of disdain in her eyes as she curtseyed to him, but it softened immediately. "You're kindly welcome, sir," she added, "and the Shenachrum shall be ready in ten minutes."

Within five minutes Mr. Fogo was seated by the corner of the hearth, and watching her as she heated the beer which, together with rum, sugar, and lemon, forms the drink known and loved by Trojans as Shenachrum. The Twins had retired to wash in the little out-house at the back, and their splashing was audible every now and again above the crackling of the wood fire, which now, as before, filled the kitchen with fragrance. Its warmth struck kindly into Mr. Fogo's knees, and coloured Tamsin's cheeks with a hot red as she bent over the flame. He watched her profile in thoughtful silence for some moments, and then fell to staring at the glowing sticks and the shadows of the pot-hooks and hangers on the chimney-back.

"So that is Shenachrum?" he said at last, to break the silence.

"Yes."

"And what, or who, is Samson?"

"Samson is brandy and cider and sugar."

"With his hair on?"

She laughed.

"That means more brandy. Samson was double as strong, you know, with his hair on."

"I see."

The silence was resumed. Only the tick-tack of the tall clock and the splashing of the Twins disturbed it. She turned to glance at him once, and then, seeing his gaze fixed upon the fire that twinkled on the rim of his spectacles and emphasised the hollows of his face, had looked for a moment more boldly before she bent over her task again.

"She is quite beautiful, but—"

He spoke in a dreamy abstracted tone, as if addressing the pot-hooks. Tamsin started, set down the pan with a clatter, and turned sharply round.

"Eh?" said Mr. Fogo, aroused by the clatter, "you were saying—?" And then it struck him that he had spoken aloud. He broke off, and looked up with appealing helplessness.

There was a second's pause.

"*You* were saying—"

The words came as if dragged from her by an effort. Her eyes were full of wrath as she stood above him and waited for his reply.

"I am very sorry," he stammered; "I never meant you to hear."

"You were talking of—?"

"Of you," he answered simply. He was horribly frightened; but it was not in the man's nature to lie, or even evade the question.

The straightforwardness of the reply seemed to buffet her in the face. She put up a hand against the chimney-piece and caught her breath.

"What is 'but'?" she asked with a kind of breathless vehemence. "Finish your sentence. What right have you to talk of me?" she went on, as he did not reply. "If I am not a lady, what is that to you? Oh!" she persisted, in answer to the swift remonstrance on his face, "I can end your sentence: 'She is quite beautiful, but—quite *low*, of course.' What right have you to call me either—to speak of me at all? We were content enough before you came—Peter and Paul and I. Why cannot you let us alone? I hate you! Yes, I hope there is no doubt now that I am low—hate you!"

She stamped her foot in passion as two angry tears sparkled in her eyes.

"Why, Tamsin!" cried Paul's voice at the door, "the Shenachrum not ready yet? I niver knawed 'ee so long afore."

She turned sharply, caught up the pan, and stooped over the fire again. But the glow on her cheeks now was hotter than any fire could bring.

"'Tes rare stuff, sir," said the Twin encouragingly, as Tamsin filled a steaming glass, and handed it, without a look, to Mr. Fogo. "Leastways, 'tes thought a deal of i' these parts by them as, wi'out bein' perlite, es yet reckoned jedges."

Mr. Fogo took the glass and sipped bravely. The stuff was so hot that tears sprang to his eyes, but he gulped it down, nevertheless.

"An' now, sir," began Peter, who had joined the group, and was looking on approvingly, "Paul an' me was considerin' in the back-kitchen, an' agreed that makin' so bold as to ax 'ee, an' hopin' 'twont' be thought over free, you must stay the night, seein' you've took this cold, an' the night air bein', as es well known, terrable apt to give 'ee inflammation."

"We'd planned," put in Paul, "to go down wi' the boat to Kit's House an' fetch up your things, and tell Caleb about et, so's he shudn' be decomposed. An' Tamsin'll tell 'ee there's a room at your sarvice, an' reckoned purty—lookin' on to the bee-skeps an' the orchard at the back," he explained with a meaning glance at Tamsin, who was silent.

"Why, Tamsin, girl, what's amiss that you don't spake?" asked Peter; and then his amazement got the better of his tact, as he added in a stage whisper, "'Tes on'y to change rooms. Paul an' me can aisy sleep down here afore the fire; an' us on'y offered your room as bein' more genteel—"

"I assure you," broke in Mr. Fogo, "that I am quite recovered of my chill, thanks to your kindness, and would rather return—much rather: though I thank you all the same." He spoke to the Twins, but kept his eyes on Tamsin.

"No kindness at all," muttered Peter. His face fell, and he, too, looked at the girl.

Finding their eyes upon her, she was compelled to speak.

"Mr. Fogo wudn' care for the likes o' what we cou'd offer him," she said. Then, seeing the pain on the men's faces, she added with an effort to be gracious, "But ef he can put up wi' us, he knows he shall be made welcome."

She did not look up, and her voice, in which the peculiar sing-song of Trojan intonation was intentionally emphasised, sounded so strangely that still greater amazement fell upon the Twins.

"Why, Tamsin, I niver knawed 'ee i' this mood afore," stammered Paul.

"I assure you," interposed Mr. Fogo, "that I value your hospitality more than I can say, and shall not forget it. But it would be absurd to accept it when I am so near home. If one of you would consent to row me down to Kit's House, it would be the exact kindness I should prefer."

The Twins assented, though not without regret at his refusal to accept more. Paul agreed to row him down, and the two started in the early twilight. As he shook Peter's hand, Mr. Fogo looked at Tamsin.

"Good-night," he said.

"Good-night, sir."

She did not offer to shake hands; she scarcely even looked up, but stood there before the chimney-place, with the fire-light outlining her form and throwing into deep shadow the side of her face that was towards him. One arm was thrown up to grasp the mantelshelf, and against this her head rested. The other hung listlessly at her side. And this was the picture Mr. Fogo carried out into the grey evening.

As the door closed upon him, Peter sank into the stiff-backed chair beside the hearth with a puzzled sigh.

"Why, Tamsin," he said, as he slowly drew out his pipe and filled it, "what ailed 'ee, girl, to behave like that?"

Looking up, he saw a tear, and then a second, drop brightly on the hearth-stone.

"Little maid!"

Before he could say more she had stepped to him, and, sitting on the chair-arm, had flung her arms around his neck and drawn his head towards her, that he might not look into her face.

"I hate him," she sobbed—"I hate him! I wish I had never seen him. He despises us, and—and I was so happy before he came."

The Twin set down his pipe upon his knee, and stared into the fire.

"As for hatin', Tamsin," he said gravely, "'tain't right. Us shud love our neighbours, Scriptur' says; an' I reckon that includes tenants. I' the matter o' hes despisin' us, I dunno as you'm right nuther. He's fash'nubble, o' cou'se; but very conformable, considerin'—very conformable. You bain't sorry us let Kit's House, eh, Tamsin? Not hankerin'—"

"No, no."

"I doubt, my dear, we'm poor hands to take care of 'ee, Paul an' me. Us talks et over togither at times, an' agrees 'twas wrong not to ha' sent 'ee away to school. Us got a whack o' handbills down, wan time, from different places. You wudn' believe et, my dear," he went on, with something like a laugh, "but Paul an' me a'most came to words over they handbills. 'Tes a curious fac', but at the places where they allowed most holidays, they was most partic'lar about takin' your own spoon and fork, an' Paul was a stickler agen that. Et grew to be a matter o' prenciple wi' Paul that wheriver you went you shudn' take your own spoon and fork. So us niver came to no understandin'. I doubt 'twas selfish an' us can't understand maidens an' their ways; but say, my dear, ef there's anything can be set right, an' us'll try—"

"No, no. Let me sit here beside you, and I shall be better presently."

She drew a low stool to his side, and sat with her head against his knee, and her dark eyes watching the fire. Peter laid one hand gently on her hair, and wound the brown locks around his fingers.

"All right now?" he asked, after several minutes had passed with no sound but the ticking of the clock.

"All right beside you, brother. It is always all right beside you."

CHAPTER XV.

HOW A LADY AND A YOUTH, BEING SEPARATED FROM
THEIR COMPANY, VISITED A SHIP THAT HELD NOTHING BUT
WATER.

Mr. Fogo and Paul performed the journey back to Kit's House in silence; for Paul was yet wondering at his sister's behaviour, and Mr. Fogo busy with thoughts he could hardly have interpreted. As they drew near the little quay, they discerned through the darkness, now fast creeping over the river, a boat pushed off by a solitary figure that jumped aboard and began to pull towards them.

"Ahoy, there!" It was Caleb's voice.

"Ahoy, Caleb!" shouted Paul in answer; "anything wrong?"

"Have 'ee seen maaster?"

"Iss, an' got un safe an' sound."

Caleb peered through the gloom and descried Mr. Fogo. Whatever relief this may have been to his feelings, it called forth no expression beyond a grunt. He turned his boat and pulled back in time to help his master ashore. Paul was dismissed with some words of thanks which he declared unnecessary. He would row back in Mr. Fogo's boat, he said, if he might be allowed, and would bring her down in the early morning. With this and a hearty "Good-night" he left the pair to walk up to the house together.

Caleb was unusually silent during supper, and when his master grew cheery and related the adventures of the day, offered no comment beyond a series of mysterious sounds expressing mental discontent rather than sympathy. Finally, when Mr. Fogo had finished he looked up and began abruptly—

"Ef you plaise, sir, I wants to gie warnin'."

"Give warning?"

"Iss, sir; notiss to go." And Caleb stared fiercely at his master.

"But, my dear Caleb, you surely don't mean—?"

"I do, tho'."

"Are you dissatisfied with the place or the wages?"

"That's et, sir—the wages."

"If they are too low—"

"They bain't; they be a darned sight too high."

Mr. Fogo leant back in his chair.

"Too high!" he gasped.

"Look 'ee here, sir: here be I, so lazy as La'rence, an' eatin' my head off 'pon a pund a week an' my small-clothes, on condishun I looks arter 'ee. Very well; what happens? 'Tes Dearlove, Dearlove, Dearlove all the time. Fust Tamsin brings 'ee back, and then Paul, an' nex' time I reckon 'twill be Peter's turn. Where-*fore*, sir, seein' I can't offer to share wages wi' the Twins, much less wi' Tamsin, I wants to go."

Caleb knocked the ashes out of his pipe, and, rising, stared at his master for some seconds and with much determination.

Mr. Fogo argued the case for some time without effect. But so sincerely did he paint his helplessness, and nervous aversion to new faces, that at length, after many pros and cons, Caleb consented to give him one more chance. "But mind, sir," he added, "the nex' time you'm brought home by a Dearlove, 'go' 's the word." On this

156

understanding they retired to rest, but it was long before Mr. Fogo could shut his memory upon the panorama of the day's experiences.

Let us return to the picnickers. After what had passed between Mrs. Goodwyn-Sandys and Mr. Moggridge on the river's bank, it may seem strange that the lady should have chosen Sam Buzza to row her home, for the two youths were now declared rivals for her goodwill. But I think we may credit her with a purpose.

At any rate, when the lengthening shadows and retreating tide hinted return, Sam, who had arrived late in a designedly small dingey, asked Mrs. Goodwyn-Sandys to accompany him, and she, with little demur, complied. It did not matter greatly, as propriety would be saved by their nearness to the larger boats; and so the party started together.

But this arrangement, though excellent, did not last long; for, curiously enough, the dingey soon began to take a formidable lead of the next boat, in which the traitorous Moggridge was pulling stroke, and gazing, with what courage he could summon, into Sophia's eyes. Indeed, so quickly was the lead increased, that at the end of two miles the larger boats had shrunk to mere spots in the distance.

The declining sun shone in Sam's eyes as he rowed, and his companion, with her sunshade so disposed as to throw her face into shadow, observed him in calm silence. The sunshade was of scarlet silk, and in the softened light stealing through it her cheek gained all the freshness of maidenhood. Her white gown, gathered about the waist with a band of scarlet, not only fitted her figure to perfection, but threw up the colour of her skin into glowing relief. To Sam she appeared a miracle of coolness and warmth; and as yet no word was spoken.

At length, and not until they had passed the Dearloves' cottage, she asked —

"Why were you late?"

"Was I missed?"

"Of course. You younger men of Troy seem strangely blind to your duties—and your chances."

The last three words came as if by after-thought; Sam looked up quickly.

"Chances? You said 'chances,' I believe?"

"I did. Was there not Miss Saunders, for instance?"

Sam's lip curled.

"Miss Saunders is not a chance; she is a certainty. Did she, for instance, announce that the beauty of the day made her sad—that even amid the wealth of summer something inside her whispered 'Autumn'?"

"She did."

"She always does; I have never picnicked with Miss Saunders but something inside her whispered 'Autumn'!"

"A small bore," suggested Mrs. Goodwyn-Sandys, "that never misses fire."

Sam tittered and resumed—

"If it comes to duties, your husband sets the example; he hasn't moved from the club window to-day."

"Oh!" she exclaimed shortly, "I never asked you to imitate my husband."

Sam ceased rowing and looked up; he was familiar with the tone, but had never heard it so emphasised before.

"Look here," he said; "something's wrong, that's plain. It's a rude question, but—does he neglect you?"

She laughed with some bitterness, and perhaps with a touch of self-contempt.

"You are right; it is a rude question: but—he does not."

There was a moment's silence, and then she added—

"So it's useless, is it not, to wish that he would?"

The blood about Sam's heart stood still. Were the words a confession or a sneer. Did they refer to her or to him? He would have given worlds to know, but her tone disclosed nothing.

"You mean—?"

She gave him no answer, but turned her head to look back. In the distant boats they had fallen to singing glees. In this they obeyed tradition: for there is one accomplishment which all Trojans possess—of fitting impromptu harmonies to the most difficult air. And still in the pauses of the music Miss Limpenny would exclaim—

"Did you ever see anything more lovely?"

And the Admiral would reply—

"Really, I never did."

Mrs. Goodwyn-Sandys could not, of course, hear this. But the voices of the singers stole down the river and touched her, it may be, with some sense of remorse for the part she was playing in this Arcadia.

"We are leaving the others a long way behind," she said irresolutely.

"Do you wish to wait for them?"

For a moment she seemed about to answer, but did not. Sam pulled a dozen vigorous strokes, and the boat shot into the reach opposite Kit's House.

"That," she said, resting her eyes on the weather-stained front of Mr. Fogo's dwelling, "is where the hermit lives, is it not? I should like to meet this man that hates all women."

Sam essayed a gallant speech, but she paid no heed to it.

"What a charming creek that is, beyond the house! Let us row up there and wait for the others."

The creek was wrapped in the first quiet of evening. There was still enough tide to mirror the tall trees that bent towards it, and reflect with a grey gleam one gable of the house behind. Two or three boats lay quietly here by their moorings; beside them rested a huge red buoy, and an anchor protruding one rusty tooth above the water. Where the sad-looking shingle ended, a few long timbers rotted in the ooze. Nothing in this haunted corner spoke of life, unless it were the midges that danced and wheeled over the waveless tide.

"Yonder lies the lepers' burial-ground," said Sam, and pointed.

"I have heard of them" (she shivered); "and that?"

She nodded towards the saddest ruin in this sad spot, the hull of what was once a queenly schooner, now slowly rotting to annihilation beside the further shore. She lay helplessly canted to starboard, her head pointing up the creek. Her timbers had started, her sides were coated with green weed; her rudder, wrenched from its pintle, lay hopelessly askew. On her stern could still be read, in blistered paint, her name, "*The Seven Sisters* of Troy." There she lay dismantled, with a tangle of useless rigging, not fit for saving, left to dangle from her bulwarks; and a quick fancy might liken her, as the tide left her, and the water in her hold gushed out through a dozen gaping seams, to some noble animal that had crept to this corner to bleed to death.

160

Mrs. Goodwyn-Sandys looked towards the wreck with curious interest.

"I should like to examine it more closely," she said.

For answer Sam pulled round the schooner, and let the boat drift under her overhanging side.

"You can climb aboard if you like," he said, as he shipped the sculls and, standing up, grasped the schooner's bulwarks. "Stop, let me make the painter fast."

He took up the rope, swung himself aboard, and looped it round the stump of a broken davit; then bent down and gave a hand to his companion. She was agile, and the step was of no great height; but Sam had to take both her hands before she stood beside him, and ah! but his heart beat cruelly quick.

Once on board Mrs. Goodwyn-Sandys displayed the most eager inquisitiveness, almost endangering her beautiful neck as she peered down into the hole where the water lay, black and gloomy. She turned and walked aft with her feet in the scuppers, and her right hand pressed against the deck, so great was the cant on the vessel. It was uphill walking too, for the schooner was sagged in the waist, and the stern tilted up to a considerable height. Nevertheless she reached the poop at last. Sam followed.

"I want to see the captain's cabin," she explained.

Sam wondered, but led the way. It was no easy matter to descend the crazy ladder, and in the cabin itself the light was so dim that he struck a match. Its flare revealed a broken table, a horsehair couch, and a row of cupboards along the walls. On the port side these had mostly fallen open, and the doors in some cases hung by a single hinge. There was a terrible smell in the place. Mrs. Goodwyn-Sandys looked around.

"Does the water ever come up here?" she asked.

Sam lit another match.

"No," he said, stooping and examining the floor.

"You are quite sure?"

Her tone was so eager that he looked up.

"Yes, I am quite sure; but why do you ask?"

She did not answer: nor, in the faint light, could he see her face. After a moment's silence she said, as if to herself—

"This is just the place."

"For what?"

"For—for an Irish jig," she laughed with sudden merriment. "Come, try a step upon these old timbers."

"For heaven's sake take care!" cried Sam. "There may be a trap-hatch where you stand, and these boards are rotten through and through. Ten minutes ago you were mournful," he added, in wonder at her change of mood.

"Was I?" She broke out suddenly into elfish song—

> "'Och! Pathrick O'Hea, but I'm sad, Bedad!
> Och! darlint, 'tis bad to be sad.'
>   'Hwat's this?' says he.
>   'Why, a kiss,' says she.
>   ''Tis a cure,' says he.
>   'An' that's sure,' says she.
> 'Och! Pat, you're a sinsible lad, Bedad!
> Troth, Pat, you're a joole uv a lad!'"

She broke off suddenly and shivered.

"Come, let us go; this place suffocates me."

She turned and ran up the crazy ladder. At the top she turned and peered down upon the dumbfounded Sam.

"Nobody comes here, I suppose?"

"I should think not."

"I mean, the owner never comes to—"

"To visit his cargo?" laughed Sam. "No, the owner is dead. He was a wicked old miser, and I guess in the place where he is now he'd give a deal for the water in this ship; but I never heard he was allowed to come back for it."

She leant her hands on the taffrail, and looked over the stern.

"Hark! There are the other boats. Don't you hear the voices? They have passed us by, and we must make haste after them."

She turned upon him with a smile. Without well knowing what he did he laid his hand softly on her arm.

"Stop, I want a word before you go."

"Well?"

Her large eyes, gleaming on him through the dusk, compelled and yet frightened him. He trembled and stammered vaguely—

"You said just now—you hinted, I mean—that you were unhappy with Mr.—with your husband. Is that so?"

It was the second time she had been asked the question to-day. A faint smile crossed her face.

"Well?" she said again.

"I mean," he answered with a nervous laugh, "I don't like to see it—and—I meant, if I could help you—"

"To run away? Will you help me to run away?" Her eyes suddenly blazed upon him, and as she bent forward, and almost hissed the words, he involuntarily drew back a step.

"Well," he stammered, "he's a good fellow, really, is your husband—he's been very good to me and all that—"

"Ah!" she exclaimed, turning away, "I thought so. Come, we are wasting time."

"Stop!" cried Sam.

But she had passed swiftly down the sloping deck and dropped into the boat without his assistance. He followed unsteadily, untied the painter, and jumped down after her. They rowed for some time in silence after the retreating picnickers. Before they came abreast of the hindmost boat, however, Sam spoke—

"Look here. I can't help myself, and that's the truth. If you want to run away I'll help you." He groaned inwardly as he said it.

She made no reply, but kept her eyes fixed on his face, as if weighing his words. Nor, beyond a cool "Good-night" at parting on the quay, did another word pass between them.

"What luck?" asked the Honourable Frederic as his wife entered the drawing-room of "The Bower." He was stretched in an arm-chair before the fire, and turned with a glance of some anxiety at her entrance.

She looked about her wearily, took off her hat, tossed it across to a table, and, sinking into the armchair opposite, began to draw off her gloves.

"I'm sick to death of all this, me dear—of 'the Cause,' of Brady, of these people, of meself."

Her face wore a grey look that made her seem a full ten years older.

"Won't you include me in the list, my love?" asked her husband amiably.

"I would," she replied, "only I've already said as much twice this very afternoon."

She laughed a fatigued little laugh, and looked around her again. The drawing-room had greatly changed since first we visited it with Admiral Buzza, and the local tradesmen regarded Mr. Goodwyn-Sandys' account with some complacency as they thought of payment after Midsummer. For the strangers were not of the class that goes to the Metropolis or to the Co-operative Stores; from the outset they had announced a warm desire to benefit the town of Troy. This pretty drawing-room was one of the results, and it only wanted a certain number of cheques from the Honourable Frederic to make the excellence of the arrangement complete.

Mrs. Goodwyn-Sandys took a leisurely survey of the room while her husband awaited information.

"The pote is hooked," she said at last, "an' so's Master Sam."

"The poet is our first card," replied her husband, searching his pocket and producing a letter. "The *Maryland* should be here to-morrow or next day. Upon my word, Nellie, I don't want to ask questions, but you've done exceedingly well."

"Better than well, me dear. I've found a *place*—an illigant hidin' in an owld schooner up the river."

"Safe?"

"As a church. I'll take yez to't to-morra. Master Sam tells me sorra a sowl goes nigh ut. He tuk me to see ut. I say, me darlint, I'd be lettin' that young fool down aisier than the pote. He's a poor little snob, but he's more like a man than Moggridge."

"He's a bad ass, is Moggridge," assented the Honourable Frederic. "Come, Nellie, we've a day's work before us, remember."

A friend of mine, the son of steady-going Nihilist parents, and therefore an authority, assures me that the Honourable Frederic cannot have been a conspirator for the simple reason that he shaved his chin regularly. Be this as it may, to-night he smiled mysteriously as he rose, and winked at his wife in a most plebeian way. I regret to say that both smile and wink were returned.

Winked … in a most plebeian way.

CHAPTER XVI.

OF STRATAGEMS AND SPOILS; AND THAT THE NOMINALISTS
ERR WHO HOLD A THING TO BE WHAT IT IS CALLED.

At two o'clock next morning Mr. Moggridge closed the door of his
lodgings behind him, and stepping out into the street stood for some
moments to ponder.

A smile sat upon his lips, witness to pleasure that underlies poetic
pains. The Collector of Customs was in humour this morning, and
had written thirty lines of Act IV. of *Love's Dilemma: a Comedy*, before
breakfast, for it was his custom to rise early and drink regularly of
the waters of Helicon before seeking his office. It is curious that the
Civil Service should so often divide its claims with the Service of the
Muse. I remember that the Honourable Frederic once drew my
attention to this, and supplied me with several instances:—"There
was What's-his-name, you know, and t'other Johnny up in the Lakes,
and a heap I can't remember at the moment—fancy it must come
from the stamps—licked off with the gum, perhaps."

Be that as it may, Mr. Moggridge had written thirty lines this
morning, and was even now, as he stood in the street and stared at
the opposite house, repeating to himself a song he had just
composed for his hero. It is worth quoting, for, with slight alteration,
I know no better clue to the poet's mood at the time. The play has
since been destroyed, for reasons of which some hint may be found
in the next few chapters; but the unfinished song is still preserved
among the author's notes, where it is headed—

A HYMN OF LOVE.

"Toiling lover, loose your pack,
     All your sighs and tears unbind;
Care's a ware may break a back,

May not bend a maiden's mind.

"Loose, and follow to a land
                Where the tyrant's only fee
Is the kissing of a hand
                And the bending of a knee.

"In that State a man shall need
                Neither priest nor lawgiver:
Those same slips that are his creed
                Shall confess their worshipper.

"All the laws he must obey,
                Now in force and now repealed,
Shift in eyes that shift as they—

"'Shift as they,' 'shift as they,'" mused Mr. Moggridge. "Let me see—"

'Till alike with kisses sealed.'

"That was it. With another verse, and a little polishing, I will take it to Geraldine and ask her—"

At this point the poet glanced down the street, and, to his surprise, beheld Mrs. Goodwyn-Sandys advancing towards him.

"Good-morning," she nodded with a charming smile, "I was coming to look for you. I have a favour to ask."

"A favour? Is it *the*—?"

"Well, it's rather prosaic for *the*—" she laughed. "In fact, it's *tea*."

"Tea?"

"Yes. It's rather a long story; but it comes to this. You see, Fred is very particular about the tea he drinks."

"Indeed?"

"It's a fact, I assure you. Well, when we were travelling in the states, Fred happened to come across some tea he liked particularly, at Chicago. And the funny thing about this tea is that it is compressed. It is called 'Wapshotts' Patent Compressed Tea;' now I daresay," added Mrs. Goodwyn-Sandys demurely, "that you wouldn't think it possible for compressed tea to be good."

"To tell you the truth," said Mr. Moggridge, "I have never given the subject a thought."

"No, of course; being a poet, you wouldn't. But it's very good, all the same: you buy it in cakes, and have to be very particular that 'Wapshott and Sons' is written on each cake: of course it isn't *really* written—"

"Of course not; but you'll excuse me if I don't yet see—"

"To be sure you don't until I have explained. Well, you see, men are so particular about what they eat and drink, and are always thinking about it—I don't mean poets, of course. I suppose you, for instance, only think about gossamer and things."

"I don't know that I think much about gossamer," said Mr. Moggridge.

"Well, moonbeams, then. But Fred is different. Ever since he left Chicago he has been talking about that tea. I wonder you never heard him."

"I have not, to my knowledge."

"No? Well, at last, finding it couldn't be bought in England, he sent across for a chest. We had the invoice a few days ago, and here it is."

Mrs. Goodwyn-Sandys produced a scrap of paper, and went on—

"You see, it's coming in a ship called the *Maryland*, and ought to be here about this time. Well, Fred was looking through his telescope before breakfast this morning—he's always looking through a telescope now, and knows, I believe, every rig of every vessel in the world—when he calls out, 'Hullo! American barque!' in his short way. Of course, I didn't know at first what he meant, and mixed it up with that stuff—Peruvian bark, isn't it?—that you give to your child, if you have one, and do not let it untimely die, or something of the sort. But afterwards he shouted, 'I shouldn't wonder if she's the *Maryland*;' and then I understood, and it struck me that it would be so nice to come to you and pay the 'duty,' or whatever you call it, on the tea, and at the same time, if you were very good, you would take me over the ship with you, and show me how you did your work. It's very complicated, I daresay: but I'll be quiet as a mouse, and won't interrupt you at all."

She paused for breath. The Collector smiled, and handed back the invoice.

"It seems all right," he said. "Let us hurry to the Custom House. An hour in your company, Geraldine, will transfigure even the dull round of duty."

Mrs. Goodwyn-Sandys smiled back divinely. She thought it extremely probable.

A few minutes later the poet sat by Geraldine's side—sweet proximity!—in the stern of one of Her Majesty's boats, while two "minions," as he was wont in verse to term his subordinates, rowed them towards a shapely barque that had just dropped anchor not far from the Bower Slip.

She flew a yellow flag in sign that she hailed from a foreign port, and as the Customs' boat dropped under her quarter Mr. Moggridge shouted—

"*Maryland*, ahoy!"

"Ahoy!" answered a gruff voice, and a red face looked over the side.

"Captain?" inquired Mr. Moggridge.

"That's me—Uriah T. Potter, Cap'n. Customs, I guess," said the red-faced man, with a slow look at Mrs. Goodwyn-Sandys.

"Clean bill of health?"

"Waal, two fo'c's'le hands down with whoopin'-cough: take it you won't keep us in quarantine for that."

The Collector helped Mrs. Goodwyn-Sandys up the ship's side. As she alighted on deck a swift glance passed between her and the red-faced man. Quite casually she laid two fingers on her chin. Uriah T. Potter did the same; but Mr. Moggridge was giving some instructions to his minions at the moment, and did not notice it.

"Anything to declare?" he asked.

"Mainly corn aboard, an' tinned fruits for Port o' London. Reas'nable deal o' tea an' 'baccy, though, for you to seal—shipped for same place. By the way, chest o' tea for party living hereabouts— Goodwyn-Sandys, friend of owner—guess that's the reason for putting in at this one-hoss place," wound up Uriah T. Potter, with a depreciatory glance at the beauties of Troy.

"This is Mrs. Goodwyn-Sandys," said the Collector.

"Proud to make your 'cquaintance, marm." The Captain held out his hand to the lady, who shook it affably.

"Let's see the cargo," said Mr. Moggridge.

The Captain led the way and they descended; Mrs. Goodwyn-Sandys full of pretty wonder at the arrangements of the ship, and slipping her fingers timidly into the Collector's hand on the dark companion stairs. He seized and raised them to his lips.

171

"Oh, you poets!" expostulated she.

"Where the tyrant's only fee," murmured Mr. Moggridge.

"Is the kissing of a hand."

"What, more verses? You shall repeat them to me."

I am afraid that in the obscurity below, Mr. Moggridge inspected the weighing of ship's stores and sealing of excisable goods in a very perfunctory manner. There were so many dim corners and passages where Mrs. Goodwyn-Sandys needed guidance; and, after all, the minions were sufficient for the work. They rummaged here and there among casks and chests, weighing, counting, and sealing, whilst the red-faced Uriah stood over them and occasionally looked from the Collector to the lady with a slow grin of growing intelligence.

They were seated together on a cask, and Mr. Moggridge had possessed himself, for the twentieth time, of his companion's hand.

"You think the verses obscure?" he was whispering. "Ah! Geraldine, if I could only speak out from the heart! As it is, 'Euphelia serves to grace my measure!'"

"Who's she?" asked Mrs. Goodwyn-Sandys, whose slight acquaintance with other poets was, perhaps, the reason why she rated her companion's verse so highly.

> "'The merchant, to conceal his treasure,
> Conveys it in a borrowed name,'"

Mr. Moggridge began to quote.—"Why, Geraldine, what is the matter? Are you faint?"

"No; it is nothing."

"I thought you seemed pale. As I was saying—"

172

'The merchant, to conceal his treasure—'

"Yes, yes, I know," said she, rising abruptly. "It is very hot and close down here."

"Then you *were* faint?"

"Here's your chest, marm," called the voice of Uriah T. Potter.

She turned and walked towards it. It was a large, square packing-case, and bore the legends—

"WAPSHOTT AND SONS',
CHICAGO,
PATENT COMPRESSED TEA,
TEN PRIZE MEDALS"—

stamped here and there about it. "I suppose," she said, turning to Mr. Moggridge, "I can have it weighed here, and pay you the duty, and then Captain Potter can send it straight to 'The Bower'?"

"Certainly," said Mr. Moggridge; "we won't be long opening it, and then—"

"Opening it!"

"Why, yes; as a matter of form, you know. It won't take a minute."

"But how foolish," said Mrs. Goodwyn-Sandys, "when you know very well by the invoice that it's tea!"

"Oh, of course it's foolish: only it's the rule, you understand, before allowing goods to be landed."

"But I don't understand. It is tea, and I am ready to pay the duty. I never thought you would be so unreasonable."

"Geraldine!"

At the utterance of Mrs. Goodwyn-Sandys' Christian name the two minions turned aside to conceal their smiles. The red-faced man's appreciation even led him to dive behind the packing-case. The Collector pulled himself up and looked confused.

"It was so small a thing I asked," said she, almost to herself, and with a heart-rending break in her voice, "so small a test!" And with a sigh she half-turned to go.

The Collector's hand arrested her.

"Do you mean—?"

She looked at him with reproach in her eyes. "Let me pass," said she, and seeing the conflict between love and duty on his face, "So small a test!"

"Damn the tea!" said Mr. Moggridge.

"I am feeling so faint," said Mrs. Goodwyn-Sandys.

"Let me lead you up to the fresh air."

"No; go and open the tea."

"I am not going to open it."

"Do!"

"I won't. Here, Sam," he called to one of the minions, "put down that chisel and weigh the chest at once. You needn't open it. Come, don't stand staring, but look alive. I know what's inside. Are you satisfied?" he added, bending over her.

"It frightened me so," she answered, looking up with swimming eyes. "And I thought—I was planning it so nicely. Take me up on deck, please."

"Come, be careful o' that chest," said Captain Uriah T. Potter to the minions, as they moved it up to be weighed.

"Heaviest tea that iver *I* handled," groaned the first minion.

"All the more duty for you sharks. O' course it's heavy, being compressed: an' strong, too. Guess you don't oft'n get tea o' this strength in your country, anyway. Give a man two pinches o' Wapshott's best, properly cooked, an' I reckon it'll last *him*. You won't find him coming to complain."

"No?"

"No. But I ain't sayin' nuthin'," added Captain Potter, "about his widder."

And his smile, as he regarded his hearers, was both engaging and expansive.

CHAPTER XVII.

HOW ONE THAT WAS DISSATISFIED WITH HIS PAST SAW A VISION, BUT DOUBTED.

Caleb Trotter watched his master's behaviour during the next few days with a growing impatience.

"I reckon," he said, "'tes wi' love, as Sally Bennett said when her old man got cotched i' the dreshin'-machine,' you'm in, my dear, an' you may so well go dro'.'"

Nevertheless, he would look up from his work at times with anxiety.

"Forty-sax. That's the forty-saxth time he've a-trotted up that blessed beach an' back; an' five times he've a-pulled up to stare at the watter. I've a-kep' count wi' these bits o' chip. An' at night 'tes all round the house, like Aaron's dresser, wi' a face, too, like as ef he'd a-lost a shillin' an' found a thruppeny-bit. This 'ere pussivantin' [1] may be relievin' to the mind, but I'm darned ef et can be good for shoe-leather. 'Tes the wear an' tear, that's what 'tes, as Aunt Lovey said arter killin' her boy wi' whackin'."

The fact is that Mr. Fogo was solving his problem, though the process was painful enough. He was concerned, too, for Caleb, whose rest was often broken by his master's restlessness. In consequence he determined to fit up a room for his own use. Caleb opposed the scheme at first; but, finding that the business of changing diverted Mr. Fogo's melancholy, gave way at last, on a promise that "no May-games" should be indulged in—a festival term which was found to include somnambulism, suicide, and smoking in bed.

The room chosen lay on the upper storey at the extreme east of the house, and looked out, between two tall elms, upon the creek and the lepers' burial-ground. It was chosen as being directly over the room occupied by Caleb, so that, by stamping his foot, Mr. Fogo could summon his servant at any time. The floor was bare of carpet, and the chamber of decoration. But Mr. Fogo hated decoration, and, after slinging his hammock and pushing the window open for air, gazed around on the blistered ceiling and tattered wall-paper, rubbed his hands, and announced that he should be very comfortable.

"Well, sir," said Caleb, as he turned to leave him for the night, "arter all, comfort's a matter o' comparison, as St. La'rence said when he turned round 'pon the gridiron. But the room's clane as watter an' scourin' 'll make et—reminds me," he continued, with a glance round, "o' what the contented clerk said by hes office-stool: 'Chairs es good,' said he, 'and sofies es better; but 'tes a great thing to harbour no dust.' Any orders, sir?"

"No, I fancy—stop! Is my writing-case here?"

Caleb's anxiety took alarm.

"You bain't a-goin' to do et in writin' sir, surely!"

Mr. Fogo stared.

"Don't 'ee, sir—don't 'ee!"

"Really, Caleb, your behaviour is most extraordinary. What is it that I am not to do?"

"Why, put et in writin', sir: they don't like et. Go up an' ax her like a man—'Will 'ee ha' me? Iss or no?' That was ould Dick Jago's way, an' I reckon *he* knowed, havin' married sax wifes, wan time an' another. But as for pen and ink—"

"You mistake me," interrupted Mr. Fogo, with a painful flush. He paused irresolutely, and then added, in a softer tone, "Would you mind taking a seat in the window here, Caleb? I have something to say to you."

Caleb obeyed. For a moment or two there was silence as Mr. Fogo stood up before his servant. The light of the candle on the chest beside him but half revealed his face. When at last he spoke it was in a heavy, mechanical tone.

"You guessed once," he said, "and rightly, that a woman was the cause of my seclusion in this place. In such companionship as ours, it would have been difficult—even had I wished it—to keep up the ordinary relations of master and man; and more than once you have had opportunities of satisfying whatever curiosity you may have felt about my—my past. Believe me, Caleb, I have noted your forbearance, and thank you for it."

Caleb moved uneasily, but was silent.

"But my life has been too lonely for me," pursued his master wearily. "On general grounds one would not imagine the life of a successful hermit to demand any rare qualifications. It is humiliating, but even as a hermit I am a failure: for instance, you see, I want to talk."

His hearer, though puzzled by the words, vaguely understood the smile of self-contempt with which they were closed.

"As a woman-hater, too, my performances are beneath contempt. I *did* think," said Mr. Fogo with something of testiness in his voice, "I should prove an adequate woman-hater, whereas it happens—"

He broke off suddenly, and took a turn or two up and down the room. Caleb could have finished the sentence for him, but refrained.

"Surely," said Mr. Fogo, pausing suddenly in his walk, "surely the conditions were favourable enough. Listen. It is not so very long ago since I possessed ambitions—hopes; hopes that I hugged to myself as only a silent man may. With them I meant to move the world, so far as a writer can move the world (which I daresay may be quite an inch). These hopes I put in the keeping of the woman I loved. Can you foresee the rest?"

Caleb fumbled in his pocket for his pipe, found it, held it up between finger and thumb, and, looking along the stem, nodded.

"We were engaged to be married. Two days before the day fixed for our wedding she—she came to me (knowing me, I suppose, to be a mild man) and told me she was married—had been married for a week or more, to a man I had never seen—a Mr. Goodwyn-Sandys. Hallo! is it broken?"

For the pipe had dropped from Caleb's fingers and lay in pieces upon the floor.

"Quite so," he went on in answer to the white face confronting him, "I know it. She is at this moment living in Troy with her husband. I had understood they were in America; but the finger of fate is in every pie."

Caleb drew out a large handkerchief, and, mopping his brow, gasped—

"Well, of all—" And then broke off to add feebly, "Here's a coincidence!—as Bill said when he was hanged 'pon his birthday."

"I have not met her yet, and until now have avoided the chance. But now I am curious to see her—"

"Don't 'ee, sir."

"And to-night intended writing."

"Don't 'ee, sir; don't 'ee."

"To ask for an interview, Caleb," pursued Mr. Fogo, drawing himself up suddenly, while his eyes fairly gleamed behind his spectacles. "Here I am, my past wrecked and all its cargo of ambitions scattered on the sands, and yet—and yet I feel tonight that I could thank that woman. Do you understand?"

"I reckon I do," said Caleb, rising heavily and making for the door.

He stopped with his hand on the door, and turning, observed his master for a minute or so without remark. At last he said abruptly—

"Pleasant dreams to 'ee, sir: an' two knacks 'pon the floor ef I be wanted. Good-night, sir." And with this he was gone.

Mr. Fogo stood for some moments listening to his footsteps as they shuffled down the stairs. Then with a sigh he turned to his writing-case, pulled a straw-bottomed chair before the rickety table, and sat for a while, pen in hand, pondering.

Before he had finished, his candle was low in its socket, and the floor around him littered with scraps of torn paper. He sealed the envelope, blew out the candle, and stepped to the window.

"I wonder if she has changed," he said to himself.

Outside, the summer moon had risen above the hill facing him, and the near half of the creek was ablaze with silver. The old schooner still lay in shadow, but the water rushing from her hold kept a perpetual music. Other sounds there were none but the soft rustling of the swallows in the eaves overhead, the sucking of the tide upon the beach below, and the whisper of night among the elms. The air was heavy with the fragrance of climbing roses and all the scents of the garden. In such an hour Nature is half sad and wholly tender.

Mr. Fogo lit a pipe, and, watching its fumes as they curled out upon the laden night, fell into a kingly melancholy. He dwelt on his past, but without resentment; on Tamsin, but with less trouble of heart. After all, what did it matter? Mr. Fogo, leaning forward on the window-seat, came to a conclusion to which others have been led before him—that life is a small thing. Oddly enough, this discovery, though it belittled his fellowmen considerably, did not belittle the thinker at all, or rather affected him with a very sublime humility.

"When one thinks," said he, "that the moon will probably rise ten million times over the hill yonder on such a night as this, it strikes one that woman-hating is petty, not to say a trifle fatuous."

He puffed awhile in silence, and then went on—

"The strange part of it is, that the argument does not seem to affect Tamsin as much as I should have fancied."

He paused for a moment, and added:

"Or to prove as conclusively as I should expect that I am a fool. Possibly if I see Geraldine to-morrow, she will prove it more satis—"

He broke off to clutch the lattice, and stare with rigid eyes across the creek.

For the moon was by this time high enough to fling a ray upon the deserted hull: and there—upon the deck—stood a figure—the figure of a woman.

She was motionless, and leant against the bulwarks, with her face towards him, but in black shadow. A dark hood covered her head; but the cloak was flung back, and revealed just a gleam of white where her bosom and shoulders bent forward over the schooner's side.

Mr. Fogo's heart gave a leap, stood still, and then fell to beating with frantic speed. He craned out at the window, straining his eyes. At the same moment the pipe dropped from his lips and tumbled, scattering a shower of sparks, into the rose-bush below.

When he looked up again the woman had disappeared.

Suddenly he remembered Caleb's story of the girl who, ages back, had left her home to live among the lepers in this very house, perhaps in the very room he occupied; and of the ghost that haunted the burial ground below. Mr. Fogo was not without courage; but the recollection brought a feeling of so many spiders creeping up his spine.

And yet the whole tale was so unlikely that, by degrees, as he gazed at the wreck, now completely bathed in moonlight, he began to persuade himself that his eyes had played him a trick.

"I will go to bed," he muttered; "I have been upset lately, and these fits of mine may well pass into hallucination. Once think of these women and —"

He stopped as if shot. From behind the wreck a small boat shot out into the moon's brilliance. Two figures sat in it, a woman and a man; and as the boat dropped swiftly down on the ebb he had time to notice that both were heavily muffled about the face. This was all he could see, for in a moment they had passed into the gloom, and the next the angle of the house hid them from view; but he could still hear the plash of their oars above the sounds of the night.

"The leper and his sweetheart," was Mr. Fogo's first thought. But then followed the reflection—would ghostly oars sound? On the whole, he decided against the supernatural. But the mystery remained. More curious than agitated, but nevertheless with little inclination to resume his communing with the night, Mr. Fogo sought his hammock and fell asleep.

The sun was high when he awoke, and as he descended to breakfast he heard Caleb's mallet already at work on the quay below. Still, anxious to set his doubts at rest, he made a hasty meal, and walked down to take a second opinion on the vision.

Caleb, with his back towards the house, was busily fitting a new thwart into Mr. Fogo's boat, and singing with extreme gaiety—

> "Oh, where be the French dogs?
>   Oh! where be they, O?
> They be down i' their long-boats,
>   All on the salt say, O!"

What with the song and the hammering, he did not hear his master's approach.

> "Up flies the kite,
> An' down flies the lark, O!
> Wi' hale an' tow, rumbleow—"

"Good-morning, Caleb."

"Aw, mornin' to 'ee, sir. You took me unawares—

> "All for to fetch home,
> The summer an' the May, O!
> For summer is a-come,
> An' winter es a-go.'"

"Caleb, I have seen a ghost."

The mallet stopped in mid-descent. Caleb looked up again open-mouthed.

"Tom Twist and Harry Dingle!"

"I beg your pardon?"

"Figger o' speech, sir, meanin' 'Who'd ha' thought et?' Whose ghost, sir, ef 'taint a rude question?"

Mr. Fogo told his story.

At its conclusion, Caleb laid down his mallet and whistled.

"'Tes the leppards, sure 'nuff, a-ha'ntin' o' th' ould place. Scriptur' says they will not change their spots, an' I'm blest ef et don't say truth. But deary me, sir, an' axin' your pardon for sayin' so, you'm a game-cock, an' no mistake."

"I?"

"Iss, sir. Two knacks 'pon the floor, an' I'd ha' been up in a jiffey. But niver mind, sir, us'll wait up for mun to-night, an' I'll get the loan o' the Dearlove's blunderbust in case they gets pol-rumptious."

Mr. Fogo deprecated the blunderbuss, but agreed to sit up for the ghost; and so for the time the matter dropped. But Caleb's eyes followed his master admiringly for the rest of the day, and more than once he had to express his feelings in vigorous soliloquy.

"Niver tell me! Looks as ef he'd no more pluck nor a field-mouse; an' I'm darned ef he takes more 'count of a ghost than he wud of a circuit-preacher. Blest ef I don't think ef a sperrit was to knack at the front door, he'd tell 'un to wipe hes feet 'pon the mat, an' make hissel' at home. Well, well, seein's believin', as Tommy said when he spied Noah's Ark i' the peep-show."

[1] I cannot forbear to add a note on this eminently Trojan word. In the fifteenth century, so high was the spirit of the Trojan sea-captains, and so heavy the toll of black-mail they levied on ships of other ports, that King Edward IV sent poursuivant after poursuivant to threaten his displeasure. The messengers had their ears slit for their pains; and "poursuivanting" or "pussivanting" survives as a term for ineffective bustle.

CHAPTER XVIII.

OF A YOUNG MAN THAT WOULD START UPON A DARK
ADVENTURE, BUT HAD TWO MINDS UPON IT.

At ten o'clock on this same morning Mr. Samuel Buzza sat by the
Club window, alternately skimming his morning paper and sipping
his morning draught. He was alone, for the habit of early rising was
fast following the other virtues of antique Troy, and the members
rarely mustered in force before eleven.

He had read all the murders and sporting intelligence, and was
about to glance at the affairs of Europe, when Mrs. Cripps, the
caretaker, entered in a hurry and a clean white apron.

"If you please, sir, there's Seth Udy's little boy below with a note for
you. I'd have brought it up, but he says he must give it hisself."

Sam, descending with some wonder, encountered Mr. Moggridge in
the passage. The rivals drew aside to let each other pass. On the
doorstep stood a ragged urchin, and waved a letter.

"For you, sir; an' plaise you'm to tell me 'yes' or 'no,' so quick as
possible."

Sam took the letter, glanced at the neat, feminine handwriting of the
address, and tore open the envelope.

"Dear Mr. Buzza,

  "If you care to remember what was spoken the other evening,
  you will to-night help a *most unhappy woman*. You will go to the
  captain's cabin of the Wreck which we visited together, and find
  there *a small portmanteau*. It may be carried in the hand, and
  holds the few necessaries I have hidden for my flight, but please
  carry it carefully. If you will be waiting with this by the sign-post

at the Five-Lanes' corner, at 11.30 *to-night*, no *words* of mine will repay you. Should you refuse, I am a wretched woman; but in any case I know I may trust you to say no word of this.

"Look out for the *closed carriage and pair*. A word to the bearer will tell me that I may hope, or that you care nothing for me.

G. G.-S.

"P.S.—Be very careful *not to shake the portmanteau*."

"What be I to say, plaise, sir?"

Sam, who had read the letter for a third time syllable by syllable, looked around helplessly.

"Ef you plaise, what be I to say?"

Sam very heartily wished both boy and letter to the devil. He groaned aloud, and was about to answer, when he paused suddenly.

In the room above Mr. Moggridge was singing a jaunty stave.

The sound goaded Sam to madness; he ground his teeth and made up his mind.

"Say 'yes,'" he answered, shortly.

The word was no sooner spoken than he wished it recalled. But the urchin had taken to his heels. With an angry sigh Sam let circumstance decide for him, and returned to the reading-room.

No doubt the consciousness that pique had just betrayed his judgment made him the more inclined to quarrel with the poet. But assuredly the sight that met his eyes caused his blood to boil; for Mr. Moggridge was calmly in possession of the chair and newspaper which Sam had but a moment since resigned.

"Excuse me, but that is my chair and my paper."

"Eh?" The poet looked up sweetly. "Surely, the Club chair and the Club paper—"

"I have but this moment left them."

"By a singular coincidence, I have but this moment taken possession of them."

"Give them up, sir."

"I shall do nothing of the kind, sir."

At this point Sam was seized with the unlucky inspiration of quoting from Mr. Moggridge's published works:

> "Forbid the flood to wet thy feet,
>   Or bind its wrath in chains;
> But never seek to quench the heat
>   That fires a poet's veins!"

This stanza, delivered with nice attention to its author's drawing-room manner, was too much.

"Sir, you are no gentleman!"

"You seem," retorted Sam, "to be an authority on manners as well as on Customs. I won't repeat your charge; but I'll be dashed if you're a poet!"

My Muse is in a very pretty pass. Gentlest of her sisterhood, she has wandered from the hum of Miss Limpenny's whist-table into the turmoil of Mars. Even as one who, strolling through a smiling champaign, finds suddenly a lion in his path, and to him straightway the topmost bough of the platanus is dearer than the mother that bare him—in short, I really cannot say how this history would have ended, had not Fortune at this juncture descended to the Club-room in form and speech like to Admiral Buzza.

The Admiral did not convey his son away in a hollow cloud, or even break the Club telescope in Mr. Moggridge's hand; he made a speech instead, to this effect:

"My sons, attend and cease from strife implacable; neither be as two ravening whelps that, having chanced on a kid in the dells of the mountain, dispute thereover, dragging this way and that with gnashing jaws. For to youth belong anger and biting words, but to soothe is the gift of old age."

What the Admiral actually said was—"Hullo! what the devil are you young cubs quarrelling about?"

And now, satisfied that no blood is to be spilt, the Muse hies gladly to a very different scene.

In the drawing-room of "The Bower" Mrs. Goodwyn-Sandys was sitting with a puzzled face and a letter on her lap. She had gone to the front door to learn Sam Buzza's answer, and, having dismissed her messenger, was returning, when the garden-gate creaked, and a blue-jerseyed man, with a gravely humorous face, stood before her. The new comer had regarded her long and earnestly before asking—

"Be you Mrs. Goodwyn-Sandys?"

"I am."

"Answerin' to name o' Geraldine, an' lawful wife o' party answerin' to name o' Honorubble Frederic?"

"Certainly!" she smiled.

"H'm. Then this 'ere's for you." And the blue-jerseyed man handed a letter, and looked at her again, searchingly.

"Is there an answer?"

"No, I reckon."

She was turning, when the man suddenly laid a finger on her arm.

"Axin' pardon, but you'll let 'un down aisy, won't 'ee? He don't bear no malice, tho' he've a-suffered a brave bit. Cure 'un, that's what I say—cure 'un: this bein', o' cou'se, atween you an' me. An' look 'ee here," he continued, with a slow nod; "s'posin' the party lets on as he's a-falled in love wi' another party, I reckon you won't be the party to hinder et. Mind, I bain't sayin' you cou'd, but you won't try, will 'ee? That's atween you an' me, o' cou'se."

The man winked solemnly, and turned down the path. Before she recovered of her astonishment he had paused again at the gate, and was looking back.

"That's understood," he nodded; "atween you an' me an' the gate-post, o' cou'se."

With that he had disappeared.

Mrs. Goodwyn-Sandys, if bewildered at this, was yet more astonished at the contents of the letter.

"Fogo?" she repeated, with a glance at the signature—"Fogo? Won't that be the name of the woman-hater up at Kit's House, me dear?"

"Certainly," answered the Honourable Frederic.

"Then I'll trouble yez to listen to this."

She read as follows:—

  "My Dear Mrs. Goodwyn-Sandys,

189

"When last you left me I prayed that we might never meet again. But time is stronger than I fancied, and here I am writing to you. Fate must have been in her most ironical mood to bring us so near in this corner of the world. I thought you were in another continent; but if you will let me accept the chance which brings us together, and call upon you as an old friend, I shall really be grateful: for there will be much to talk about, even if we avoid, as I promise to do, all that is painful; and I am very lonely. I have seen your husband, and hope you are very happy.—Believe me, verysincerelyyours,

Philip Fogo."

"What does it mean?" asked Mrs. Goodwyn-Sandys helplessly.

"It means, Nellie, that we have just time enough, and none to spare; in other words, that 'Goodwyn-Sandys' has come near to being a confoundedly fatal—"

"Then he must have known—"

"Known! My treasure, where are your wits? Beautiful namesake— jilted lover—'hence, perjured woman'—bleeding heart—years pass— marry another—finger of fate—Good Lord!" wound up the Honourable Frederic. "I met the fellow one day, and couldn't understand why he stared so—gave me the creeps—see it all now."

He lay back in his chair and whistled.

There was a tap at the drawing-room door, and the buttoned youth announced that Mrs. Buzza was without, and earnestly begged an interview with Mrs. Goodwyn-Sandys. The Honourable Frederic obligingly retired to smoke, and the visitor was shown in.

Her appearance was extraordinary. Her portly figure shook; her eyes were red; her bonnet, rakishly poised over the left eye, had dragged askew the "front" under it, as though its wearer had parted her hair

190

on one side in a distracted moment. A sob rent her bosom as she entered.

"My poor soul!" murmured Mrs. Goodwyn-Sandys, "you are in trouble."

Mrs. Buzza tried to speak, but dropped into a chair and nodded instead.

"What *is* the matter?"

"It's—it's *him.*"

"The Admiral?"

Mrs. Buzza mopped her eyes and nodded again.

"What has he done now?"

"S-said his bu-bu-breakfast was cold this mo-horning, and p-pitched the bu-bu-breakfast set over the quay-door," she moaned. "Oh! w-what shall I do?"

"Leave him!"

Mrs. Buzza clasped her hands and stared.

"You could see the m-marks quite plain," she wailed.

"What! Did he strike you?"

"I mean, on the bo-bottom of the c-cups. They were real W-worcester."

"Leave him! Oh! I have no patience," and Mrs. Goodwyn-Sandys stamped her little foot, "with you women of Troy. Will you always be dolls— dolls with a painted smile for all man's insane caprices? Will you never—?"

"I don't paint," put in Mrs. Buzza feebly.

"Revolt, I say! Leave him this very night! Oh! if I could—"

"If you please 'm," interrupted the page, throwing open the door, "here's Mrs. Simpson, an' says she must see you partic'lar."

Mrs. Buzza had barely time to dry her eyes and set her bonnet straight, before Mrs. Simpson rushed into the room. The new comer's face was crimson, and her eyes sparkled.

"Oh! Mrs. Goodwyn-Sandys, I must—"

At this point she became aware of Mrs. Buzza, stopped abruptly, sank into a chair, and began aimlessly to discuss the weather.

This was awkward; but the situation became still further strained when Mrs. Pellow was announced, and bursting in with the same eagerness, came to a dead halt with the same inconsequence. Mrs. Saunders followed with white face and set teeth, and Mrs. Ellicome-Payne in haste and tears.

"Pray come in," said their hostess blandly; "this is quite like a mothers' meeting."

The reader has no doubt guessed aright. Though nobody present ever afterwards breathed a word as to their reasons for calling thus at "The Bower," and though the weather (which was serene and settled) alone supplied conversation during their visit, the truth is that the domestic relations of all these ladies had coincidently reached a climax. It seems incredible; but by no other hypothesis can I explain the facts. If the reader can supply a better, he is entreated to do so.

At length, finding the constraint past all bearing, Mrs. Buzza rose to go.

"You will do it?" whispered her hostess as they shook hands.

She could not trust herself to answer, but nodded and hastily left the room. At the front door she almost ran against a thin, mild-faced gentleman. He drew aside with a bow, and avoided the collision; but she did not notice him.

"I will do it," she kept repeating to herself, "in spite of the poor girls."

A mist swept before her eyes as she passed down the road. She staggered a little, with a vague feeling that the world was ending somehow; but she repeated—

"I will do it. I have been a good wife to him; but it's all over now— it's all over to-night."

The mild-faced gentleman into whom Mrs. Buzza had so nearly run in her agitation was Mr. Fogo. A certain air of juvenility sat upon him, due to a new pair of gloves and the careful polish which Caleb had coaxed upon his hat and boots. His clothes were brushed, his carriage was more erect; and the page, who opened the door, must, after a scrutiny, have pronounced him presentable, for he was admitted at once.

Undoubtedly the page blundered; but the events of the past hour had completely muddled the poor boy's wits, and perhaps the sight of one of his own sex was grateful, coming as it did after so many agitated females. At any rate, Mr. Fogo and his card entered the Goodwyn-Sandys' drawing-room together.

I leave you to imagine his feelings. In one wild instant the scene exploded on his senses. He staggered back against the door, securely pinning the retreating page between it and the doorpost, and denuding the Goodwyn-Sandys' livery of half a dozen buttons. The four distracted visitors started up as if to escape by the window. Mrs. Goodwyn-Sandys advanced.

She was white to the lips. A close observer might have read the hunted look that for one brief moment swept over her face. But when she spoke her words were cold and calm.

"You wish to see my husband, Mr.—?" She hesitated over the name.

"Not in the least," stammered Mr. Fogo.

There was an awful silence, during which he stared blankly around on the ladies.

"Then may I ask—?"

"I desired to see Gerald—I mean, Mrs. Goodwyn-Sandys—but—"

"I am Mrs. Goodwyn-Sandys. Would you mind stating your business?"

Mr. Fogo started, dropped his hat, and leant back against the door again.

"*You!*"

"Certainly." Her mouth worked slightly, but her eyes were steady.

"You are she that—was—once—Geraldine—O'Halloran?"

"Certainly."

"Excuse me, madam," said Mr. Fogo, picking up his hat and addressing Mrs. Simpson politely, "but the mole on your chin annoys me."

"Sir!"

"Annoys me excessively. May I ask, was it a birth-mark?"

"He is mad!" screamed the ladies, starting up and wringing their hands. "Oh, help! help!"

Mr. Fogo looked from one to another, and passed his hand wearily over his eyes.

"You are right," he murmured; "I fancy—do you know—that I must be— slightly—mad. Pray excuse me. Would one of you mind seeing me home?" he asked with a plaintive smile.

His eyes wandered to Mrs. Goodwyn-Sandys, who stood with one hand resting on the table, while the other pointed to the door.

"Help! help!" screamed the ladies.

Without another word he opened the door and tottered out into the passage. At the foot of the stairs he met the Honourable Frederic, who had been attracted by the screams.

"It's all right," said Mr. Fogo; "don't trouble. I shall be better out in the open air. There are women in there"—he pointed towards the drawing-room—"and one with a mole. I daresay it's all right— but it seemed to me a very big mole."

And leaving the Honourable Frederic to gasp, he staggered from the house.

What happened in the drawing-room of "The Bower" after he left it will never be known, for the ladies of Troy are silent on the point.

It was ten o'clock at night, the hour when men may cull the bloom of sleep. Already the moon rode in a serene heaven, and, looking in at the Club window, saw the Admiral and Lawyer Pellow—"*male feriatos Troas*"—busy with a mild game of *ecarte*. There were not enough to make up a loo to-night, for Sam and Mr. Moggridge were absent, and so—more unaccountably—was the Honourable Frederic. The moon was silent, and only she, peering through the blinds of "The Bower," could see Mr. and Mrs. Goodwyn-Sandys hastily packing their boxes; or beneath the ladder, by the Admiral's quay-door, a figure stealthily unmooring the Admiral's boat.

To say that Sam Buzza did not relish his task were but feebly to paint his feelings, as, with the paddles under one arm, and the thole-pins in his pocket, he crept down the ladder and pushed off. Never before had the plash of oars seemed so searching a sound; never had the harbour been so crowded with vessels; and as for buoys, small craft, and floating logs, they bumped against his boat at every stroke. The moon, too, dogged him with persistent malice, or why was it that he rode always in a pool of light? The ships' lamps tracked him as so many eyes. He carried a bull's-eye lantern in the bottom of his boat, and the smell of its oil and heated varnish seemed to smell aloud to Heaven.

With heart in mouth, he crossed the line of the ferry, and picked his way among the vessels lying off the jetties. On one of these vessels somebody was playing a concertina, and as he crept under its counter a voice hailed him in German. He gave no answer, but pulled quickly on. And now he was clear again, and nearing Kit's House under the left bank. There was no light in any window, he noticed, with a glance over his shoulder. Still in the shadow, and only pulling out, here and there, to avoid a jutting rock, he gained the creek's mouth, and rowed softly up until the bulwarks of the old wreck overhung him.

The very silence daunted him now; but it must be gone through. Thinking to deaden fear by hurry, he caught up the lantern, leapt on board with the painter, fastened it, and crept swiftly towards the poop.

He gained the hatch, and paused to turn the slide of his lantern. The shaft of light fell down the companion as into a pitch-dark well. He could feel his heart thumping against his ribs as he began the descent, and jumping with every creak of the rotten boards, while always behind his fright lurked a sickening sense of the guilty foolishness of his errand.

At the ladder's foot he put his hand to his damp brow, and peered into the cabin.

In a moment his blood froze. A hoarse cry broke from him.

For there—straight ahead—a white face with straining eyes stared into his own!

And then he saw it was but his own reflection in a patch of mirror stuck into the panel opposite.

But the shock of that pallid mask confronting him had already unnerved him utterly.

He drew his eyes away, glanced around, and spied a black portmanteau propped beside a packing-case in the angle made by the wall and the flooring. In mad haste to reach the open air, but dimly remembering Geraldine's caution, he grasped the handles, flung a look behind him, and clambered up the ladder again, and out upon deck.

The worst was over; but he could not rest until again in his boat. As he untied the painter, he noticed the ray of his lantern dancing wildly up and down the opposite bank with the shaking of his hand. Cursing his forgetfulness, he turned the slide, slipped the lantern into his pocket, and, lowering himself gently with the portmanteau, dropped, seized the paddles, and rowed away as for dear life.

He had put three boats' lengths between him and the hull, and was drawing a sigh of relief, when a voice hailed him, and then—

A tongue of flame leapt out, and a loud report rang forth upon the night. He heard something whistle by his ear. Catching up the paddles again, he pulled madly out of the creek, and away for the opposite bank of the river; ran his boat in; and, seizing the portmanteau, without attempt to ship the oars or fasten the painter, leapt out; climbed, slipped, and staggered over the slippery stones; and fled up the hill as though a thousand fiends were at his heels.

CHAPTER XIX.

THAT A SILVER BULLET HAS VIRTUE:
WITH A WARNING TO COMMODORES.

"Well, sir," remarked Caleb at ten o'clock that evening, after an hour's watching had passed and brought no sign of a ghost, "I wish this 'ere sperrit, ef sperrit et be, wud put hissel' out to be punkshal. They do say as the Queen must wait while her beer's a-drawin'; but et strikes me ghost-seein' es apt to be like Boscas'le Fair, which begins twelve an' ends at noon."

Caleb caressed a huge blunderbuss which lay across his knee, and caused Mr. Fogo no slight apprehension.

"Et puts me i' mind," he went on, as his master was silent, "o' th' ould lidden [1] as us used to sing when us was tiny mites: —"

> Riddle me, riddle me, riddle me right,
> Where was I last Sat'rday night?
> I seed a chimp-champ champin' at his bridle,
> I seed an ould fox workin' hissel' idle.
> The trees did shever, an' I did shake,
> To see what a hole thic' fox did make.

"Now I comes to think 'pon et, 'tes Sat'rday night too; an' that's odd, as Martha said by her glove."

Still Mr. Fogo was silent.

"As for the blunderbust, sir, there's no call to be afeard. Tes on'y loaded wi' shot an' a silver shillin'. I heerd tell that over to Tresawsen, wan time, they had purty trouble wi' a lerrupin' big hare, sir. Neither man nor hound cud cotch her; an' as for bullets, her tuk in bullets like so much ballast. Well, sir, th' ould Squire were out wi' his gun wan day, an' 'way to track thicky hare, roun' an' roun', for up ten mile; an' the more lead he fired, the better plaised her seemed. 'Darn et!' says the old Squire at las'. "'Tes witchcraf; I'll try a silver bullet.' So he pulls out a crown-piece an' hammers 'un into a slug to fit hes gun. He'd no sooner loaded than out pops the hare agen, not twenty yards off, an' right 'cross the path. Th' ould man blazed away, an' this time hit her sure 'nuff: hows'ever, her warn't too badly wounded to nip roun' the knap o' the hill an' out o' sight. 'I'll ha' 'ee!' cries the Squire; an' wi' that pulls hot foot roun' the hill. An' there, sir, clucked in under a bit o' rock, an' pantin' for dear life, were ould Mally Skegg. I tell 'ee, sir, the Squire made no more to do, but 'way to run, an' niver stopped till he were safe home to Tresawsen. That's so. Mally were a witch, like her mother afore her; an' the best proof es, her wore a limp arter this to the day o' her death."

Mr. Fogo roused himself from his abstraction to ask—

"Do you seriously believe it was a ghost that I saw last night?"

"That's as may be. Ef 'taint, 'tes folks as has no bus'ness hereabouts. I've heerd tell as you'm wi'in the law ef you hails mun dree times afore firin'. That's what I means to do, anyway. As for ghostes, I do believe, an' I don't believe."

"What? That a man's spirit comes back after death to trouble folks?"

"I dunno 'bout sperrit: but I heerd a tale wance 'bout a man's remains as gi'ed a peck o' trouble arter death. 'Twas ould Commodore Trounce as the remains belonged to, an' 'tes a queer yarn, ef you niver heerd et afore."

Caleb looked at his master. Mr. Fogo had not yet told the story of his call at "The Bower"; but Caleb saw that he was suffering, and had planned this story as a diversion.

The bait took. Mr. Fogo looked up expectant, and lit a fresh pipe. So Caleb settled himself in his corner of the window-seat, and, still keeping an eye on the old schooner, began—

"THE COMMODORE'S PROGRESS.

"You've heerd me spake, sir, o' Joe Bonaday, him as made poetry 'long wi' me wan time when lying becalmed off Ilfrycombe?"

"Certainly."

"Well, this Joe were a Barnstaple man, bred an' born. But he had a brother—Sam were hes name—as came an' settled out Carne way; 'Ould These-an'-Thicky,' us used to call 'n. Sam was a crowder, [2] you must knaw, an' used to play the fiddle over to Tregarrick Fair; but he cudn' niver play more'n two tunes. 'Which'll 'ee ha',' he used to say, 'which'll 'ee ha'—these or thicky?' That's why, tho' he was christened Sam, us used to call 'n These-an'-Thicky for short."

"I see."

"This 'ere Sam Bonaday, tho' he came an' settled down i' these parts, was a bettermost body i' some ways, an' had a-seen a heap o' life 'long wi' ould Commodore Trounce. Sam was teetotum to the Commodore, an' acted currier when th' ould man travelled, which he did a brave bit—brushin' hes clothes, an' shinin' hes boots, an' takin' the tickets, an' the res'. The Commodore were mighty fond o' Sam: an' as for Sam, he used to say he mou't ha' been the Commodore's brother— on'y, you see, he warn't."

"I think I understand," said Mr. Fogo.

"Iss, sir. Well, t'ward the end o' hes days the Commodore were stashuned out at Gibraltar, an' o' cou'se takes Sam. He'd a-been ailin' for a tidy spell, had the Commodore, an' I reckon that place finished 'un; for he hadn' been there a month afore he tuk a chill, purty soon Sam saw 'twas on'y a matter o' time afore th' ould man wud go dead.

"Sam kep' hes maaster goin' 'pon brandy an' milk for a while; but wan day he comes in an' finds 'un settin' up in bed an' starin'. The Commodore was a little purgy, [3] bustious [4] sort o' man, sir, wi' a squinny eye an' mottles upon hes face pretty near so thick as the Milky Way; an' he skeered Sam a bit, settin' up there an' glazin'.

"Th' ould man had no more sproil [5] nor a babby, an' had pretty nigh lost hes mouth-speech, but he beckons Sam to the bed, and whispers—

"' Sam, you've a-been a gude sarvent to me.'

"'Gude maasters makes gude sarvents,' says Sam, an' falls to cryin' bitterly.

"'You'm down i' my will,' says the Commodore, 'so you've no call to take on so. But look 'ee here, Sam; there's wan thing more I wants 'ee to do for your old maaster. I've a-been a Wanderin' Jewel all my life,' says he, '—wanderer 'pon the face o' the earth, like—like—'

"'Cain,' says Sam.

"'Well, not azackly. Hows'ever, you an' me, Sam, have a-been like Jan Tresize's geese, never happy unless they be where they bain't, an' that's the truth. An' now,' says he, 'I've a-tuk a consait I'd like my ould bones to be carr'd home to Carne, an' laid to rest 'long wi' my haveage. [6] All the Trounces have a-been berried in Carne Churchyard, Sam, an' I'm thinkin' I'd like to go back to mun, like the Prodigious Son. So what I wants 'ee to do es this:—When I be dead an' gone, you mus' get a handy box made, so's I shall carry aisy, an' take me back to England. You'll find plenty o' money for the way i' the skivet [7] o' my chest there, i' the corner.'

"''Tes a brave long way from here to England,' says Sam.

"'I knaws what you be thinkin' 'bout,' says the Commodore. 'You'm reckonin' I'll spile on the way. But I don't mean 'ee to go by say. You mus' take me 'cross the bay an' then ship aboard a train, as'll take 'ee dro Seville, an' Madrid, an' Paris, to Dover. 'Tes a fast train,' says he, 'as trains go i' these parts; but I'm doubtin' ef et starts ivery day or

201

only dree times a week. I reckon, tho', ef you finds out, I can manage so's my dyin' shan't interfere wi' that.'

"Well, Sam was forced to promise, an' the Commodore seemed mighty relieved, an' lay still while Sam read to 'n out o' the books that th' ould man had by 'n. There was the Bible, and the Pellican's Progress, an' Philip Quarles, an' Hannah Snell, the female sodger. Sam read a bit from each, an' when he comes to that part about Christ'n crossing the river, th' ould man sets up sudden an' calls, 'Land, Sam, land! Fetch a glass, lad!'—just like that, sir; an' wi' that falls back dead.

"Well, sir, Sam was 'most out o' hes wits, fust along, for grief to lose hes maaster; but he warn't the man to go back 'pon hes word. So he loses no time, but, bein' a handy man, rigs up a wooden chest wi' the help o' a ship's carpenter, an' a tin case to ship into this, an' dresses up the Commodore inside, an' nails 'un down proper; an' wi'in twenty-four hours puts across in a boat, 'long wi' hes charge, for to catch the train.

"He hadn' barely set foot on shore, an' was givin' orders about carryin' the chest up to the stashun, un' thinkin' 'pon the hollerness o' earthly ways, as was nat'ral, when up steps a chap in highly-coloured breeches an' axes 'un ef he'd anything to declare.

"Sam had disremembered all 'bout the Customs, you see, sir.

"Hows'ever, et mou't ha' been all right, on'y Sam, though he could tackle the lingo a bit—just enough to get along wi' on a journey, that es—suddenly found that he disknowledged the Spanish for 'corpse.' He found out, sir, afore the day was out; but just now he looks at the chap i' the colour'd breeches and says—

"'No, I ha'nt.'

"'What's i' that box?' says the chap.

"Now this was azackly what Sam cudn' tell 'un; so, for lack of anything better, he says—

"'What's that to you?'

"'I reckon I must ha' that chest open,' says the chap.

"'I reckon you'll be sorry ef you do,' says Sam.

"'Tell me what's inside, then.'

"'Why, darn your Spanish eyes!' cries Sam, 'can't 'ee see I be tryin' to think 'pon the word for corpse?'

"But the chap cudn', of cou'se; so he called another in breeches just as gay as hes own, on'y stripier; and then for up ten minutes 'twas Dover to pay, all talkers an' no listeners. I reckon 'twas as Sal said to the Frenchman, 'The less you talks, the better I understands 'ee.' But Sam's blud were up by this time. Hows'ever, nat'rally he was forced to gi'e way, and they tuk the box into the Custom House, an' sent for hammer an' screw-driver.

"'Seems to me,' says the chap, prizin' the lid open a bit, an' snifnn', 'et smells oncommon like sperrits.'

"'I'm thinkin',' says Sam, ef *you'd* been kep' goin' on brandy-an'-milk for a week an' more, *you'd* smell like sperrits.'

"'I guess 'tes sperrits,' says wan.

"'Or 'baccy,' says anuther.

"'Or furrin fruits,' says a third.

"'Well, you'm wrong,' says Sam, "cos 'tes a plain British Commodore; an' I reckon ef you taxes *that* sort o' import, you dunno what's good for 'ee.'

"At las', sir, they prizes open the chest an' the tin case, an' there, o' cou'se, lay th' ould man, sleepin' an' smilin' so paiceful-like he looked ha'f a Commodore an' ha'f a cherry-bun."

"I suppose you mean 'cherubim,' Caleb?" corrected Mr. Fogo.

"I s'pose I do, sir; tho' I reckon th' ould man seemed happier than he were, havin' been a 'nation scamp in hes young days, an' able to swear to the las' so's t'wud pretty nigh fetch the mortar out'n a brick wall. Hows'ever, that's not to the p'int here.

"Aw, sir, you may fancy how them poor ign'rant furriners left that Custom House. Sam told me arterwards 'twere like shellin' peas—spakin' in pinafores—"

"Metaphors," said Mr. Fogo.

"That's et—met-afores. Anyway, they jest fetched a yell, an' then *went*, sir. I guess Sam knawed the Spanish for 'corpse' afore they was gone. In less 'n a minnit not a pair o' coloured breeches cud you find, not ef you wanted them fancy articles ever so. Sam chuckles a bit to hissel', fas'ens down the lid so well as he cud, h'ists the Commodore aboard a wheelbarrer, an' trundles 'un off to the train.

"He cotches the train jest as 'twere startin', an' sails away in a fust-class carr'ge all to hissel', wi' the Commodore laid 'long the seat opposite; 'for,' said Sam, 'drat expense when a fun'ral's goin'!' An' all the way he chuckles an' grins to hissel', to think o' the start he'd gi'ed they Custom House rascals; an' at las' he gets that tickled he's bound to lie back an' fairly hurt hissel' wi' laffin'.

"I reckon, tho', he laffed a bit too early; for jest then the train slowed down, and pulled up at a stashun. Sam looked out an' saw a dapper little man a-bustlin' up an' down the platform, like a bee in a bottle, an' pryin' into the carr'ge windeys same as ef the train were a peep-show. Presently he opens the door of Sam's compartment, an' axes, holdin' up a tellygram—

"'Be you the party as es travellin' wi' a dead man?'

"He spoke i' Spanish, o' cou'se, sir; but, not knowin' the tongue, I tells et to you in English."

"I had guessed that to be the reason," replied Mr. Fogo.

"Well, Sam were a bit tuk aback, but he answers—

"'Iss, I be. Why?'

"'Want 'un berried?'

"'Why, no, not partic'lar. Sooner or later, o' cou'se; but, thank'ee all the same, I'm thinkin' to do et a bit furder on.'

"'Then,' says the dapper man, 'I'll trouble you to hand over the berryin' fees for this parish.'

"'But I baint goin' to berry deceased i' this parish.'

"'That don't matter. Ef a corpse has use o' this parish, he's got to pay fees.'

"'How's that?'

"'Why, a corpse es dead,' says the chap; 'you'll allow that, I s'pose?'

"'Iss,' says Sam, 'I reckon I'll allow that.'

"'An' ef a corpse es i' this parish, he's dead i' this parish?'

"'Likely he es,' admits Sam.

"'Well, 'cordin' to law, anybody dead i' this parish es boun' to be berried i' this parish, an' therefore to pay fees,' says the man; 'and now I hopes you'll hand over the money, 'cos the train's waitin'.'

"Sam was for a raisin' a rumpus, an' gathered a crowd roun' the door; but they all sided wi' the dapper man, and said 'twas Spaniards' law, an' ef he wudn' pay, he must get out an' berry the Commodore there an' then. So he gi'ed in and pulled out the money, an' off they starts, the dapper man standin' an' bowin' 'pon the platform.

"Well, Sam leant back an' ciphered et out, an' cudn' see the sense o't. 'But,' says he, 'when you'm in Turkey you do as the Turkeys do, 'cordin' to the proverb, so I guess 'tes all right; an' ef et 'pears wrong, 'tes on'y that I bain't used to travellin' wi' corpses;' an' wi' that he settles down an' goes to sleep.

"He hadn' been long sleepin' when the train pulls up agen, an' arter a minnit in comes anuther chap wi' a tellygram.

"'Deceased?' axes the chap, pointin' to the chest.

"'Mod'rately,' says Sam.

"'Wants berryin' p'raps?' says the chap.

"'I reckon he'll hold on a bit longer.'

"'Next parish, likely?'

"'Why, iss,' says Sam, 'or next arter that.'

"'Ah, what et es to be rich!' says the man, kind o' envious-like.

"'What do 'ee mean by that?' Sam axes.

"'Niver mind,' answers the man. ''Twarn't no bus'ness o' mines. Wud 'ee kindly hand me the fees for this parish?'

"Well, Sam argeys the matter agen, but i' the end he pays up: 'Tho',' says he, 'I'd a notion travellin' were costly afore this, but darn me! you've got to be dead afore you sizes et. I've heerd as a man can't take nuthin' out o' this world, but blest ef I iver got the grip o' that tex' till I travelled i' Spain.'

"Well, sir, purty soon the same thing happened agen, an', to shorten the yarn, ivery time they got into a new parish an' pulled up, in walked a chap wi' a tellygram an' axed for berryin'-fees. Luckily, there was money to pay mun, for the Commodore had left a bravish sum for travellin' expenses, and by-'m-by Sam begins to take a sort o' pride in pullin' out hes purse.

"'Talk 'bout fun'rals!' says he, 'I reckon this es suthin' *like*. Adm'ral Nelson! why, Adm'ral Nelson didn' cost ha'f so much! An' you ain't but a Commodore,' says he. 'Devil fly away wi' 'ee, maaster, but so long as the coin lasts Sam won't cry 'Woa!''

"The words warn't fairly out o' hes mouth, sir, when the train draws up, an' in steps another man. He comed in so quiet that Sam didn' see 'un at first; but when he turned roun', there was the man standin' an' starin' at 'un. 'Twas a strange-looking party, dressed i' black—a better-most body, like.

"'Aw, good eveling!' says Sam.

"'Good eveling,' says the man i' black, an' nods t'wards the chest. 'How's deceased?'

"'Gettin' a bit costly,' answers Sam, 'but doin' purty well, consederin'. You'm wantin' more fees, I reckon'; an' wi' that he dives hes hand into hes trowsy-pocket.

"'I don't want no fees,' says the man.

"Sam was knacked 'pon a heap wi' this.

"'Well, then, you'm the fust man I've a-met in Spain as doesn',' he says.

"That ain't onlikely,' says the man; and Sam noticed for the fust time that he'd a-been speakin' English all along. 'I be a-travellin', same as you,' he adds.

"'You'll 'scuse me, sir, but this compartment es resarved.'

"'That's a pity,' says the stranger, "cos the train's a-started.'

"So 'twas. Sam hadn' a-noticed et, but they was movin' on. Hows'ever, he detarmined to make the best o't; so he ups and says, perlite-like—

"'Terrable hot weather this, ain't et, sir?' Somehow et seemed to Sam as ef et had got hotter sence the stranger comed in.

"'I don't feel so mighty hot,' says the man. 'But there, I've a-been a gude deal in hot countries. How's deceased takin' the journey?' says he.

"'He ain't complainin'; but, then, in life he warn't a complainin' sort. Aw, sir, but a man must be over-nice ef a fun'ral like thes don't satisfy 'n. Phew! but 'tes awful!'

"'What's awful?'

"'The heat,' answers Sam, moppin' his forehead; 'but I s'pose you'm a traveller, an' 'customed to heat.'

"'Why, iss,' says t'other, 'I do travel a purty passel to an' fro 'pon th' earth. Few folks travels more'n me.'

"Well, et kep' gettin' hotter an' hotter; an' Sam cussed an' mopped, an' mopped an' cussed, an' all the time the stranger were cool an' aisy. He kep' axin', too, 'bout th' ould Commodore an' hes past life, an' 'peared to take interes' in Sam, an' altogither seemed a proper gen'l'm'n. An' all the time et kep' gettin' hotter an' hotter, till Sam were fairly runnin' to waste wi' sweatin'. At las' he pops hes head out'n the windey for fresh air, an' cries out—

"'Hulloa! here's a stashun.'

"Well, the train pulls up, an' Sam says to the stranger—

"'Look 'ee here. Wud 'ee mind keepin' your eye 'pon th' ould man while I runs out to get a drink? I reckoned I knawed thirst afore this,' he says, 'but I were mistook.'

"The stranger was very willin', and away Sam goes.

"He warn't away more'n a minnit; but when he comes back an' takes a look at the platform, my! Sir! there warn't no trace of the train to be seen—not a vestment. You see, they don't blaw no whissle in Spain when the train goes; an' there was poor Sam left stranded.

"Well, he tellygrafs o' cou'se to the nex' stashun, an' in less 'n an hour back comes an answer to say as they searched the train when et stopped, an' there warn't no corpse there, nor chest, nor nuthin'. An' ef you'll believe me, sir," concluded Caleb, bending forward and touching his master's knee, "th' ould Commodore ha'n't niver been found fro' that day to this. Et 'most broke Sam's heart; an', as he said to me wan time, 'For all I knaws 'twas the devil; and for all I knaws th' ould maaster be travellin' roun' Spain to this day; but ef so,' says he, 'I reckon by this time he's like Patty Ward's pig—no lavender.'"

"That's a very curious tale," said Mr. Fogo, as Caleb leant back in the window-seat and awaited its effect.

"'Tes so true, sir, as I'm here—or so Sam used to say. An' the moral goes agen talkin' lightly o' what a man don't understand," he added reflectively. "But forebodin' es so bad as witch-craf', an' 'tes more'n likely they won't come to-night; but if they does, 'tes on'y fair to ax mun who they be dree times afore firin'. What's fair for man es fair—
"

He broke off and clutched his master by the arm.

"Look, sir—look!"

About the deck of the old schooner a shaft of light was dancing fitfully—now here, now there, up and down—and all without visible source or guidance.

The two watchers leapt to their feet and peered out at the window.

The strange brilliance flickered to and fro, falling even on the further bank, and threading with a line of yellow the silver-grey of the moonlight. Then it ceased suddenly.

Caleb and his master waited breathlessly. Half a minute passed without further sign. Then they heard a light splash or two, and Mr. Fogo pointed frantically at the line of the moon's reflection on the creek.

"There! Look—the boat!"

Caleb whipped the blunderbuss up to his shoulder and shouted—

"Who be 'ee? Darn 'ee, here goes—wan, two, dree, all to wanst!"

He pulled the trigger. A tongue of flame leapt forth and burst upon the night with a terrific explosion; and as Caleb fell backwards with the shock, the clumsy engine slipped from his fingers and fell with a clatter upon Mr. Fogo's instep.

When the pair recovered and looked forth again, the echoes had died away, and once more the night was tranquil.

[1] A monotonous chant or burthen.
[2] A fiddler.
[3] Thick-set.
[4] Stout.
[5] Strength.
[6] Kin.
[7] A concealed compartment or drawer.

CHAPTER XX.

HOW CERTAIN CHARACTERS FOUND THEMSELVES,
AT DEAD OF NIGHT, UPON THE FIVE LANES ROAD.

Panting, slipping, with aching sides, but terror at his heels, Sam Buzza tore up the hill. Lights danced before him, imaginary voices shouted after; but he never glanced behind. The portmanteau was monstrously heavy, and more than once he almost dropped it; but it was tightly packed, apparently, for nothing shook inside it. Only the handles creaked in his grasp.

He gained the top, shifted the load to his left hand, and raced down the other side of the hill. How he reached the bottom he cannot clearly call to mind; but he dug his heels well into the turf, and arrived without a fall. At the foot of the slope a wire fence had to be crossed; next the railway line, then, across the embankment, another fence, which kept a shred of his clothing. A meadow followed, and then he dropped over the hedge into the high road.

Here he stopped, set down the portmanteau, and looked about him. All was quiet. So vivid was the moonlight that as looking down the road he could mark every bush, every tuft of grass almost, on the illumined side. Not a soul was in sight.

The night was warm, and his flight had heated him intolerably. He felt for his handkerchief to mop his brow, but snatched his hand away.

His coat was burning. It was the lantern. Like a fool he had forgotten to blow it out, and an abominable smell of oil and burning cloth now arose from his pocket. He stifled the smouldering fire, pulled out the lantern, and looked at his watch.

It wanted twenty minutes to eleven.

He had plenty of time; so, having extinguished the lantern, and bestowed it in another pocket, he caught up his burden and began to walk up the road at a leisurely pace.

His terrors had cooled, but nevertheless he wished himself well out of the scrape. The report of the gun still rang in his ears and in fancy he could hear again the buzz of that bullet by his ear. More than once a shadow lying across the white road gave him a twinge of fear; and when a placid cow poked its nose over the hedge above him, and lowed confidentially, he leapt almost out of his skin.

The task before him, too, gave him no small anxiety. The directions in the letter were plain enough, but not so the intention of Mrs. Goodwyn-Sandys. Did she mean him to elope with her? He did not care to face the question. The Admiral, though an indulgent father, was not extravagant; and Sam had but seven-and-sixpence in his pocket. This was an excellent sum for long whist at threepenny points, but would hardly defray the cost of an elopement. Besides, he did not want to elope.

"No *words* of mine will repay you." Now he came to consider, these words wore an awkward look. Good Heavens! he had a mind to drop the portmanteau and run home. What had he done to be tempted so? And why had these people ever come to Troy?

Ah! Sam, that was the question we should have asked ourselves months ago. Some time before, at a concert in the Town Hall, I remember that Mr. Moggridge sang the line—

"Too late the balm when the heart is broke!"

And a Trojan voice at the back assented—

"A durn sight."

Why had we been denied that perspicacity now?

So with a heavy burden, and heavier conscience (both of Mrs. Goodwyn-Sandys' packing), he trudged forward, kicking up clouds of dust that sparkled in the moonlight. Presently the ascent grew more gradual, the hedges lower, and over their tops he could feel the upland air breathing coolly from the sea. And now the sign-post hove in sight, and the cross-roads stretching whitely into distance.

If we take the town of Troy as a base, lying north and south, this sign-post forms the apex of a triangle which has two high-roads for its remaining sides—the one road entering Troy from the north by the hill which Sam had just ascended, the other running southwards and ending with a steep declivity at no great distance from "The Bower."

It was by this southern road, of course, that Mrs. Goodwyn-Sandys would come. Sam looked along it, but all as yet was silent. He pulled out his watch again, and, finding that he had still twenty minutes to spare, set down his load at the foot of the signpost, and began to walk to and fro.

So gloomy were his reflections that, to soothe his nerves, he pulled out a cigar, lit it, and then, for lack of anything better to do, rekindled his lantern, and resumed his walk.

The cigar was barely half smoked when he heard a noise in the distance.

Yes, there was no doubt. It was the sound of horses. Sam caught up the portmanteau, and stared down the highway. For a full minute he listened to the advancing clatter, and presently, around an angle of the road, a chaise and pair broke into view, and came up at a gallop.

Sam advanced a step or two; a white handkerchief was thrust out at the window, and the driver pulled up suddenly. Then the face of Mrs. Goodwyn-Sandys looked anxiously out.

"Ah! you are there," she exclaimed with a little cry of relief. "I have been so afraid. Have you got it?"

In the moonlight, and that pretty air of timidity on her face, she was more ravishing than ever. Her voice called as a siren's; her eyes drew Sam irresistibly. In a second all his fears, doubts, scruples, were flung to the winds. He held up the portmanteau, and advanced to the carriage door.

"Here it is. Geraldine—"

"Oh! thanks, thanks. How can I show my thanks?"

The perfume of her hair floated out upon the night with the music of her tone until they both fairly intoxicated him.

He opened the door of the chaise.

"Where shall I stow it?" he asked.

"Here, opposite me; be very careful of it."

In the darkness he saw a huge bundle of rugs piled by Geraldine's side.

"Where am I to sit?" he asked, as he bestowed the portmanteau carefully.

He looked up into her face. The loveliest smile rested on him, for one instant, from those incomparable eyes. She did not answer, but held out her hand with the grace of a maiden confessing her first passion. He seized the ungloved fingers, and kissed them.

"Geraldine!"

At this moment a low chuckle issued from the bundle of rugs. Sam dropped the hand, and started back as if stung. A hateful thought flashed upon him.

"Moggridge? But no—"

He seized his lantern, and turned the slide. A stream of light shot into the corner of the chaise, and revealed—the bland face of Mr. Goodwyn-Sandys!

There was an instant of blank dismay. Then, with a peal of laughter, Geraldine sank back among the cushions.

"*Good*-night!" said the Honourable Frederic with grim affability; then, popping his head out at the further window, "Drive on, John!"

The post-boy cracked his whip, the horses sprang forward, and Sam, with that pitiless laugh still pealing in his ears, was left standing on the high-road.

In the tumult of the moment, beyond a wild sense of injustice, it is my belief that his brain accomplished little. He stared dully after the retreating chaise, until it disappeared in the direction of Five Lanes; and then he groaned aloud.

There was a patch of turf, now heavy with dew, beside the sign-post. Upon this he sat down, and with his elbows on his knees, and head between his hands, strove to still the giddy whirl in his brain. And as his folly and its bitterness found him out, the poor fool rocked himself, and cursed the day when he was born. If any one yet doubt that Mr. Moggridge was an inspired singer, let him turn to that sublime aspiration in *Sophronia: a Tragedy*—

"Let me be criminal, but never weak;

For weaklings wear the stunted form of sin

Without its brave apparel"—

and considered Sam Buzza as he writhed beneath the sign-post.

Pat, pat, pat!

It was the muffled sound of footsteps on the dusty road. He looked up. A dark figure, the figure of a woman, was approaching. Its air of timorous alertness, and its tendency to seek the shadow of the hedge-row, gave him some confidence. He arose, and stepped forward into the broad moonlight.

The woman gave a short gasp and came to a halt, shrinking back against the hedge. Something in her outline struck sharply on Sam's sense, though with a flash of doubt and wonder. She carried a small handbag, and wore a thick veil over her face.

"Who are you?" he asked gently. "Don't be afraid."

The woman made no answer—only cowered more closely against the hedge; and he heard her breath coming hard and fast. Once more—and for the third time that night—Sam pulled the slide of his lantern.

"*Mother!*"

"Oh! Sam, Sam, don't betray me! I'll go back—indeed I'll go back!"

"In Heaven's name, mother, what are you doing here?"

The retort was obvious, but Mrs. Buzza merely cried—

"Dear Sam, have pity on me, and take me back! I'll go quietly—quite quietly."

The idea of his mother (who weighed eighteen stone if an ounce) resisting with kicks and struggles might have caused Sam some amusement, but his brain was overcrowded already.

"It's a judgment," she went on incoherently, wringing her hands; "and I thought I had planned it so cleverly. I dressed up his double-bass, Sam, and put it in the bed—oh! I am a wicked woman—and pinned a note to the pin-cushion to say he had driven me to it, throwing the breakfast things over the quay-door—real Worcester,

216

Sam, and marked at the bottom of each piece; and a carriage from the Five Lanes Hotel to meet me at twelve o'clock; but I'd rather go home, Sam; I've been longing, all the way, to go back; it's been haunting me, that double-bass, all the time—with my nightcap, too—the one with real lace—on the head of it. Oh! take me home, Sam. I'm a wicked woman!"

Sam, after all, was a Trojan, and I therefore like to record his graces. He drew his mother's arm within his with much tenderness, kissed her, and began to lead her homewards quietly and without question.

But the poor soul could not be silent; and so, very soon, the whole story came out. At the mention of Mrs. Goodwyn-Sandys Sam shut his teeth sharply.

"I shall never be able to face her, Sam."

"I don't think you need trouble about that, mother," he answered grimly.

"But I do. It was she—"

But at this moment, from the hedge, a few yards in front, there issued a hollow groan.

They halted, and questioned each other with frightened eyes.

"Geraldine!" wailed the voice. "Cruel, perjured Geraldine!"

"It was going on just like this," whispered Mrs. Buzza, "when I came along. I shut my eyes, and ran past as hard as I could; but my head was so full of voices and cries that I didn't know if 'twas real or only my fancy."

"Geraldine!" continued the voice. "Oh! dig my grave—my shroud prepare; for she was false as she was fair. Geraldine, my Geraldine!"

"Moggridge, by all that's holy!" cried Sam.

It was even so. They advanced a few yards, and to the right of the road, beside a gate, they saw him. The poet reclined limply against the hedge, and with his head propped upon a carpet-bag gazed dolefully into the moon's face.

"Thou bid'st me," he began again, "thou bid'st me think no more about thee; but, tell me, what is life without thee? A scentless flower, a blighted—"

At the sound of their footsteps he looked round, stared blankly into Sam's face, and then, snatching up the carpet-bag, leapt to his feet and tore down the road as fast as he could go.

Sam paused. They had reached the brow of the steeper descent, where the road takes a sudden determination, and plunges abruptly into the valley, Below, the roofs of the little town lay white and sparkling, and straight from a wreath of vapour the graceful tower of St. Symphorian leapt into the clearer heaven. Beyond, a network of lights glimmered, like fire-flies, from the vessels at anchor in the harbour. The Penpoodle Hill, on the further shore, wore a tranquil halo; and to the right, outside the harbour's mouth, the grey sea was laced with silver.

"Did you ever see anything more lovely?"

Mrs. Buzza murmured the words with no desire to be answered. It was the old Trojan formula, and there was peace in the sound of it.

"Do you know," she cried, turning to Sam, "we were very happy before these people came. We shall never be the same again—never. Sam, I feel as if our innocence had ended, Oh! I am a wicked woman. Look below, Sam dear, I have never thought of it before, but how sweet it would have been to have enclosed the old town in a ring-fence, and lived our days in quiet! It is too late now; more will come, and they will build and alter, and no one will be able to stop it. Even if these people should go, it will never be the same again. Oh! I am a sinful woman."

Sam looked at his mother. Something familiar, but hitherto half-comprehended, spoke to him in her words. He drew her arm once more within his own, and they descended the hill together.

Stealing like ghosts into the front hall of No. 2, Alma Villas, they were startled to perceive the dining-room door ajar, and a light shining out into the passage. Creeping forward on tip-toe, they peeped in.

Beside the table and with his back towards them, sat the Admiral in his dressing-gown. His right hand grasped the throat of the double-bass, on the top of which nodded Mrs. Buzza's night-cap. His left fumbled with a large miniature that lay on the table before him—a portrait of Mrs. Buzza, taken in the days when she was still Emily Rogers and the Belle of Portsmouth; and from this to the instrument and back again the Admiral's gaze wandered, as if painfully comparing the likeness.

"Hornaby!" This was the Admiral's Christian name.

"Emily!"

He turned and stared at her stupidly. The look was pitiful. She flung herself before him.

"Forgive me, Hornaby! I never thought—I mean, it was all a—"

"Practical joke," suggested Sam.

"No, no. I meant to go, but I have come back. Hornaby, can you forgive me?"

He raised her up, and drew her towards him very tenderly.

"I—I thought it had *killed* me," he muttered hoarsely. "Emily, I have treated you badly."

Sam discreetly withdrew.

With his back towards them sat the Admiral.

CHAPTER XXI.

THAT A VERY LITTLE TEA MAY SUFFICE TO ELEVATE A MAN.

Next morning Mr. Fogo was aroused from sleep by the rattle of breakfast-cups, and the voice of Caleb singing below—

> "O, Amble es a fine town, wi' ships in the bay,
> An' I wish wi' my heart I was on'y there to-day;
> I wish wi' my heart I was far away from here,
> A-sittin' in my parlour, an' a-talkin' to my dear."

This was Caleb's signal for his master to rise; and he would pipe out his old sea-staves as long as Mr. Fogo cared to listen. Often, of an evening, the two would sit by the hour, Caleb trolling lustily with red cheeks, while his master beat time with his pipe stem, and joined feebly in the chorus—

> "Then 'tes home, dearie, home—O, 'tes home I wants to be!
> My tawps'les are h'isted, an' I must out to sea.
> Then 'tes home, dearie, home!"

Mr. Fogo arose and looked forth at the window. The morning was perfect; the air fresh with dew and the scent of awakening roses. Across the creek the old hull lay as peacefully as ever.

"I will explore it this very morning," thought Mr. Fogo to himself.

The resolve was still strong as he descended to breakfast. Caleb was still singing—

> "O, ef et be a lass, she shall wear a goulden ring;
> An' ef et be a lad, he shall live to sarve hes king;
> Wi' hes buckles, an' hes butes, an' hes little jacket blue,

He shall walk the quarter-deck, as hes daddy used to do.
Then 'tes home—"

"Mornin', sir, an' axin' your pardon for singin' o' Sunday. How be feelin' arter et?—as Grace said to her cheeld when her rubbed in the cough-mixtur' an' made 'un swaller the lineament."

"Do you mean after the ghost?"

"Iss, sir. There's no dead body about, so ghost et were. I were a-thinkin', wi' your lave, sir, I'd go down to Troy to church this mornin'; I wants to be exercised a bit arter all this witchcraf'."

Mr. Fogo wondered at this proposal to go to church for exercise, but readily granted leave. Nor was it until Caleb had departed that "exorcised" occurred to him as a *varia lectio*.

Left to himself, Mr. Fogo spent a tranquil hour among his roses; and then, remembering his determination, unmoored his boat and prepared to satisfy his doubts.

The tide was low—so low that on the further side of the old wreck his paddles plunged once or twice into mud. Nor was it easy to swing himself on board; but a rusty chain helped him, and after one or two failures he stood upon deck.

All was desolation. He peered down into the hold, where the water lay deep and still; crawled forward, and peeped through a shattered deadlight into the forecastle. The water was here, too, though it had drained somewhat, owing to the depression amidships; but nothing to explain the mystery.

Mr. Fogo crept aft with better hopes of success, gained the poop, and peered down the companion. The light was too dim to reveal anything. Nothing daunted, he crawled down the ladder and into the captain's cabin.

The first thing to catch his eye was an empty packing-case, with a heap of shavings and cotton-wool beside it. On the side of the case was printed in blue letters—" *Wapshott and Sons. Chicago. Patent Compressed Tea. With Care.*" Mr. Fogo poked his nose inside it. A faint smell of tea still lingered about the wood.

Next he inspected the cupboards. Some were open and all unlocked. He went over them all. At the end he found himself the richer by—

A watch-glass.
Three brass buttons (one bearing the initials P. J., and all coated with verdigris).
A pair of nut-crackers.
Several leaves of a devotional work entitled "Where shall I be To-morrow? or, Thoughts for Mariners."
A key.
An oily rag.
The cap of a telescope.
An empty bottle, labelled, and bearing in faded ink: "Poison. For Dick Collins, when his leg is bad."

On the whole this was not encouraging. Mr. Fogo was turning to abandon the search, when something upon the cabin-floor caught his eye.

He stooped and picked it up. It was a lady's glove.

Mr. Fogo turned it over in his hand. It was a dainty six-buttoned glove, of a light tan colour, and showed scarcely a trace of wear.

"This is very odd," muttered he; "I can hardly fancy a smuggler wearing this, still less a ghost."

With his thoughts still running on the woman he had seen upon the deck, he advanced to the packing-case again, and was beginning absently to kick aside the heap of shavings and cotton-wool, when his foot encountered some hard object. He bent down and drew it forth.

It was a small tin case or canister, of oblong shape, and measured some four inches by two. It was perhaps two inches in depth. On the cover was a label, and on the label the legend—

"WAPSHOTTS' PATENT COMPRESSED TEA."

Beware of Imitations."

The lid was lightly soldered, and the canister remarkably heavy.

Mr. Fogo pulled out his pocket-knife, sat down on the edge of the packing-case, and began to open his prize.

He had broken one blade in trying to unfasten the solder, and was beginning with the second, when it occurred to him to cut through the soft metal of the canister. In a few minutes he had worked a considerable hole in the lid.

"Very curious tea this," remarked Mr. Fogo. "It's a deal more like putty—or Californian honey."

The light in the cabin was faint; he determined to carry the canister on deck and examine it in the sunlight.

He picked his way up the ladder, and was just emerging from the hatch, when the sudden glare of the sun caused him to blink and then sneeze. He caught his toe on the last step, stumbled, dropped his prize, and fell forward on to the deck. The canister struck the step, jolted twice, plunged to the bottom with a smart thud—

There was a flash of jagged flame, a loud roar, a heave and crash of riven timbers—and the old hull had passed from decay to annihilation.

This would seem a convenient moment for regulating our watches, which have gained considerably, and putting back the hands to half-past ten, at which hour the bells of St. Symphorian's, Troy, began to summon the town to worship.

A few minutes later the town sallied forth in pairs and decorous excitement. It was dying to see Mrs. Goodwyn-Sandys' costume, and marched churchwards in haste. But to-day it halted for the most part at the church-porch, and went no further.

Who first whispered the news is disputed. It is conjectured that Mrs. Tripp, whose cow supplied "The Bower" with milk, learnt the facts from the buttoned youth when she paid her professional call at 7.30 a.m.; but none knew for certain. I might here paint Mrs. Tripp full of tongues, and dress her up as "Rumour," after the best epic models; but in saying that she had the usual number of lips and hands, that her parents were respectable, and that she never shrieked from a lofty tower in her life, I only do her the barest justice.

This much is sure—that among the knot of loungers at the church-gate such sentences as the following passed from mouth to mouth—

"Es et true, do'ee think?"

"Certain—carr'ge an' pair from Five Lanes las' night—not a word said."

"My!"

"Ef so, this town's been purtily robbed."

"That's a true word."

Then this happened—

The Trojan in broadcloth heard, as he passed, the words of the Trojan in corduroy; inquired, shook his head, and walked on; doubted; turned back to hear more; consulted his wife; and decided to go and see.

The consequence was that at ten minutes to eleven the stream of church-goers descending along the Parade was met by another stream rolling towards "The Bower" and every moment gathering volume. As there was no place of worship in this direction, a conference followed the confluence. The churchgoers turned, joined the larger stream, and the whole flood poured uphill.

Outside "The Bower" they halted for a moment. One tradesman, a furniture dealer, bolder than the rest, advanced to the front-door and knocked.

The boy in buttons answered with a white face. In a moment the truth was out.

This whisper among the crowd grew to a murmur, the murmur to a roar. In vain the church-bell tolled out the single note that summons the parson. The dismay of the cheated town waxed to hot indignation. Even Miss Limpenny, issuing from her front door, heard the news, and returned in a stupor to watch matters from her bedroom window. She had not missed a morning service for fourteen years.

Then as if by one impulse passion gave way to action. Like an invading army the townspeople poured in at the gate, trampling the turf and crushing the flower-beds. They forced the front door (whence the page fled, to hide in the cellar), pushed into the hall, swarmed into the drawing-room—upstairs—all over the house.

Only in the bedrooms were there signs of a hasty flight; but they were enough. The strangers had decamped. There was a pause of indecision, but for no long time.

"Sunday or no Sunday," screamed the choleric upholsterer, "every stick of mine will I take off this morning!"

He tucked up his sleeves, and, flinging open the French window of the drawing-room, caught up an arm-chair, and began to drag it out towards the lawn.

A cheer followed. The Trojan blood was up.

It was the signal for a general sack. Flinging off his Sunday coat, each deluded tradesman seized upon his property, or ransacked the house until he found it. The ironmonger caught up his fire-irons, the carpenter pulled down his shelves, the grocer dived into the pantry and emerged with tea and candles. It is said that the coal-merchant— who was a dandy—procured a sack, and with his own hand emptied the coal-cellar within half an hour.

As each fresh article was confiscated, the crowd cheered anew.

Never was such a scene in Troy. Even the local aristocracy— the *Cumeelfo*—mingled with the throng and watched the havoc as curiously as their neighbours.

No member of the Buzza family was there, nor Mr. Moggridge. But few others did Miss Limpenny fail to perceive as she sat with hands hanging limply and mourned to Lavinia—

"What disgrace! What a lasting blemish upon our society! There goes Hancock with the music-stool. To run away just before quarter-day, and they so refined to all appearance, so—My dear, they will have the house down. Papa told me once that during the Bristol riots— I declare, there's the Doctor looking on! I wonder how he *can*."

And the poor lady hid her face in her hands.

By half past twelve all was over, and "The Bower" stripped of every article of furniture or consumption for which the money was owing. And yet, to the honour of Troy, no single theft or act of wanton destruction was perpetrated. Save for the trampled flowers and marks of dusty boots upon the carpets, the house was left as it stood on the day when Mr. and Mrs. Goodwyn-Sandys arrived. It should be mentioned, perhaps, that Seth Udy's little boy was detected with his fist in a jar of moist sugar; but Mrs. Udy, it was remarked, was a Penpoodle woman.

The sack was accomplished; and the crowd, heated but conscious of a duty done, was returning with the spoil, when towards the north a white glare leapt into the heaven and as suddenly vanished. In a moment or so a dull roar followed, and the earth shuddered underfoot.

Troy trembled. It remembered its neglected Sabbath, and trembled again.

CHAPTER XXII.

IN WHICH SEVERAL ATTEMPTS ARE MADE
TO PUT A PERIOD TO THIS HISTORY.

The congregation at St. Symphorian's on this memorable Sunday morning numbered nine persons. Possibly this was the reason why, against all precedent, the Vicar's sermon terminated at "thirdly."

Woman has been stated so often, and by such capable observers, to be more inquisitive than man, that I will content myself with establishing an exception. Of these nine persons, five were women, and the remainder held the salaried posts of organist, organ-blower, pew-opener, and parish-clerk. Of the women, one was Tamsin Dearlove. It is noteworthy that Caleb spent his morning at "The Bower."

Service was over, and Tamsin was rowing homewards. She was alone; for Troy was not the Dearloves' parish, and the Twins attended their own church—being, indeed, churchwardens. As she pulled quietly upwards, a shade of thought rested on her pretty face. I do not know of what she was thinking; and may add that if I did, I should not tell you. I would as lief rob a church.

She had passed the jetties, and was pulling her left paddle to turn the corner off Kit's House, when a flash crossed the heaven from behind her, and in an instant followed that rending explosion which (at different distances) has been twice presented to the reader, and with pardonable pride; for the story of Troy has now a catastrophe as well as episodes, and is vindicated as a theme.

As soon as the throbbing of the atmosphere and the buzzing in her ears began to die away, two swift thoughts crossed her brain. Oddly enough, the first was for the safety of Kit's House. She glanced over her shoulder. A mere film of smoke hung over the creek, and to the right of this she saw the house standing, seemingly unharmed. Then came the second thought—

If the explosion came from the creek, where the light smoke hung, there would be a wave.

She half turned on the thwart and looked intently.

Yes. It was curling towards her, widening from the creek's mouth, and arching with a hateful crest. On it came, a dark and glossy wall; and she knew that if it broke or caught her boat in the least aslant, she must be either swamped or overset.

With a sound that was half a sob and half a prayer she grasped her paddles and, still looking over her shoulder, gently moved the boat's nose to face it.

A moment, and it rose above her, hissing death; another, and the boat was caught high in air, tottered on the summit, and then with a shiver shot swiftly down into the trough beyond—safe.

A second wave followed, and a third, but with less peril. She was still tossed, but as she saw that mass of water hurled upon the shore, and sweeping angrily but with broken force towards the harbour, she knew that she could thank Heaven for her escape.

She pulled towards the creek. Already the air was clear; but as she glanced again her eye missed something familiar. And then it struck her that the old schooner had gone. At that instant, as if in confirmation, a shattered board bumped against the boat's side. She looked, and noticed that far and near the water was strewn with such fragments.

She was pausing for a second to consider, when she caught sight of a black object lying on the mud beside the shore, and with a short cry fell to rowing with all her strength. She guided the boat as nearly up to it as the mud allowed, and then, catching up her skirts, jumped into the ooze and waded.

It was Mr. Fogo; but whether dead or alive she could not say. Down on the mud she knelt, and, turning him gently over, looked into his face. It was streaked with slime, and powdered with a yellowish flake, as of sand. His locks were singed most pitifully. She started up, took him by the shoulders, and tried to drag him up to the firmer shingle.

Mr. Fogo opened his eyes and shut them again, feebly.

"Not dead! Oh! thank Heaven you are not dead."

With a sob she dropped again beside him, and brushed the flaked powder from his eye-lashes.

He opened his eyes again.

"Would you mind speaking up? I—I think I am a little deaf."

"I thought you were dead," she cried, in a louder tone.

"No-o, I am not dead. Oh! no; decidedly I am not dead. It—it was the Tea, I fancy."

He added this apologetically, much as some gentlemen are wont to plead "the salmon."

Apparently believing the explanation sufficient, he shut his eyes again, and seemed inclined to go to sleep.

"The Tea?" questioned Tamsin, chafing his hands.

"Or the Honey, perhaps—or the Putty," he answered drowsily. Then, opening his eyes and sitting up with a start, "Upon my soul, I don't know which. It *called* itself Tea, but I'm—bound—to— admit—
"

He was nodding again. Utterly perplexed, Tamsin leant back and regarded him.

"Can you walk, if you lean on my arm?"

"Walk? Oh! yes, I can walk. Why not?"

But it seemed that he was mistaken; for, in attempting to start, he groped about for a bit and then sat down suddenly. Tamsin helped him to his feet.

The reader has long ago guessed the cause of the catastrophe. It was dynamite—conspirators' dynamite, and therefore ill-prepared. Now dynamite, when it explodes, acts, we are told, with "local partiality"; and of this term we may remark—

> That it is given as an explanation by men of science,
> Without being a "scientific" explanation;
> But is, in fact, a "metaphysical" explanation,
> And therefore no explanation at all of
> The astonishing fact that dynamite hits one thing and does not
> hit another.

In the case of Mr. Fogo, his top-hat had vanished, but the brim still clung to his head, like a halo. His spectacles and one boot had gone; the other boot was unlaced. His coat was split up the back, and his collar had broken away, but his tie was barely disarranged. He has since declared that he left the schooner with two-and-sixpence in his trowser pocket, and came ashore with two-and-a-penny; but this was in an account delivered to a scientific audience, and is thought to have been a joke.

From head to foot he was besmeared with black mud; for the rotten stern must have parted and fallen with the first touch of the explosion, so that the wave caught him as he toppled out, and flung him at once upon the shallows. But Tamsin's Sunday frock was already ruined. She made him rest his hand on her shoulder, and so, with one arm thrown round him for steadiness, led him down the beach, and with infinite difficulty got him across the mud and into the boat.

With infinite difficulty got him across the mud.

She managed to push off at last, and pulled rapidly across for Kit's House. Hitherto Mr. Fogo's condition had slightly resembled a drunken stupor; but now he shivered violently and looked about him.

"Where am I?"

"Safe and sound, I hope."

He passed his hand over his eyes and shivered again.

"I remember. Something—blew up, did it not? The canister, I think."

She nodded encouragingly.

"Where did you come from?" he asked abruptly.

"From church."

"Oh! from church. Do you know, I'm very glad to see you—I am, indeed, I hope you'll come often, now that—Excuse me," he broke off with a weak smile, "but I fancy I'm talking nonsense."

She nodded again.

"I am aching all over," he added with a shiver.

She pulled the boat up to the little quay. "Now I wonder where Caleb is," she said to herself, as she stood up and looked around; "but he's like most men, always in the way or out of the way." She turned suddenly with a white face. "Caleb was not with you?"

To her hearty relief Mr. Fogo understood the question and shook his head. She helped him ashore. Though he walked with pain, he made an obvious effort to lighten his weight on her shoulder; and this returning bashfulness was a good sign, she thought. They passed slowly up the steps; at the top he acknowledged her help with a grateful look, but neither spoke until he was seated in a chair by the kitchen fireplace.

Then she withdrew her attention for a moment to glance round upon the clumsy appliances and masculine untidiness of the place. She noticed that fully half the window-panes had been shattered by the explosion; but otherwise the house had barely suffered.

"Is there any brandy or whiskey in the house?"

He shook his head.

"If you want to drink—" he began, but stopped hastily and added, "I beg your pardon."

"Is there any tea?"

He pointed to the cupboard, but dropped his arm with a groan. She was at his side in a moment.

"Now, listen to me. You are not to stir or speak, but only to nod or shake your head when I ask a question. Do you understand?"

He nodded.

"That's right."

She stepped to the cupboard, produced the tea and a box of matches; then, stooping down, rekindled the fire with the help of some sticks which she found in the oven, and put the kettle on the flame. This done, she sought and found the tea-things.

"Milk?" she asked.

He nodded towards a blue jug on the mantel-shelf.

"Milk on the mantel-shelf! That's like a man."

But at this point the kettle began to boil. She filled the tea-pot, and replaced the kettle on the hob. As she turned, she was aware of a clearer look in Mr. Fogo's eyes. She smiled and nodded.

"You are better."

"Much. I can remember it all, after a fashion. Did I talk nonsense?"

"A little." She smiled again.

His eyes followed her as she moved about the kitchen. Presently he said—

"You are very good to me."

"I think I am."

"Tamsin—"

She turned suddenly to the table, and caught up the teapot.

"Do you know," she asked, "that tea is worthless if it stands for more than five minutes?"

She filled a cup, and gave it to him with a hand that trembled slightly. He sipped, and scalded his lip.

"Tamsin—"

"My name is Dearlove," she said shortly, "and you are spilling the tea."

There was silence for a minute or so. Mr. Fogo stirred his tea abstractedly. Tamsin, whose shoes were soaked, put one foot upon the fender, and bent her gaze upon the fire.

"I would give something," observed Mr. Fogo suddenly, in desperate reverie, "to know how other people manage it. It was moonlight when I proposed to Geraldine. I began by squeezing her hand, if I remem —"

He looked up, and found her regarding him with eyes ablaze.

But luckily at this moment the door opened, and Caleb appeared. He was evidently much agitated; but at sight of Tamsin and the woeful figure in the armchair, he halted on the threshold and stared dumbly.

"I think," said Tamsin, "you had better put your master to bed."

"Mussy 'pon us, what's been doin'?"

Briefly she told as much as she knew. With each successive sentence Caleb's mouth and eyes opened wider.

"And now," she ended, "as Peter and Paul have been waiting for their dinner this half-hour, I will be going. Don't trouble to come with me; but attend to your master. Good-morning, sir."

She dropped him a low curtsey and was gone. He started up.

"Where be goin', sir? Sit down; you'm not fit to stir."

But Mr. Fogo had passed him, and was out of the room in a moment. In spite of the pain that racked every limb, he overtook Tamsin in the porch.

"What are you doing?" she cried. "Go back to bed."

As she faced him, he could see that her eyes were full of angry tears. The sight checked him.

"It's—it's of no consequence," he stammered, "only I was going to ask you to be my wife."

For answer she turned on her heel, and walked resolutely down the steps.

Mr. Fogo stood and watched her until she disappeared, and then crawled painfully back into the house.

"An' now, sir," said Caleb, as he led his master to bed, "warnin' et es. This day month, I goes, unless—"

"Unless what, Caleb?"

"Well, sir, I reckons there be on'y wan way out o't, as the cat said by the sausage-machine, an' that es—to marry Tamsin Dearlove."

"My dear Caleb," groaned Mr. Fogo, "I only wish I could! But I will try again to-morrow."

CHAPTER XXIII.

HOW ONE LOVER TOOK LEAVE OF HIS WITS,
AND TWO CAME TO THEIR SENSES.

But Mr. Fogo was not to try again on the morrow.

For Caleb, stealing up in the grey dawn to assure himself that his master was comfortably asleep, found him tossing in a high fever, and rowed down to Troy for dear life and the Doctor. Returning, he found that the fever had become delirium. Mr. Fogo, indeed, was sitting up in bed, and rattling off proposals of marriage at the rate of some six a minute, without break or pause. He was very red and earnest, rolled his eyes most strangely, and wandered in his address from Tamsin to Geraldine, and back again with a vehemence that gravelled all logic.

"Lord ha' mussy!" cried Caleb at last. "Do 'ee hush, that's a dear. 'Tes sinful—all these gallons o' true affecshun a-runnin' to waste. You'm too lovin' by half, as Sam said when hes wife got hugged by a bear. What do 'ee think, sir?"

The last sentence was addressed to the little Doctor, who, after staring at the patient for some minutes without noticeable result, nodded his head, announced that the fever must run its course, and promised to send a capable nurse up to Kit's House without delay.

"Beggin' your pard'n, Doctor," interposed Caleb with firmness, "but I've a-got my orders."

"Eh?"

"I've a-got my orders. Plaise God, an' wi' plenty o' doctor's trade, [1] us'll pull 'un round: but nobody nusses maaster 'ceptin' you an' me—leastways, no womankind."

"This is nonsensical."

"Nonsensical, do 'ee say? Look 'ee here, Doctor; do 'ee think I'd trust a woman up here wi' maaster a-makin' offers o' marriage sixteen to the dozen? Why, bless 'ee, sir, her'd be down an' ha' the banns called afore night, an' maaster not fit to shake hes head, much less say as the Prayer Books orders—'I renounce mun all.' That's a woman, Doctor, an' ef any o' the genteel sex sets foot on Kit's beach I'll—I'll *stone* her."

The Doctor gave way in the end and withdrew, promising another visit before evening. When he returned, however, at five in the afternoon, he found, with some wonder, a woman quietly installed in the sick-room. It happened thus:—

Barely an hour after the Doctor's departure, Caleb, sitting at his master's bedside, heard footsteps on the gravel walk, and looked out of window.

"Hist!" he called softly; and Peter Dearlove, followed by Paul, stepped round the angle of the house into sight. The Twins bore a look of the gravest perplexity and a large market basket.

"Hulloa!" said Caleb, "what's up?"

The pair looked at each other. At length Peter began with a serious face and unwonted formality of tone—

"Es Mr. Fogo wi'in?"

"Why, iss," Caleb allowed, "he's inside."

"We was a-wishin' to request o' the pleasure"—here Peter looked at Paul, who nodded—"the pleasure o' an interval o' five minnits."

"Interview," corrected Paul.

"I misdoubts," answered his brother, "that you are wrong, Paul. I remember the expresshun 'pon the programme o' a Sleight o' Hand Entertainment, an' there et said 'Interval'—'An Interval o' Five Minnits.'"

"Ef that's so," broke in Caleb from above with fine irony, "p'raps you wudn' mind handin' up your visitin' cards an' doin' the thing proper. At present maaster's busy."

"Busy?"

"Iss. A-makin' proposals o' marriage—which es a serious thing, an' not to be interrupted."

The Twins set down the basket and stared at each other. Paul was the first to recover.

"Ef 'tes fully allowable to put the question, Peter an' me wud like to knaw the young leddy's name. 'Tes makin' bould to ax, but there's a reason."

"Well," said Caleb, disappearing for a moment and then poking his head forth again, "at the present moment 'tes a party answerin' to the name o' Geraldin'. A minnit agone 'twas—But maybe you'd better step up an' see for yoursel'."

"What!"

"Step up an' see."

"Now, Peter," said the Twin, turning from Caleb to contemplate his brother, "puttin' the case (an' far be et from me to say et cudn' be) as you was payin' your addresses to a young leddy answerin' to the name o' Geraldin' (which she wudn' be call'd that, anyway), an' puttin' the case as you was a-makin' offers o' marriage, an' a pair o' twin-brothers (same as you an' me might be) walked up to the front door an' plumped in afore you'd well finished talkin' o' the weatherprospec's (bein' a slow man, though a sure)—now, what I wants to knaw es, wud 'ee like et yoursel'?"

"No, I shudn'."

"Well, I reckon'd not. An' that bein' so, Go's the word."

"Afore Peter talks 'bout gettin' a wife," broke in Caleb, "he'd better read 'bout Peter's wife's mother. She was sick wi' a fever, I've heerd, an' so's maaster. Ef you don't believe, walk up an' see; 'cos 'tain't good for a sick man to ha' all this palaverin' outside hes windey."

The Twins stared, whispered together, took off their boots, and softly entered the house. At the door of the sick-room Caleb met them.

"Brain fever," he whispered, "which es on'y catchin' for them as has brains to catch et wi'."

The trio stood together at the foot of the bed on which Mr. Fogo tossed and chattered. Peter and Paul looked from the sick man to their hats, and back again in silence. At length the elder Twin spoke—

"I' the matter o' behavin' rum, some folks does it wi' cause an' others not so. But I reckons ef you allows as there's likely a cause, you'm 'pon the safe side—'speshully wi' Mr. Fogo. Wherefore, Caleb, what's the meanin' o' this here?"

"Tamsin!"

The answer came so pat from the sick man's lips that Peter fairly jumped. Caleb looked up with finger on lip and a curious smile on his weather-tanned face.

"Don't leave me! Look! There are devils around me—cold white devils—devils with blank faces—no features, only flesh. Look! Sunday, Monday, Tuesday—every day with a devil, every day in the year—look, look!"

"Pore soul!" whispered Paul; "an' 'tes Leap Year, too, which makes wan extry."

"Don't leave me, Tamsin—don't leave me!"

The sick man's voice rose to a scream. Caleb bent forward and tried to soothe him. The mahogany faces of the Twins were blanched. They whispered apart—

"You was right, Peter."

"Aye, more's the pity. I thought the lass misliked 'un—the bigger fool I. 'Twas on'y yestiddy I guessed more was troublin' her than her soiled gown, an' tax'd her wi' et. We used to pride oursel' on knawin' her wants afore her spoke—an' now—"

Peter weakly concluded with a sigh.

"Bring Tamsin down an' help me here," said Caleb, from across the room.

The pair started.

"That es," he went on, "ef she'll come. You heerd maaster? Well, he said purty much the same to her yestiddy; so her won't be frightened. Leastways, go an' say you'm comin' yoursel' to help nuss; 'cos ef you won't I'll nuss 'un alone, an' ef that's the case, you'm a queer pair o' Christians, as the Devil said to the two black pigs."

"Fact es," hesitated Peter, "I'd a-larnt so much las' evenin' from Tamsin, though she were main loth to tell; an' Paul agreed as we'd call this mornin' an' tell Mr. Fogo as 'twarn't right for 'n to set hes thoughts 'pon Tamsin, who isn' a leddy, nor to put notions in her head as'll gi'e her pain hereafter. An' that's all 'bout et; an' us brought a whack o' vegetable produce 'long wi' us, jes' to show there was no ill-feelin's. But as et turns out, neither argyment nor vegetables bein' acceptable to a party that's sick wi' a fever, I be clane floored for what to do."

"Well, now, I've a-told 'ee. An' don't let the grass grow 'neath your feet, 'cos 'twill grow fast enough over your heads some day."

The Twins, unable to cope with Caleb's determination, stole noiselessly out. And thus it was that when, late in the afternoon, the little Doctor returned, he found Peter and Paul, in large blue aprons, busily helpless downstairs, and Tamsin, bright-eyed and warm of cheek, seated by the sick man's bedside.

On the following morning, which the reader, should he care to calculate, will find to be Tuesday, Admiral Buzza dropped his newspaper with a start, and glared across the breakfast-table.

"What is it, my love?" inquired his wife. "Nothing wrong, I hope?"

"Wrong? Oh! no," replied the Admiral grimly, "nothing—wrong. Oblige me by listening to this, madam." He took up the paper and read aloud:

"ANOTHER DYNAMITE PLOT.
A WHOLE TOWN DECEIVED—EXTRAORDINARY
PROCEEDINGS.
ESCAPE OF THE SUSPECTED PERSONS.
THE DYNAMITE FIENDS STILL AT LARGE.

"The existence of another of these atrocious conspiracies aimed at the security of our public buildings and the safety of peaceful citizens, has been brought to light by certain recent occurrences at the romantic little seaport town of Troy. We have reason to believe that the suspicions of the police have been for some time aroused; and it is to their unaccountable dilatoriness we owe it that the conspirators have for the time made good their escape and still continue to menace our lives and property. It appears that some months back a couple, giving the names of the Honourable Mr. and Mrs. Goodwyn-Sandys—"

["Really, Samuel, if you cannot eat an ordinary egg without clattering the spoon in that unseemly manner, I must ask you to suspend your meal until I have finished."]

"appeared at Troy as tenants of one of the most fashionable villa residences in that town. The *elite* [ahem] of the neighbourhood, too easily cajoled [h'm], and little suspecting their villainous designs, received the newcomers with open arms and a lamentable lack of inquisitiveness."

"Well, really," put in Mrs. Buzza, "I don't know what they call 'inquisitiveness'; if a brass telescope—Why, Sam, dear, how pale you are!"

"Through the gross carelessness, we can hardly bring ourselves to say the connivance, of the Custom House officials, they were allowed to land with impunity a considerable quantity of dynamite, with which on Saturday night they decamped. Their disappearance remained unsuspected up to a late hour on Sunday morning, when 'The Bower' was visited, and (to borrow the words of the great master of prose) *non sunt inventi*. The neatness with which the escape was executed points to the disquieting conclusion that they did not want for assistance."

"I'll ask you to excuse me," said Sam, rising abruptly and leaving the room. A sick terror possessed his heart; visions of the dock and the felon's cell followed him as he picked up his hat and crept into the street. Outside, the morning was serene, with the promise of a broiling noon; but as far as Sam was concerned, Egyptian darkness would have been better. He shivered: at the corner of the street he met the local policeman and winced.

But far, far worse was it with Mr. Moggridge, to whose lodgings his steps were bending. The Poet, as Sam entered, was seated as nearly as possible on the small of his back before the breakfast table. If mental anguish can be expressed by unkempt hair and a disordered cravat, that of Mr. Moggridge was extreme; and the untasted bloater, pushed aside and half concealed by the newspaper, was full of lurid significance.

Sam paused at the door. The two friends had barely spoken for more than a month. Three days ago they had all but fought. All this, however, was forgotten now.

"Is that you, Sam? Come in."

Then, having displayed the olive-branch, the Poet waved the newspaper feebly, and groaned.

"Moggridge, old man—"

"Sam!"

"What a pair of asses we have been!"

"The Poet moaned, and pointed to the paper.

"I know," nodded Sam; "is it true, d'ye think?"

"My heart forebodes," said Mr. Moggridge, collapsing still further— "my heart forebodes 'tis true, 'tis true; then deck my shroud about with rue, and lay me 'neath the dismal—"

"Pooh!" broke in Sam; "stuff and nonsense, man! It's bad for you, I know, but after all *I'm* the sufferer."

The Collector of Customs turned a glassy stare upon him.

"*I* carried the bag up to Five Lanes; *I* put the infernal stuff into her very hands; *I*—"

"*You?*"

Sam nodded desperately. "She asked me to elope with her—to meet her at Five Lanes."

Mr. Moggridge staggered up to his feet, and fumbled in his waistcoat pocket.

"You are mad!" he gasped. "She asked *me* to elope with her—*me* to meet her at the top of Troy Hill. Look here!" He held out a crumpled letter. Sam took it, glanced at it, produced an exactly similar note, and handed it to his friend.

They read each the other's letter sentence by sentence, and in doleful antiphon. At the conclusion they looked up, and met each other's gaze; whereat Mr. Moggridge smote his brow and cried—

"False, false!"

While Sam pushed his hands deep into his trouser-pockets and emitted a long breath, as though, his cup being full, he must needs blow off the froth.

"Do you mean to say," he asked, after a pause, "that you helped her to land the stuff?"

"I thought it was Tea."

"And you never examined it?"

"She told me it was Tea."

"Moggridge, you have been given away, as the Yankees put it. I have been sold, which is bad; but you have been 'given away,' which is worse."

"You were sold for 'love,' which is pretty much the same, I take it, as being given away," objected the Poet testily.

"Not at all the same, Moggridge, as being given away—with half a pound of Tea."

[1] Medicine. (return)

CHAPTER XXIV.

OF THE BEST HELLEBORE; AND AN EXPERIMENT
IN THE ENTERTAINMENT OF TWINS.

For three days Mr. Fogo continued to propose. On the evening of the
third day the little Doctor shook his head. After this, for about a
week, Mr. Fogo proposed and the Doctor shook his head at intervals.
Finally, and in the middle of a sentence, the patient fell into a deep
slumber.

When he awoke, it was to the conviction that he, Mr. Fogo, being a
bolster, had been robbed of his rightful stuffing by some person or
persons unknown. He had lain for some time pondering this
situation with a growing resentment, when he was aware of some
one sitting between him and the sunshine.

"Who are you?" he asked.

"I am Tamsin Dearlove."

The remark made by Diogenes under somewhat like circumstances
would have been ungallant. In the process of searching for a better
the sick man fell asleep again.

What happened on his next return to consciousness shall be given in
his own words. He told me the story last autumn:—

"You see," he explained shyly, "I have not, my dear young friend,
that ingenuity of phrase which I so admire in you" (I protest I have
not the heart to suppress this tribute), "but seeing that, in such a
case, experience counts for something—and naturally, at your age,
you have yet to learn what it is to propose to a woman—I think I had
better tell you exactly what happened, the more so as it is a matter
which, if, as you assure me, necessary to your chronicle, I desire to
be related with accuracy. I am not, you understand, in the least

reflecting on your love of truth, but, after all, I *did*, as the obnoxious phrase has it, 'propose' to Tamsin, whereas you—ahem—did *not*."

I am convinced my friend meant to say "would not have had the infernal impudence," but softened the expression, being habitually careful of the feelings of others.

"When I awoke again," he went on, "she was seated in the window, knitting. I lay for a long while watching her—indeed, this is my first impression—before I made any sign. The sunshine—it was morning—fell on her head as she bent over her needles, and emphasised that peculiar bloom of gold which (you may have noticed) her brown locks possess. Her lashes, too, as they drooped upon a cheek pale (as I could perceive) beyond its wont, had a glimmer of the same golden tint. Altogether I thought her more beautiful than I ever imagined; and to this day," he added in an outburst of confidence, "I frequently decoy her to a seat in the sunlight, that I may taste a renewal of the sensations I enjoyed that morning. Some day, perhaps, you will be better able to sympathise with this caprice.

"I had been lying thus for some time, luxuriously drinking in her loveliness, when her eyes lifted and met mine. And then—well, I can hardly tell you what happened then, except that I do not believe a word was spoken on either side. I suppose our eyes had told enough. Anyhow, the next thing I remember is that my dear girl's head was on my breast, and one arm flung across the pillow that supported my head. I have a dim recollection, too, of trying to smooth her hair, and finding my strength too feeble even for that. That is all, I think; except that we were ludicrously happy, of course—Tamsin smiling with moist eyes, while I lay still and let the joy of it trickle in my veins. I am extremely obliged to you, my dear young friend, for not laughing outright at this confession. It encourages me to add, for exactness, that Tamsin kept putting her hand up to the back of her head. She has since explained that she felt sure her 'back-hair' was coming down. Women are curious creatures.

"Let me resume. In the midst of what used to be called a 'love passage,' the door opened, and in walked Peter Dearlove with a basin of beef-tea. So quietly did he enter, that the first announcement of his presence was a terrific sound which my experience can compare with nothing unless it be whooping-cough—the whooping-cough of a robust adult.

"'This,' he remarked, setting down the tray and eyeing Tamsin severely, 'ain't nussin' properly so called.'

"I do not think we made any answer to this.

"'Ef a name es to be found for 't, 'tain't so much 'nussin'' as 'goin's on.''

"'Your sister has promised to be my wife,' I ventured.

"'Beggin' your pard'n, sir, but the Catechism has summat to say to that.'

"'The Catechism?'

"'Iss, sir—'that stashun o' life.' An' not a word 'bout raisin' et, even by th' use o' globes—which some considers unekalled.'

"I put out my hand to cover Tamsin's, and looked up into her face before I answered him with some heat—

"'I won't affect to misunderstand you. You mean that I am marrying beneath me?'

"He hesitated.

"'There's two meanin's to 'beneath''

"'Ah!' I cried, 'I am glad you see that.'

"He looked at me slowly and continued—

250

"'Second p'int. Not so long agone you was talkin' of a Geraldin.'"

"I glanced at Tamsin again and comprehended.

"'I have been talking—?'

"She nodded.

"'And you know it all—the whole story?'

"She nodded again, with a world of healing pity in her eyes. Then, with a swift glance at her brother, she stooped and kissed me.

"'Oh!' said Peter, very shortly; 'I'm thinkin' I'd best see Paul 'bout this;' and with that he disappeared.

"Whereupon," concluded Mr. Fogo, "I think I must have dropped asleep again, for I remember nothing after this—at least, nothing that is worth mention."

It is quite true that Mr. Fogo dropped asleep. He slept, moreover, for a considerable time, and awoke to find Caleb seated beside the bed.

"Where is Tam—Miss Dearlove?" he asked.

"There ain't no Dearlove, as I knaws by, called Tammis. The males was chris'n'd Peter an' Paul, the female Thomasina: an' they'm gone."

"Gone?"

"Gone, an' left we like Hocken's duck, wi'out mate or fellow."

"How long?"

"Matter o' five hour'."

There was a long silence.

"Caleb!"

"Aye, aye, sir."

"How long do you think it will be before I can get about—be fit to go downstairs, I mean?"

"Well, sir, I reckon et depends on yoursel'. Try, an' 'twill come, as the Doctor said when Bill swallered 'arf-a-crown an' wanted to get et up agen by Lady-Day, rent bein' doo."

"Do you think a week would do it?"

"Better say a fortni't, sir."

"What day is it to-day?"

"Thursday."

"Have I been ill for two days?"

"For a fortni't an' two days."

"Bless my soul!"

"Amen, sir."

"Caleb, would you mind writing a letter for me?"

Caleb had no objection; and the composition that followed may be given in full, for works of divided authorship have always possessed an interest of their own from the days of Homer, Homer and Homer downwards:—

"Hond Twins,—"

"Mr. Fogo's complements to the pare of You not forgetting Miss Thomasina and shall be glad if you will all Dine with me at 7 p.m. in the evening precisely on This day (Wensdy) fortunite. You will be glad to heer that I am recuvering fast thanks to your care and kindness which Is his own words and Gospel truth and so No more at present from yours to command"

"P. Fogo, Esq."

"per C. Trotter."

"Knowing whats up with the kitchin range you wont look for much of A dinner."

The answer was brought up by Paul Dearlove early, next morning. It ran:—

"Respectd Sir,—"

"This is thanking you for your kind and welcome letter just recd, and shall be proud to accept of the invitation in the spirit in which it is given you must not mind the kitchin range please as between them that knows all about it having difficulties at times with the beef tea which trusting you will overlook we remain"

"Your obedt servts"

(signed)   "Peter Dearlove."

"Paul Dearlove."

"Thomasina has gone into Troy or would have signed too."

To a certain extent this was satisfactory; and Mr. Fogo endeavoured to possess his soul in patience, and recover with all speed. It was weary work at first, but as the sick man really began to mend he found much interest in discussing with Caleb the preparations for the feast.

"We must not be too ambitious, Caleb. Let the fare be simple—'Persicos odi, puer, apparatus'—as long as it is well cooked and neatly served."

"I dunno what you means by 'pure apparatus,'" answered Caleb. "There's a flaw in the range, as you knaw; but 'tes so clane as scrubbin' 'll make et."

And, indeed, when the evening arrived with the mellow twilight of July, and the Twins with a double knock, the arrangement of the table, as well as the smell of cooking which pervaded the front hall, did Caleb all credit. The dining-room was bare alike of carpet and pictures, but the floor had been scoured until the boards glistened whitely; and two red ensigns, borrowed by Caleb from the British mercantile marine, served to hide certain defects in the wallpaper.

Here Mr. Fogo sat awaiting his guests; for the preparation of the drawing-room would have overtaxed Caleb's resources.

"Miss Thomasina Dearlove, and Messrs. Peter and Paul ditto!"

Mr. Fogo arose with a flush on his wasted cheek, held Tamsin's hand for a moment, and then, bending, kissed it with grave courtesy. She had removed her hat and cloak in the passage, and now stood before him in a plain white frock—short-waisted, and of antique make, perhaps, but little the worse for that. She wore no ornament but a red rose on her bosom; and if, as I do not believe, a shade of apprehension had troubled Mr. Fogo, it would have taken flight as she stood before him, challenging his eyes.

But the Twins!

Like the Austrian army, they were "awfully arrayed." So stiff and shiny indeed was their apparel, and such mysterious sounds did the slightest movement draw from their linen, that the beholder grew presently as uneasy as the wearer. Each wore a high stock and a collar that cut the ears. The neck-cloth of Peter was crimson; of Paul, vivid amber. The waistcoats of both bore floral devices in primary colours, and the hands of both were encased in gloves of white cotton.

Mr. Fogo took heart of grace and bade them welcome.

"'Tes a warm evenin'," ventured Paul, rubbing a forefinger round the inside of his collar.

"Uncommon," responded Peter, addressing his brother.

Whereupon, as if by preconcerted signal, they faced about and made for the two most distant chairs, on the edges of which they took an uneasy rest. Peter had brought his hat into the room, and now, after gazing at it reproachfully for some moments, began to stow it away beneath him, doing violence to its brim with the air of one who does not count the cost. He was relieved by Caleb, who bore it off with the pleasant remark—

"Now, then, remember what the old leddy said to make her guests aisy, 'I'm at home, an' I wish you all were.'"

"Silence, Caleb!" said his master. "I—I think, as dinner is ready, we may as well be seated at once. Will you take the head of the table?" he asked, turning to Tamsin.

She blushed faintly and moved to her place. The Twins leapt up, performed a forced march, and took the table in flank from opposite quarters. Mr. Fogo looked around.

"If one of you would say Grace—"

"Tamsin says it at home. I taught her mysel'," said Peter. "Now, then, little maid, 'For what we'm about—'"

She spoke the simple Grace and the company sat down—with the exception of Paul.

Now, Paul's position at table faced the fireplace, and as he raised his head after Grace a large text in red and blue upon the mantelshelf caught his eye, and held him spell-bound.

"'Paice on Earth an' Goodwill to-ward Men!'" he read. "Excuse me, sir, but nothin' more appropriate to the occashun can I imagine. Et does 'ee credit—ef I may say so."

He dropped into his seat, and taking off his gloves laid them beside his glasses. Peter, more ceremonious, retained his throughout the meal.

"I am afraid," explained their host, "that the credit belongs to Caleb, who insisted upon placing the text there; and as he had obtained it with considerable trouble from the Vicar (it was used, I believe, to decorate St. Symphorian's last Christmas), I had not the heart to deny him. But for what are we waiting?"

He was answered by the appearance of Caleb, who marched up to Tamsin with a woeful face, and announced in a loud whisper that "Suthin' was up wi' the soup."

"I think," said she, rising, "if you will let me help—"

"Sutt'nly," assented Peter in a loud tone. "To be sure—that es, beggin' your pard'n, sir," he added apologetically.

"It is very good of you," said Mr. Fogo.

"I should like to help," she explained, and followed Caleb to the kitchen.

Somehow, with her absence, an oppressive silence fell on the three men. Peter coughed at intervals, and once even began a sentence, but stopped halfway. Mr. Fogo did not heed him, but had fallen to drumming softly with his spoon upon the table. A full five minutes passed thus, and then he started to his feet.

"Must you really be going?"

"Eh?"

"It is early yet; but I suppose you have some distance to go?"

"What?"

"Let me, at least, help you on with your coats."

They stared blankly at him. There was a faraway look in his eyes, but his speech was quiet and distinct enough. Like lambs they obeyed, and marched out into the hall.

"I am afraid I am too weak to offer much assistance—"

"Don't 'ee menshun et."

They resumed their coats, and groped for hats and sticks. A deep and awful wonder possessed them both.

"The night is fine," observed their host, as he opened the door: "you will have a pleasant journey home. *Good*-night!"

He shook them by the hand as they staggered out, shut the door upon them, and returned pensively to the dining-room.

As the door closed behind them, the brothers looked into each other's eyes. Paul gave a short gasp, and leant against a pillar of the verandah.

"Peter!"

"Paul!"

"Wud 'ee mind pinchin' me i' the ca'f o' the leg, jes' to make sure?"

"I was a-goin' to ax the same favour, Paul."

"Well, churchwarden or no churchwarden, I reckon I *am* damned!"

"What I complains of in this 'ere fash'nubble life," said Peter slowly, "es this—'tes too various—by a sight, too various."

"Arter eatin' next door to nuthin' all day, so's we mou'tn' be behindhand in tacklin' the vittles!"

There was an interval of painful stupor.

"Paul!"

"Peter!"

"I'm reckonin' up what my hunger's wuth at this moment. I dunno as I'd take twenty pund for 't."

Inside the house Mr. Fogo had sunk into an armchair, and was regarding the ceiling with thoughtful attention. He was aroused by steps in the hall, and Tamsin re-entered the room, followed by Caleb with the soup-tureen.

"Hulloa! where's the Twins?"

"Eh?"

"Es this a round game, or a conjurin' trick?"

"I beg your pardon?" Mr. Fogo turned a dull gaze upon him. Caleb set down the tureen with a crash, and rushing up shook his master gently, but firmly, by the collar.

"Where—be—they—Twins?"

"Oh! The Twins? They have gone—gone some five minutes. I saw them out. It's all—Bless my soul, how extraordinary, to be sure!"

Caleb did not wait for the end of the sentence, but darting out, discovered the brothers in the porch, and haled them back.

"I beg your pardon most heartily," said Mr. Fogo, as they appeared; "the fact is—"

"There's no call, sir. I reckon us'll get the grip o't wi' time an' practice; on'y bein' new to the ropes, so to spake—"

Mr. Fogo looked at Tamsin. She broke into a merry laugh.

It snapped the spell. The Twins, who had been waiting on each other for a lead with the first spoonful of soup, set down their spoons and joined in, at first decorously, then with uproar.

"Talk 'bout fun!" gasped Peter at length, with tears in his eyes, "Bill Stickles at the Market Ord'nary can't match et—an' he's reckoned a tip-topper for fun. An' this es fash'n! Well, I never did. Ho, ho, ho!"

From this moment the success of the dinner was assured. All talked, and talked with freedom. The brothers threw off their restraint, and were their natural and well-mannered selves. It is true that Peter would pause now and again to slap his thigh and renew his mirth; it is true also that he continued to wear his white gloves throughout the meal. But he pocketed them when Caleb removed the cloth, and the company fell into more easy postures.

It was late that evening when the Twins consulted their watches and rose to go, and as yet nothing had been said on the subject nearest to Mr. Fogo's heart. He motioned them back to their seats.

"There is still one more question that I must ask you," he said, rising and stepping to Tamsin's side. "You guess what it is?"

"I mou't," admitted Peter slowly.

"I ask you, then, if Tamsin has your leave to make me happy. Knowing what it costs you—"

"No cost, sir, where our little maid's happiness es consarned. Tamsin knaws that, but 't 'as been the harder to talk wi' her as us shud ha' wished, an' that there's no denyin'. Us knawed all along she'd be leavin' us some day, an' oft'n Paul an' me have a-made up each other's mind to 't. I misdoubts, sir—I misdoubts sorely— seein' 'tes *you* her heart es set to marry—meanin' no offence, sir. But as *'tes* set—Tamsin, girl, we'll be goin', I reckon. I'm thinkin' I've a-parted wi' enough o' my heart's blud for wan night."

He moved towards the door, but came back again to shake hands, with a word of self-reproach for his lack of courtesy. Then, with a tenderness almost motherly on his mahogany face—

"Be gentle wi' her," he said. "She's quick to larn—an' takes cold aisy, which, ef seen to early, a little nitre will a'most al'ays pervent. Come 'long, Tamsin."

CHAPTER XXV.

WHICH ENDS THE STORY OF TROY.

The wedding took place in less than two months after Mr. Fogo's dinner-party. A longer interval would have proved, I believe, fatal to both Peter and Paul, who wore themselves thin over small anxieties, from the trousseau to the cake.

Three days before the wedding, for instance, they rowed down to Kit's House and awoke Caleb at 4.30 a.m. by throwing gravel against his window.

"Oh, 'tes you," said Caleb, as he thrust open the lattice; "what's amiss now?"

"We have been considerin' which of us two es to gi'e Tamsin away."

"Toss up."

"We *have* tossed up—scores o' times."

"Well?"

"The results," said Peter gravely, "es versified."

"What?"

"Otherwise, various. The results es various—inclinin' to Paul."

"Well, let Paul do it."

"Peter es oulder," objected Paul.

"By dree minnits—which don't fairly count," put in Peter.

"Peter," observed Caleb, "looks th' oulder—by full dree minnits."

"Paul went to school afore me," said Peter, "by two days—along o' measles."

"Look 'ere," decided Caleb, "let Paul gi'e her away, an' you, bein' the better spokesman, can propose th' health o' the bride an' bridegroom."

This satisfied them, and so it was arranged at the wedding. I am not going to describe the ceremony—at which I had the privilege of holding my friend's hat—beyond saying that woman, as is usual on these occasions, was a success, and man a dismal failure. There was one exception. When little Susie Clemow, who at Mr. Fogo's express desire was one of the bridesmaids, identified the bridegroom with the strange gentleman who had frightened her in the lane, and burst into loud screams in the middle of the service, I could not sufficiently admire the readiness with which Peter Dearlove produced a packet of brandy-balls from his tail-pocket to comfort her, or the prescience which led him to bring such confectionery to a wedding.

At the breakfast, too, which, owing to the dimensions of the Dearloves' cottage, was perforce select, Peter again shone. In proposing the health of Mr. and Mrs. Fogo, he said—

"On an occasion like the present et becomes us not to repine. These things es sent us for our good" (here he looked doubtfully at the cake), "an' wan man's meat es t'other's p'ison, which I hopes" (severely) "you knawed wi'out my tellin' 'ee; an' I shudn' wonder ef Paul an' me was to draw lots wan o' these fine days as to which o' us shud take the pledge—I means, the plunge—an' go an' scarify hissel' 'pon the high menial altar."

Immense excitement at this point prevailed among certain elderly spinsters present.

"That was a joke," explained the speaker, with a sudden and stony solemnity, "an' I hopes 'twill be tuk in the sperrit in which 'twas meant. An' wi' that I gi'es Tamsin's health an' that o' P. Fogo, Esquire, to whom she has been this day made man an' wife; an' bless them an' their dear offspring!"

At this point he was sitting down when Paul leant across and whispered in his ear.

"You are right, Paul," said the orator—"or offsprings. Bless their dear offspring *or* offsprings—as the case may be."

And with this he resumed his seat amid frantic applause.

The Twins alone escorted the bride and bridegroom to the railway-station; and with the accident that there befell, the chronicle of Mr. Fogo's adventures may for the present close. While the brothers saw Tamsin to her carriage, and with their white waistcoats and gigantic favours planted awe in the breast of the travelling public, the bridegroom dived into the Booking Office to take the tickets for London; for Mr. and Mrs. Fogo were to spend some days in the Metropolis before crossing the Channel.

Now it so happened that in the Booking Office there hung a gorgeous advertisement of one of the principal Steamship Companies, representing a painted ship, the S.S. *Popocatepetl*, upon a painted ocean, with a deckload of passengers in all varieties of national and fancy costume. Mr. Fogo, as his eye rested on this company, halted and looked more closely.

"That Highlander," he said, "is out of drawing."

Purse in hand, he paused before the advertisement and slowly yielded to its spell. His eyes grew fixed and glassy: tickets, train, and waiting bride had passed out of his mind. Mr. Fogo's fit was upon him.

Meanwhile the Twins, unconscious of the flight of time, and untutored in the ways of locomotives, were loading their sister with parting advice.

"This 'ere," remarked Peter, pulling a bulky parcel from his pocket, "contains a variety o' useful articles for travellin', which I've a-reckoned up durin' the past week an' meant to hand 'ee at the las' moment. There's a wax candle an' a box o' lucifers for the tunnels, an' a roll o' diach'lum plaister in case o' injury, an' 'Foxe's Book o' Martyrs,' ef you shud tire o' lookin' out at the windey, an' Thorley's-Food-for-Cattle Almanack for the las' thirteen year all done up separate, an' addressed to 'Mr. P. Dearlove, juxty Troy.' 'Bout this last, I wants Mr. Fogo to post wan at ivery stashun where you stops, so's we may knaw you've got there safe."

"I see," broke in Paul, who had been spelling through the notices with which the carriage was adorned, "there's a fine not exceedin' saxty shillin' ef you communicates wi' the guard wi'out reason, an' wuss ef you cuts the cush'ns or damages the compartment. You'd bes' call Mr. Fogo's 'tention to that."

"An' warn 'un not to get out while the train's i' motion; but you was al'ays thoughtful, Tamsin. God bless thee, little maid! Et makes my head swim o' whiles to think 'pon the times I've a-danced 'ee 'pon my knee, an' now you'm a married woman!"

"God bless you both, my dear brothers!"

"Amazin'," said Paul; "I see the Cumpenny won't hold itsel' liable for—"

There was a slamming of doors, a shriek of the whistle, and the train began to move away. At the same moment Mr. Fogo darted out of the Booking Office, and came tearing up the platform.

"Where's my wife?" he cried. "Which carriage—?"

It was too late. The carriage was already beyond the platform, and the train had gathered speed. But presence of mind belongs not to experience only. At the end of the train was hitched an empty clay-truck, bound on a return journey to Five Lanes Junction. Quick as thought the Twins, as Mr. Fogo rushed up to them, caught him by the coat collar and seat of his trousers, and with one timely heave sent him flying into this. When he staggered to his feet— hatless, without spectacles, and besmeared with clay from head to foot—the train was fifty yards beyond the station. And so, staring back mournfully at the little group upon the platform, he vanished from their sight.

"That," said Peter, turning slowly to his brother, "was nibby-gibby."

"Tamsin mou't ha' communicated wi' the guard," responded Paul, "on'y that, wi'out sufficient reason, wud ha' been not exceedin' saxty shillin'. Do 'ee think 'twud ha' been held sufficient reason?"

"I dunno. I reckon they mou't ha' made et two-pund-ten, all things conseddered," said his brother thoughtfully, "but there's no knawin'."

It is always hateful to say good-bye to friends, and here, with his leave, the reader shall be left to guess on the later fortunes of Tamsin and Mr. Fogo, the Twins and Caleb. It may be, if he care, and the Fates so order it, he shall some day follow them through new adventures; but it will be far from Troy Town. And for the present they shall fare as his imagination pleases.

Of Tamsin, however, who is thus left with her good or sorry fortune before her, something shall be hinted. Public opinion at Troy condemned her marriage. As Miss Limpenny neatly asked, "If we were all to marry beneath us, pray where should we stop?" "We should go on," replied the Admiral, "*ad libitum.*" I am inclined to think he meant "*ad infinitum;*" but the argument is quite as cogent as it stands.

And yet, since they returned to Kit's House, which they did after an absence of three years, Mr. and Mrs. Fogo have been called upon by the *Cumeelfo.* Some months ago the Admiral button-holed me in the street.

"I say, who are all those people staying with—with your friends? I mean, the strangers I saw in Church yesterday—a very creditable lot, upon my word."

"I am glad you approve of them," I answered gravely. "The lady with the spectacles is Miss Gamma Girton, the Novelist of Agnosticism; the tall man in black, Thomas Daniel, the critic—"

"Oh, literary people."

"Quite. Then there is Sir Inchcape Bell, the great Engineer; and Lady Judy Twitchett—her husband (the young man with the bald head) sits for Horkey-boro', you know, and will be in the Cabinet with the next—"

But the Admiral was already hurrying down the street. That very afternoon he took his family up to Kit's House, to call; and has been calling at short intervals ever since.

The Goodwyn-Sandys, unless we are sharper than the police, we shall never see again. So close was the pursuit, however, that they were forced to leave the portmanteau in the cloak-room at Paddington Station, where it was discovered and opened. It contained a highly curious clock-work toy, and enough dynamite to raze St. Paul's to the ground. Even without exploding, it converted three statesmen to Home Rule.

Mr. Moggridge's resignation of his post in the Customs was received without expressed regret. He has since married Sophia Buzza, and edits a Conservative paper in Wales. I see that another volume of his verse is in the press. It is to be called "Throbs: and other Trifles," and will include the epithalamium written by him for his own nuptials, as well as his "Farewell to Troy!"—a composition which Mrs. Buzza said she defied "you to read without feeling as if geese were walking over your grave."

Sam Buzza has gone to College.

And what of Troy Town? By degrees the old phrases, old catch-words, and old opinions have come to reign again. Troy's unchanged loveliness too, the daily round full of experiences familiar as old friends, the dear monotony of sight and sound in the little port—all have made for healing and oblivion. If you question us on a certain three months in our life, the chances are you will get no answer. We have agreed to forget, you see; and so we are beginning to persuade ourselves, almost, that those months have never been.

Almost. But, as a fact, Mrs. Buzza had been right. "It will never be the same again-never!" Something we have lost, and I think that something is Troy. For strangers have come amongst us, and have formed a society of their own. The Town is grown out of our knowledge. They have built, and are building, mansions of stucco, and a hotel of hideous brick; a fifth-rate race-meeting threatens the antique regatta; and before all this the savour of Trojan life is departing. Ilion is down, and by no assault of war.

And yet—

The evening before last I passed up the road in front of No. I, Alma Villas. The air was warm, and through the half-opened window a voice stole out—

"In the Great Exhibition of 1851, my dear, Her Majesty the Queen, while partaking of luncheon—"